HER
FORBIDDEN
KNIGHT

HER
FORBIDDEN
KNIGHT

by **Rex Stout**

CARROLL & GRAF PUBLISHERS, INC.
NEW YORK

Carroll & Graf Publishers, Inc.
A Division of Avalon Publishing Group
19 West 21st Street
New York, NY 10010-6805

ISBN 0-7394-1087-3

Manufactured in the United States of America

CHAPTER I.

The Champion and the Lady.

"Young man," said Tom Dougherty, "that'll do. Remove yourself."

"What do you mean?" said the person addressed, pugnaciously.

Dougherty regarded him with stern disfavor.

"You know what I mean. Go over and talk to Venus at the cigar stand. But as for that"—he nodded toward the telegraph desk, where sat Lila Williams, the operator, her face reddened by the impertinent gaze of the young man—"nothing doing. Stay away, and far away."

"Private, eh?" the young man grinned.

Dougherty's face became sterner still.

"You say one more word," he said calmly, "and I'll punch your face. Now clear out."

At this threat the young man raised his brows in a sort of pained surprise.

"I say," he protested, "that isn't necessary. When

you talk about punching my face you offend my sensibilities. I regard it as impolite. Nevertheless, I'm a good fellow, and I'll be glad to seek fresh pastures on your assurance that the little brunette yonder, who is somewhat of a peach, belongs to you. If she does, I wish to congratulate you on having—''

But the voluble young man's oration met with a sudden and effectual interruption. Staggered, but not floored, by the scientific blow that Dougherty planted on his jaw, he fell a step or two backward, involuntarily raising his hands to a posture of defense. Then, as his face colored with anger, he recovered himself and glared at Dougherty with an almost joyous hostility.

"In that case," he said calmly, "where shall we go?"

"To the billiard room," said Dougherty in a pleased tone. There was something to this young fellow, after all, he thought.

The affair was not without its audience. A half-dozen loungers who had observed the clash in the lobby followed on their heels, and the attendant and one or two players looked up curiously as they entered the billiard room.

In the lobby the Venus at the cigar stand, otherwise known as Miss Hughes, stretched her neck to an unbelievable length in an effort to look round two corners at once, and Lila Williams, the innocent cause of the battle, trembled in her chair and covered her face with her hands.

Dougherty soon discovered that there was, indeed, "something to this young fellow." No sooner had he squared off and assumed his favorite guard—for Dougherty had at one time been a prizefighter—than he suddenly felt himself in the midst of a mad, breathless whirlwind.

A thousand arms and fists seemed to be revolving crazily about his head and shoulders. This was bewildering.

And what was worse, sometimes they landed. Nothing more unscientific could possibly be imagined; Dougherty felt aggrieved. This was no man, but a windmill.

Dougherty struck out blindly with both arms, then suddenly felt himself propelled backward by some jolting force, while he clutched frantically at a table to save himself from falling.

He opened his eyes. Before him stood the young man, smiling pleasantly; on either side a knot of lobby loungers, on their faces an expression of amused surprise.

"This is where Tom gets his," observed Billy Sherman.

At this remark Dougherty's strength returned. He leaped at his opponent fiercely and by the mere force of impact bore him to the floor; then, as they both rose, he landed a free swing on the young man's ear.

But the windmill proved too much for him. A succession of jolts on the nose and mouth rattled and unnerved him; his hands waved wildly in the air; and when, after a feeling of delicious repose and a succeeding blackness, he found himself lying flat on his back on the floor, he decided to remain there.

"How about it, old man?" came a voice.

Dougherty opened his eyes and smiled weakly.

"Hello, Dumain! Oh, all right. Only he don't know how to fight. Does he think he's a semaphore? What was it he hit me with?"

Dumain stooped down, placed his hands under

Dougherty's shoulders and helped him to his feet. One or two of the others approached and offered assistance, but Dougherty shook them off with a gesture.

"Here, brace up," said Dumain. "What was zee quarrel?"

"Woman, lovely woman," chirped Harry Jennings.

"Shut up," growled Dougherty. "It was Miss Williams," he added, turning to Dumain. "The puppy insulted her."

"My dear fellow," came a voice, "how can you call me that after what has just happened? Do you require additional demonstration?"

Dougherty turned and glared at his late opponent.

"No, thanks," he said dryly. "You've already proved you're one. Just because I've lost my wind is no sign you're a man. And anybody who insults Miss Lila Williams is a puppy, and remains so till he apologizes."

"You are, I take it, the young lady's champion," the young man observed.

"Call it anything you like. But I'm her friend," said Dougherty.

"And I," said Dumain.

"And I," came in a chorus from the loungers, who had remained to support Dougherty.

The young man whistled expressively.

"So many! She is a lucky woman. And surely she could use one more."

"Zee next time," Dumain observed significantly, "there will be five of us, or seex. I imagine you will have rather a lively time of it. And be good enough to refrain from remarks such as zee one you have just made. They displease us."

"But what the deuce!" the young man exclaimed. Then he hesitated and appeared to consider.

"Now, listen here," he continued finally; "you can't frighten me. I'd take you all on in a minute. But I'm a good fellow. I would rather walk on my own feet than somebody else's toes.

"As far as your Miss Williams is concerned, I'm interested in her. But if you chaps have any reason, philosophical, domestic, or amatory, which might cause me to smother my inclinations, I'm willing to hear it. I put it up to you."

"Indeed!" said Dumain contemptuously. "And who are you?"

"Let him alone," said Dougherty. "I like him. Moreover, I'll talk to him.

The young man smiled.

"My name is Driscoll—Bub Driscoll," he said, holding out his hand to Dougherty.

"Tom Dougherty," said that gentleman, taking the hand.

They found chairs in a corner of the billiard room, and Dougherty began his tale. Some of the others gathered round—for Dougherty's tongue was famous—and divided their attention between the narration and a game of billiards begun by Harry Jennings and Billy Sherman.

Driscoll, during the readjustment, found opportunity for the first time to take note of his surroundings.

Filled with stale tobacco smoke, poorly ventilated, and receiving constantly the heterogeneous fumes from the bar adjoining, the most noticeable thing about the room was the odor which pervaded it. To an ordinary human being this atmosphere is vitiating: but the sport and the tenderloin loafer thrive and grow fat on it. They breathe it as the salamander does the flame.

The room, long and narrow, was lined along either side with chairs with raised seats, the better to overlook the five or six billiard tables which ranged along the center from end to end. On the walls were hung pictures of racehorses and actresses, and copies of the rules of the National Billiard Association; at intervals a cue rack. A wide arch at one end led into the main half of the hotel; a small door at an opposite corner connected with the bar.

Here and there were small tables ready to hold whatever might be deposited on them by the white-coated attendants, at the request of those made thirsty by the exercise and mental strain occasioned by the classic and subtle game of billiards.

The occupants were few. This was not the result of any lack of popularity for the Lamartine, being on the Madison Square section, in the Nineties, was at the height of its career. The fact is, it was only ten o'clock; an hour when any sensible man—according to the view of the Broadway sport—should be trying to decide whether to turn over for another snatch of sleep or to get up and give his serious consideration to the question of breakfast. Therefore was the billiard room by no means filled.

The game just begun by Harry Jennings and Billy Sherman was the only one in progress, and the spectators were few in number.

In the farthest corner the white-coated attendant was replacing some chairs that had been overturned during the late unpleasantness. Driscoll, observing this, smiled at some inward recollection and turned to Dougherty who was seated at his side.

"Really," said Dougherty, "there's nothing to it. We're Miss Williams's friends, and we don't intend to let anyone annoy her. That's all."

"But it's not enough," declared Driscoll. "We've agreed to argue this out as man to man. Very well.

Now, I'll leave it to you: If, in my wanderings through the highways and byways of existence, I suddenly find a young woman who causes my heart to jump from side to side like the pendulum of an eight-day clock, what is there to keep me from telling her so? The mere fact that she possesses friends? Hardly."

Dougherty observed him with a new interest.

"That was exactly how I felt," he observed.

"How? What?"

"Like the pendulum of an eight-day clock."

"Oh! Well?"

"Well"—Dougherty hesitated—"it's like this: I suppose I must begin at the beginning. If I didn't you wouldn't understand how we feel. Anyway, there's not much to tell.

"It was about two months ago that we first saw Miss Williams. We all hang out here in the Lamartine—that is, Dumain, Booth, Sherman, Jennings, myself, and one or two others. Well, one day, coming in the lobby, what do I see? I see what I call the Queen of Egypt sitting at the telegraph desk.

"'Aha!' says I, 'a new one.' Without loss of time I proceed to skirmish. The enemy ignores me. I advance right up to the fortifications. Still no sign. I prepare to turn loose with my artillery, and at that point am interrupted by Dumain and Jennings entering the lobby.

"As soon as they observe me they hasten up with reenforcements. 'Who is it?' says Jennings. 'The Queen of Egypt,' says I, 'and no time to be lost.' Then we begin in earnest.

"Dumain had a roll—some rich guy wanted to find out who to give it to (you know, Dumain's a palmist)—and that day we must have sent something like five million telegrams, having found her silent on all other topics. It wasn't easy. Did you ever try to write a telegram when you had nothing to say and nobody to say it to? And still we never got across the trenches. It went something like this:

" 'How much?' says I, handing over for the ninth time a telegram to my brother in Trenton, telling him I was well and hoping he was the same.

" 'Sixty cents,' says the Queen of Egypt.

" 'Now,' says I, 'that's what I don't like. I don't mind paying out five for a dinner or tickets to a show, but I do hate to spend money on telegrams. But as I say, I'd just as soon buy tickets to a show as not—any show.'

" 'Sixty cents,' says the Queen of Egypt.

" 'And so far as dinner is concerned—why, I hardly consider ten dollars too much for a good dinner,' says I.

" 'Sixty cents, please,' says she.

"And that was the way it went all day. Not a word could we get. It appeared to be hopeless. Jennings got disgusted.

" 'You've made a mistake, Dougherty,' says he. 'She belongs to Egypt all right, but she's not the queen. She's the Sphinx.' I was inclined to agree with him.

"The time passed quicker than we thought. We were sitting over in the corner, trying to think up one more telegram, when we heard somebody stop right in front of us. It was the Queen of Egypt, with her hat and coat on, ready to go home. Before we could say a word she spoke.

" 'Gentlemen,' she says, 'you must pardon me for speaking to you. I do it because I believe you are gentlemen. I suppose you have been trying to joke with me today; and I am sure that when I tell you it disturbs me and makes me unhappy, you will promise not to do it any more. For if you continue, I must give up my position.'

"You can imagine—maybe—how we felt. Dumain stammered something, and I choked, and the next minute we saw the door close behind her. I guess she realized our condition.

"Well, the next day we had to catch Booth and train him. And the day after that, Sherman. He was the hardest of all. About every day it happens that some stranger suddenly finds himself de trop, though we don't usually interfere unless he insists. And now you get us. She is no longer the Queen of Egypt. She is Miss Lila Williams—which is to say, she's better than any queen."

"But still," persisted Driscoll, "by what right do you interfere with me?"

"Well," Dougherty appeared to reflect, "perhaps none. But there's one or two things we've found out that I haven't told you. One is that she has no father or mother. She's all alone.

"Very well. One thing a mother does is this: if some guy comes round with a meaning eye, she hauls him up short. She says to him: 'Who are you, and what are you good for, and what are your intentions?' Well, that's us. As far as that part of it's concerned, we're mama."

"But I have no intentions," said Driscoll.

"That's just the point. You have no intentions. Then hands off."

Dougherty at this point glanced aside at a shout from the billiard players. When he turned back he found Driscoll standing before him with outstretched hand.

"You're on," said Driscoll briefly. "Shake."

"You're a gentleman," said Dougherty, grasping the hand.

"And now—will you introduce me to Miss Williams?"

Dougherty looked somewhat taken aback.

"I want to apologize to her," Driscoll explained.

"Why, sure," said Dougherty. "Of course. I forgot. Come on."

Halfway to the door they were intercepted by Dumain.

"Well?" said he.

"Oh, it's all right," said Dougherty. "Driscoll's a gentleman."

"*Mon Dieu!*" exclaimed the little Frenchman. "Eet ees not surprising. For zee little Miss Williams—she ees irresistible."

He returned to the game, and Driscoll and Dougherty passed down the hall and thence into the lobby.

The lobby, more ornate and pretentious than the billiard room, was at the same time more typical. With Driscoll, we shall pause to observe it in detail.

There were two entrances: the main one on Broadway, and a side door leading to a crosstown street not far from Madison Square. On the right, entering, were the hotel desk and the cigar stand; beyond, the hall leading to the bar and billiard room. Further on came the telegraph desk and the elevators. Along the whole length of the opposite side was a line of leather-covered lounges and chairs, broken only by the side entrance.

At one time the Lamartine had been quiet, fashionable, and exclusive. Now it was noisy, sporty, and popular; for fashion had moved north.

The marble pillars stood in lofty indifference to the ever-changing aspect and character of the human creatures who moved about on the patterned floor; subtly time had imprinted the mark of his fingers on the carvings, frescoes, and furniture. From magnificent the lobby had become presentable; it was now all but dingy.

With its appearance and character, its employees had changed also. The clerks were noisy and assertive, the bell boys worldly-wise to the point of impudence, and the Venus at the cigar stand needs no further description than the phrase itself.

But what of the girl at the telegraph desk? Here, indeed, we find an anomaly. And it is here that Driscoll and Dougherty stop on their way from the billiard room.

As Lila Williams looked up and found the two men standing before her, her face turned a delicious pink and her eyes fell with embarrassment. Before Dougherty spoke Driscoll found time to regard her even more closely than he had before, in the light of the new and interesting information he had received concerning her.

Her figure was slender and of medium height; exactly of the proper mold and strength for her small, birdlike head, that seemed to have fluttered and settled of itself on the white and delicate neck. Her lips, partly open, seemed ever to tremble with a sweet consciousness of the mystery she held within her—the mystery of the eternal feminine.

Her hands, lying before her on the desk, were very white, and perhaps a little too thin; her hair a fluffy, tangled mass of glorious brown.

"Altogether," thought Driscoll, "I was not mistaken. She is absolutely a peach."

"Miss Williams," Dougherty was saying, "allow

me to introduce a friend. Mr. Driscoll—Miss Williams.''

Lila extended a friendly hand.

"A little while ago,'' said Driscoll, "I was presumptuous and foolish. I want to ask you to forgive me. I know there was no excuse for it—and yet there was—''

He stopped short, perceiving that Lila was not listening to him. She was gazing at Dougherty with what seemed to Driscoll an expression of tender alarm.

"Oh!'' she exclaimed suddenly. "Mr. Dougherty!''

That gentleman appeared startled.

"What is it?''

"Your—your—why, what has happened to your nose?''

"My nose?'' he repeated, puzzled.

"Yes. What has happened?''

Dougherty raised his hand and roughly grasped that rather prominent feature of his face; then his hand suddenly fell and he made a grimace of pain. Then he remembered.

"Oh,'' he said, as carelessly as possible, "a mere nothing. I fell. Struck it against a billiard table.''

Driscoll was doing his best to keep a straight face.

"Mr. Dougherty,'' said Lila, shaking a finger at him solemnly, "tell me the truth. You have been fighting.''

The ex-prizefighter and Broadway loafer, blushing like a schoolboy, gathered himself together as though about to attack the entire heavyweight division.

"Well,'' he demanded with assumed bravado, "and what if I have been fighting?''

"You promised me you wouldn't,'' said Lila. "That is, you said you wouldn't—anyone—who annoyed—about me.''

"It wasn't his fault, Miss Williams,'' said Driscoll,

coming to his friend's assistance. "The blame is mine. It is for that I want to apologize. I can't say how sorry I am, and I hope you'll forgive me, and if there's any——I mean——"

Driscoll, too, found himself hopelessly confused by the frank gaze of those brown eyes.

"Anyway," he ended lamely, "I'll renew his promise for him. He'll never do it again."

"No, you won't do anything of the kind!" exclaimed Dougherty, who, during the period of relief offered by Driscoll, had fully recovered himself—"nobody shall promise anything for me. And, Miss Williams, I am very sorry I ever made that promise to you. I take it back. What has happened today is proof that I would never be able to keep it, anyway."

"But you must keep it," said Lila.

"I can't."

"Mr. Dougherty!"

"Well, I'll try," Dougherty agreed. "I promise to try. But there are some things I can't stand for; and we all feel the same way about it. You leave it to us. We know you don't like us much, and we don't blame you. But any guy that tries to get into informal communication with your eyes is going to see stars—and that's no pretty speech, either."

Lila opened her mouth to renew her protest, but someone approached to send a telegram, and she contented herself with a disapproving shake of the head.

Driscoll touched the ex-prizefighter on the arm.

"Dougherty," he said, "you're enough to frighten a chorus girl; and that's going some. Come on, for Heaven's sake, and do something to that nose!"

Dougherty allowed himself to be led away.

CHAPTER II.

THE RECRUIT.

IT WAS THREE OR FOUR DAYS LATER, ABOUT ONE o'clock in the afternoon, that Pierre Dumain and Bub Driscoll, seated in the lobby of the Lamartine, beheld a sight that left them speechless with astonishment.

They saw Tom Dougherty enter the hotel by the Broadway door, carrying a bouquet of roses—red roses. They were unwrapped, and he bore them openly, flamboyantly, without shame. An ex-prizefighter carrying roses on Broadway in the light of day!

" 'Mother, Mother, Mother, pin a rose on me!' " they sang in unison.

Dougherty ignored them. He scowled darkly at the hotel clerk, who grinned at him delightedly, and walked boldly down the center of the lobby, past a score of curious eyes. At the telegraph desk he halted and accosted the messenger boy. Lila had gone to lunch.

"Got a vase?" Dougherty demanded.

The boy gaped in complete bewilderment.

"Don't you know what a vase is?" said Dougherty sarcastically. "V-a-s, vase. Get one."

"They ain't any," said the boy.

"Then get one!" Dougherty roared, producing a dollar bill. "Here, run around to Adler's. They keep all kinds of 'em. Get a pretty one."

The boy disappeared. In a few minutes he returned, bearing a huge, showy, glass vase, the color of dead leaves. During his absence Dougherty had kept his back resolutely turned on Dumain and Driscoll, who received only silence in return for their witty and cutting remarks.

"Fill it with water," commanded Dougherty.

The boy obeyed.

"Now," said Dougherty, arranging the roses in the vase and placing it on the top of Lila's desk, "see that you leave 'em alone. And don't say anything to Miss Williams. If she asks where they came from, you don't know. Understand?"

The boy nodded an affirmative. Dougherty stepped back a pace or two, eyed the roses with evident satisfaction, and proceeded to the corner where the others were seated.

"Do you know who that is?" said Driscoll in a loud whisper as the ex-prizefighter approached.

"No," said Dumain. "Who ees eet?"

"Bertha, the flower girl," Driscoll replied solemnly.

"Oh, shut up!" growled Dougherty. "You fellows have no sentiment."

Dumain lay back in his chair and laughed boisterously.

"Sentiment!" he gasped. "Dougherty talking of sentiment!"

Then suddenly he became sober.

"All the same, you are right," he said. "Miss Williams should get zee roses. They seem made for her. Only, you know, eet is not—what you say—correct. We can't allow it."

"How?" said Dougherty. "Can't allow it?"

"Positively not," put in Driscoll. "Too much of a liberty, my dear fellow. 'Tis presumptuous. You know your own views on the subject."

This staggered Dougherty. Without a word he seated himself, and appeared to ponder. Dumain and Driscoll, after trying vainly to rouse him by sarcastic observations and comments, finally tired of the sport and wandered over to throw Indian dice for cigars with Miss Hughes. That lady, being wise in her manner, separated them from two or three dollars in as many minutes with ease, complacency, and despatch.

They were rescued by Dougherty, who came bounding over to them with the grace of a rhinoceros.

"I have it!" he exclaimed triumphantly.

"Then hold onto it," said Driscoll, setting the dice box far back on the counter with an emphatic bang. "You have what?"

"About the roses. See here, Miss Williams ought to have 'em. Dumain said so. Well, why can't we take turns at it? Say, every day we fill up the vase, each one in his turn. She'll never know where they come from. Are you on?"

"Wiz pleasure," said Dumain. "And I'll tell Booth and Sherman and the others. We'll have to let them in."

"Ordinarily," said Driscoll, "I would be compelled
to refuse. Being an actor, and, I think I may add, an
artist, my normal condition is that of flatness. But at
the present time I have a job. I'm on."

Thus it was that Lila, on her return from lunch, was
surprised by the sight of a floral offering which flamed
like a beacon on the top of her desk. She regarded it
in wonder while taking off her coat and hat, and
glanced up in time to receive a knowing smirk from
the hotel clerk. Then she saw the three conspirators
observing her furtively with self-conscious indifference. She smiled at them pleasantly, reached up for
the vase, and buried her face in the velvet petals. Then,
replacing the vase, she seated herself at her desk and
picked up a book.

"Gad!" exclaimed Dougherty in high delight. "She
kissed 'em! D'ye see that? And say, d'ye notice how
they match the pink on her cheeks?"

"My dear fellow," said Driscoll, "that won't do.
It's absolutely poetical."

"Well, and what if it is?" Dougherty was lighting
a cigarette at the taper at the cigar stand. "Can't a
prizefighter be a poet?"

"If you are talking of the poetry of motion, yes. But
this is the poetry of e-motion."

Miss Hughes, the Venus at the cigar stand, tittered.

"You Erring Knights are funny," she observed.
"Who bought the roses?"

"Us what?" said Dougherty, ignoring the question.
"What kind of knights did you say?"

"Erring Knights."

"She means knights errant," put in Driscoll.

"I do not," denied Miss Hughes.

"It's a pun. Erring Knights."

"Well," said Dougherty, "and why not? I like the title."

And the title stuck. The lobby loungers of the Hotel Lamartine, purveyors of roses and protectors of beauty in distress, shall henceforth be designated by it.

They formed a curious community. What any one of them might have attempted but for the restraining presence of the others may only be conjectured. Collectively, they became the bulwark of innocence; individually, they were—almost anything.

There was Pierre Dumain, palmist and clairvoyant, with offices just around the corner on Twenty-third Street, a little garrulous Frenchman who always had money.

Tom Dougherty, ex-prizefighter, bookmaker, and sport, who was generally understood to be living under the shadow of a secret.

Bub Driscoll, actor and philosopher, about whom there was known just one fact: he had floored Tom Dougherty.

Billy Sherman, newspaper reporter (at intervals), who was always broke and always thirsty.

Sam Booth, typewriter salesman, who was regarded as somewhat inferior because he rose every morning at nine o'clock to go to work.

Harry Jennings, actor, who was always just going to sign a contract to play leads for Charles Frohman.

What a collection of Broadway butterflies for a young girl to accept as protectors and friends! And yet—you shall see what came of it.

For something over a month the roll of membership remained as given above; then, on a day in October, a candidate presented himself for election.

The corner of the lobby preempted by the Erring Knights was that farthest from the Broadway entrance, opposite the telegraph desk. It was partially hidden from the front by two massive marble pillars, and contained an old worn leather lounge, three or four chairs, and a wide window seat.

This corner had been so long occupied by a dozen or so of the oldest habitués that the advent of a stranger within its sacred precincts was held to be an unwarranted intrusion. This opinion was usually communicated to the stranger with speed and emphasis.

Here it was, at about two o'clock in the afternoon, that Driscoll, Sherman, and Dougherty were seated, discoursing amiably.

Sherman, a tall, dark man, with a general air of assertiveness, was explaining the deficiencies and general inutility of the New York press.

The door opened; Dumain approached. At his side was a stranger, whom he introduced to the others as Mr. Knowlton.

"I believe I've met Mr. Knowlton before," said Sherman, extending a hand.

"You have the advantage of me," said the newcomer politely.

Sherman was silent, but gazed at him curiously as he turned to Driscoll.

They conversed. Knowlton appeared to be educated, well informed, and a good fellow. He also possessed an indefinable air of good breeding—lacking in the others.

Driscoll proposed a game of billiards.

"You're on," the others agreed.

"As for me," said Knowlton. "I'll be with you in a minute. Want to send a telegram."

They nodded and proceeded to the billiard room, while Knowlton approached Lila's desk.

Lila was reading a book, and handed him a pad of

blanks absently, without looking up; and when he
pushed the telegram across the counter she took it and
counted the words, still without looking at him. It was
signed "John Knowlton."

"Eighty cents, please," said Lila.

As she raised her head and met the eyes of the
stranger she was conscious of a distinct and undenia-
ble shock.

Why, she could not have told. There was nothing
alarming in the young man's appearance; he had a
very ordinary face and figure, though the former was
marked by an unusually genial and pleasing pair of
gray eyes, and bore an expression of uncommon frank
good nature. Lila, feeling that she was staring at him,
flushed and turned aside, and the gray eyes twinkled
with an amused smile as their owner took a ten-dollar
bill from his wallet and held it out to her.

"Is this the smallest you have?" asked Lila, opening the cash drawer.

"I believe it is," said Knowlton. "Sorry; but you
see, being a millionaire, I never care to be bothered
with anything smaller. Can you make it?"

Lila examined the contents of the drawer.

"If you'll take some silver."

"Anything," Knowlton smiled.

Lila handed him his change.

"You will send it at once?" asked Knowlton.

She nodded. Knowlton appeared to be in no hurry
to leave.

"I suppose that since my business is over I should
make my bow and depart," he said finally. "But I like
to talk and I hate billiards."

"Then why do you play?" Lila asked.

"Why? Oh, why do we do anything? I suppose
merely to kill time."

"But that is wrong. A man ought to do something—something worth while. He should never want to kill time, but to use it."

"A sermon?" Knowlton smiled.

"I beg your pardon," said Lila, coloring.

"But I was joking."

"I know—of course—and it was very silly of me. Only I do believe that what I said is true. I have always wished to be a man."

"Motion denied," said Knowlton.

"And that means?"

"That it is impossible. That is to say, my guess is that you are thoroughly a woman. Am I right?"

"Do I look so old?"

"Oh, I didn't mean that! Then we'll say girl. You are—let's see—nineteen."

"Twenty," Lila declared.

"Well, that leaves one for safety. It really wasn't a bad guess. It's always best to—"

"Are you coming, Knowlton?" came a voice.

Billy Sherman was standing in the hall leading to the billiard room, regarding them with a sinister frown.

"Right away," Knowlton answered. "Didn't know you were waiting."

He lifted his hat to Lila and joined Sherman. The two disappeared within.

Lila began humming a tune softly under her breath. She picked up her book and turned to the page she had marked, then suddenly let it fall to the desk, gasping with amazement. She had been conversing familiarly, even intimately, with a man she had never before seen—an utter stranger! And at first she had not even realized it! What had she been thinking of? It was incredible.

"Of course," she thought, "there was really nothing wrong about it. I suppose I am silly. And yet—how did it happen? He is certainly different from other men. And, oh, what will he think of me? I hope he will understand that I don't talk to everybody."

Again she picked up the book and tried to read, but the printed words were blurred and meaningless to her eyes. She was saying to herself over and over: "I wonder what he is thinking of me?"

The truth is, that just at that moment Knowlton was not only thinking of her, but was also talking about her.

On entering the billiard room with Sherman he had found the others waiting. Two or three other games were in progress, and the room was filled with men and smoke, the clicking of balls, and the clinking of glasses. Dumain was sitting on a billiard table to preserve their claim to its use.

"Come on!" called Dougherty; "get a cue!"

Knowlton took one from a rack, tested its weight, and chalked it.

"How do we play?" he asked.

"You and Dougherty, Dumain and I," said Driscoll. "Sherman's out."

The game proceeded. They had run through the first frame and begun on the second before Knowlton found opportunity to put his question.

"Who is she?" he said to Dougherty.

Dougherty stared at him.

"Who?"

"The girl at the telegraph desk."

"None of your business," said the ex-prizefighter.

"Why," said Knowlton, surprised at his bruskness, "I meant no offense, I'm sure."

"That's all right," said Dougherty, "but we don't

allow anybody to talk about Miss Williams who doesn't know her. Perhaps you'll have that honor—some day.''

"Your shot, Knowlton!" called Driscoll.

Knowlton made a try at a cushion-carrom and missed badly. Dumain, who followed, nursed the balls into a corner and seemed in for a run.

"So her name is Miss Williams?" said Knowlton, returning to Dougherty.

Dougherty turned on him sharply.

"See here," he said, "I told you not to talk about her."

"Who's talking about her? I merely asked her name. Is that an insult?"

"Perhaps not," Dougherty admitted. "But it's too familiar. And I don't like your tone."

Knowlton assured him that if he read anything but the deepest respect in his tone he was mistaken. This somewhat mollified Dougherty, and he ended by reciting the tale of the Erring Knights.

"I fancied it was something like that," said Knowlton when he had finished. "And she appears to be all you say she is. But it is really rather amusing. A Broadway gang acting chaperon for a pretty girl! Who would believe it?"

"It's the hardest job I ever had," said Dougherty. "See this nose? I got that from a guy that was making eyes at her just the other day—Driscoll yonder. He's one of us now."

"And how may one be elected a member of this club?"

"Nothing doing. We're full up."

"But I want to join. Really—I'm serious about it. To tell the truth"—Knowlton hesitated—"it's been such a deuce of a time since I've done anything really decent that the idea appeals to me. How about it?''

''Oh, stick round if you want to,'' said Dougherty. ''If you feel that way about it, I have no objections. And anytime you want to know—''

''Your shot, Dougherty,'' called Dumain. ''I just ran thirty-two. Zat win zee game. You haven't got a chance.''

And they hadn't. Driscoll completed the frame in the next inning, and the game was ended.

''Enough!'' said Dougherty. ''Dumain ought to be ashamed of himself. He's a blooming professional. It's time to eat, anyway. Come on.''

The others trooped out in a body, while Knowlton remained behind to pay for the game. He had just pocketed his change and was turning to follow, when he heard his name called. At his elbow was Billy Sherman, who had remained seated in a corner while the others were playing.

''Did you call me?'' asked Knowlton.

''Yes,'' said Sherman. ''I want a word with you— alone.''

His eyes glittered with hostility and with a certain air of command as he turned to leave the room with a gesture to Knowlton to follow.

Knowlton appeared surprised, but obeyed with a shrug of the shoulders. ''Another of Miss Williams's chaperons,'' he thought. ''Jove, they're worse than a pack of women!''

Sherman led the way down the hall, round a corner, and into a small room containing a table or two, some chairs, and a sofa—evidently a private parlor. When Knowlton had followed him inside he locked the door. Then, motioning Knowlton to a chair, he stood before him with his hands in his pockets, looking down on him with an insolent leer.

But Knowlton refused to be impressed. "This air of mystery appeals to me," he smiled. "Is it murder or merely a sermon? Now that you have aroused my expectations, I shall expect you to satisfy them."

Sherman, disregarding him, came directly to the point. "You were talking with Miss Williams," he said abruptly.

Knowlton, with a smile of amusement, admitted it.

"Well, you'll have to cut it," said Sherman calmly.

"But why?"

"No questions. I say cut it."

"Mr. Sherman"—Knowlton's voice remained calm—"you are impudent. This thing is no longer amusing. It is decidedly tiresome. I shall talk to whomever I please."

Sherman nodded.

"I expected you to say that. Very well. In that case, I have a story to tell you." He leaned forward, and continued in a tone of sneering insult: "I lived for ten years in a little town called Warton. Does that interest you?"

Knowlton turned suddenly pale, and appeared to control himself with an effort.

"Well?" he said finally.

"Well," repeated Sherman, with a smile of satisfaction at having touched his man, "isn't that enough? If it isn't, listen to this. You don't need to talk; I'll spare you the trouble.

"In the first place, there's the Warton National Bank. I know they're done with you; but it shows I know what I'm talking about.

"I know why you left Warton. I know why you came to New York, and I know who brought you. I ˙now why you call yourself John Knowlton instead ˙—you know what. I know why you choose a new hangout every week, and I know where you get the coin. Is that enough?''

''I haven't the slightest idea what you are driving at,'' said Knowlton, with a light laugh. If it was acting, it was cleverly done. ''I do come from Warton, and my name is not John Knowlton; but anybody is welcome to that information. As for the rest—is it a puzzle?''

Sherman grinned.

''You do it very well,'' he admitted. ''But it's no go. I'm on. That's what I know. Now, here's what I want:

''Today I saw you talking to Miss Williams; and, frankly, I don't like the way she looked at you. These other guys are dubs. They don't bother me. They can buy roses forever if they want to. But that little Williams girl looks good to me, and it's me for her.

''If I can't get her one way, I'll take her another. But I'll get her. As I said, these other guys don't count. But you do. I don't like the way she looked at you. And it's your move.''

''You mean?''

''I mean just this—beat it.''

''And if I don't?''

''The cops.''

Knowlton rose to his feet, smiling.

''Stand away,'' he said pleasantly. Sherman, unsuspecting and wondering a little at the request, obeyed it.

Then, like a leaping flame, Knowlton's fist shot forth straight from the shoulder. With terrific force it caught Sherman full in the face. He staggered, fell against a table, then dropped to the floor in a heap.

Knowlton, with the light of battle in his eyes, stood above him with clenched fists. Then, without a word he turned, unlocked the door, and disappeared into the hall.

Sherman sat up, lifted his hand gingerly to his face, and let out a volley of curses.

"Well," he muttered, "I made a bad guess. And yet—I can't be wrong. He's crooked and I'll get him. And when I do I'll pay him for this."

He rose to his feet painfully and made his way unobserved to the street.

CHAPTER III.

HIDDEN WIRES.

ON THE FOLLOWING MORNING KNOWLTON WAS formally enrolled as a member of the Erring Knights.

"The qualifications," said Tom Dougherty, "are a good pair of biceps and a boundless esteem for Miss Lila Williams. The dues are two dozen roses each week. A fresh bouquet every morning. Your day will be Saturday."

Dumain was really not quite easy about it. He himself had introduced Knowlton to the Lamartine, and he knew nothing whatever about him, having picked him up in a Broadway café by accident. But, as was quite right for a palmist and clairvoyant, he trusted to Providence for justification of his action.

From that day forth Knowlton took his place and held it. In spite of his superior education and breeding, he seemed exactly to fit, and within a week had earned quite a reputation as a good fellow. He always ha money, and leisure and willingness to spend it.

Nothing came of the encounter with Sherman. A day or two afterward they had met in the billiard room. Dumain and Knowlton were playing.

"Take a cue, Sherman?" Dumain had said.

"If Knowlton doesn't object," Sherman replied.

"Not I," laughed Knowlton. "You can't bluff in billiards, you know. It's either hit or miss."

The significance of this remark was not lost on Sherman.

No one knew anything of the nature of Knowlton's occupation, or even if he had any. He was in the Lamartine at all hours of the day, and he always had leisure to perform any favor or meet any engagement.

He had one habit that aroused some comment. Two or three times each week he sent a telegram at Lila's desk. It always bore the same address.

Laughingly alluding to their first meeting, he always insisted on paying with a ten-dollar bill, and the state of Lila's cash drawer became a standing joke between them. Lila wondered a little about the mysterious telegrams; in fact, she wondered about everything connected with him—and knew nothing.

She even wondered why she was interested in him; why she looked forward to the sight of his face and the sound of his voice. For her innocence was that of inexperience and ignorance—the purest if not the best. It led her into a score of charming deceptions, of which, however, she herself was always the victim.

One of these had to do with the bouquet of roses.

In the first place, no girl likes to receive flowers unless she knows who gives them to her. So, on the first appearance of the glorious vase, Lila had set about discovering its source.

Let us not be too harsh on the poor little messenger

boy. It is true that he had promised Dougherty not to tell, but if you blame him severely for his betrayal of the confidence it merely proves that you know nothing of the charm of Lila's smile.

It would have coaxed a secret from the Sphinx herself. Thus she became aware that the roses were the gift of the Erring Knights, furnished by each in his turn.

Then one morning, about a week after the first appearance of Knowlton, she decided that her information was not sufficiently definite. Observe the effect of love! Ordinarily Lila was the most open and straightforward creature in the world. But see the cunning of her procedure!

"Jimmie," she said to the messenger boy, "the roses yesterday were the most beautiful shade I have ever seen. Do you know who got them?"

"What's today—Saturday?" Jimmie asked.

"Yes. Yesterday was Friday."

"Then it was Mr. Driscoll."

"Oh!" Lila hesitated. "And who—who gets them on Thursday?"

"Mr Dumain—Frenchy."

"And on Wednesday?"

Jimmie remained silent and eyed her keenly.

"Mr. Knowlton's day is Saturday," he said finally. "That's today."

Lila blushed a rosy pink.

"Jimmie!" she exclaimed.

"Aw, come off! Don't you think I know nothin'?" said the boy. Only a boy—or a woman—could have guessed it.

Lila was silent. But that evening she took the bouquet of roses home with her. As to what she did wit' them after she got them there, you must guess yourself. Unlike Jimmie, I can keep a secret.

A month passed uneventfully.

Dumain improved his play at billiards till he threatened to take part in a tournament; Jennings reported daily concerning his contract with Charles Frohman; Knowlton continued to spend his ten-dollar bills on telegrams at Lila's desk, and Driscoll spouted the classics on all occasions. Dougherty and Booth held down their chairs and talked philosophy.

Since the day of Knowlton's introduction, Sherman, who had always been barely tolerated by the others, had increased his attentions to Lila to a point where they were noticed by several of the others. But, as Driscoll said, they regarded him as harmless.

Had Lila cared to speak she could have told them that which would have caused them to think differently; but she bore his troublesome attentions in silence. And if she had but known the depth of his treachery and the strength of his passion for her, she would have feared him, instead of merely despising him, and avoided many a poignant hour of sorrow and anxiety.

But Sherman cleverly concealed his real nature and treacherous designs under an appearance of blunt frankness. It must be admitted that the others were easily deceived. But then what cause had they for suspicion? We learn of the presence of the deadly rattlesnake only when we hear his warning rattle, and Sherman, like the serpent, was waiting silently for the time to spring.

It was Dumain who first noticed that Lila carried home the bouquet of roses on Saturday evening. These Frenchmen have an eye for such things. He watched and discovered that this compliment was paid on Saturdays only.

Now Dumain was not exactly jealous. The mere fact that Lila exhibited a preference for Knowlton's roses did not disturb him; but the question was, what had Knowlton done to bring about such a state of affairs? For it was evident to Dumain that Knowlton must have done or said something thus to have installed himself in the first place in Lila's affections.

Of course, Dumain was mistaken. A girl gives her heart not to a man's actions or words, but to the man himself. Knowlton was innocent of any treachery to the Erring Knights. He was not to blame for the vagaries of Dan Cupid.

But when, for the fourth Saturday in succession, he saw Lila carefully place the roses in a large paper bag and leave the hotel with the bag under her arm, he could contain himself no longer. He called to Knowlton, who was talking with the Venus at the cigar stand.

Knowlton walked over to him in a secluded corner of the lobby.

"I want to talk to you," said Dumain.

"Fire away!" said Knowlton.

"It is about zee roses."

"Roses?"

"Yes. Zee roses you gave to Miss Williams."

"What about them?"

Dumain pointed toward Lila's desk.

"You see. Zee vase is empty."

"Why, so it is," said Knowlton. "I wonder—that's funny."

"Very funny." said Dumain sarcastically. "Now, where are they?"

"I have no idea."

"Do you mean to say you don't know?"

"I don't know."

Dumain eyed him incredulously.

"Well, zen, I tell you," he said finally. "Miss Williams took zem home."

Knowlton seemed surprised.

"Miss Williams took them home?" he repeated.

"Yes."

"Well, they are hers, aren't they? Hasn't she a right to do as she pleases with them? Why do you trouble me about it?"

"Because she pay zat compliment to no one but you," said Dumain impressively.

"What? How—only to me?"

"She never take any roses home but yours. She does it now for—oh, a month. And what does zat mean? It means you're a traitor. It means you've deceived us. It means you are trying to make zee impression on Mees Williams, and I am afraid you succeed."

Knowlton appeared to be touched. His face colored, and he seemed to be at a loss for words. Was it possible that this evidence of an interest in him on the part of Miss Williams found a corresponding thrill in his own breast?

Suddenly he smiled—a smile of genuine amusement.

"Dumain," he said, "you fellows are the limit. You're not only amusing—you're extremely dense. I would be very happy indeed if I could believe that Miss Williams had singled me out for the distinction you mention; but the real cause of her seeming preference is only too evident."

"Well?"

"Every evening," Knowlton continued, "Miss Williams's roses are left to adorn the lobby of this hotel. It is by her order, as you know. But as she is at home Sunday she wants them on that day for herself.

"So every Saturday evening she takes them home. That must be the correct explanation. She can't even know that I bought them."

Dumain's little round face was filled with light.

"Of course!" he exclaimed. "What an ass am I! Forgive me, Knowlton. Zen she doesn't care for you?"

"I'm afraid not." Knowlton smiled. But the smile was not an easy one.

"And you haven't been trying to—"

"My good fellow," Knowlton interrupted him, "as long as I am an Erring Knight I shall act only in the role of protector."

At that moment Driscoll approached and the interview was ended. Knowlton wandered over to the cigar stand, bought a packet of cigarettes, and, lighting one, transferred the remainder to a silver-mounted leather case. Then strolling past Lila's desk with a nod, he stopped in front of the lounge in the corner and exchanged the time of day with Harry Jennings and Billy Sherman.

After a few minutes of desultory conversation with Jennings, during which Sherman sat noticeably silent, Knowlton, glancing at his watch and observing that he had an engagement, left the lobby of the hotel, and started up Broadway.

He had no sooner disappeared than Sherman sprang up from the lounge, left by the side door, and followed him some twenty paces in the rear.

Broadway was crowded and Sherman was forced to keep close to his quarry in order not to lose sight of him. Knowlton walked with a swinging, athletic stride, looking neither to right nor left—ordinarily the gait of a man who has nothing to fear and nothing to be ashamed of. Now and then the pressure of the crow caused him to make a detour, and Sherman dodged in and out behind him.

At Madison Square Knowlton stopped abruptly and looked first to one side, then the other. On account of the congested traffic at that point the action was perfectly natural, and Sherman, who had darted quickly behind a standing cab, was convinced that he had not been seen. After a short wait Knowlton stepped off the curb, crossed the square, and proceeded up Broadway.

At Twenty-eighth Street he turned suddenly and disappeared through the swinging doors of a café.

Sherman approached, and halted a foot from the door.

"Now," he muttered, "if I only dared go in! I'd give a ten-spot to know who he's with in there. That would settle it. But they'll probably come out together, anyway." He retired to a doorway nearby and waited.

In a few minutes Knowlton emerged alone. Sherman, cursing under his breath, hesitated and appeared ready to give it up; then, with a gesture of decision, he resumed the chase with an air of determined resolve. Knowlton had quickened his step, and Sherman had to move swiftly to overtake him.

At Thirtieth Street Knowlton turned westward. At once the pursuer's task became more difficult. There was no crowd of pedestrians here, as on Broadway, and there was imminent danger of discovery. Twice when Knowlton halted he was forced to dodge aside into a doorway.

At Sixth Avenue Sherman found his passage obstructed by a passing cab. It was empty. Struck by a sudden thought, he sprang inside and, thinking thus to lessen the chances of detection, pointed to Knowlton and instructed the driver to follow him.

The driver grinned, wheeled his cab sharply, and turned down Thirtieth Street.

They crossed Seventh Avenue and Eighth, past rows of five-story apartment houses, with their narrow brass-railed stoops and air of dingy respectability. Straight ahead at a distance the Hudson could be seen shimmering in the light of the winter sun; from the rear came the sounding rumble and rattle of an Elevated train above the low, never-ceasing hum of the great city.

Knowlton continued his rapid stride to Ninth Avenue, and beyond, while the cab followed cautiously. Then suddenly he turned in at the entrance of one of a row of apartment houses. By the time the cab approached he had disappeared within.

Sherman ordered the driver to halt in front of the entrance, while a look of disappointment and chagrin covered his face. "Well, I'll be hanged," he said finally. "I thought sure I had him this time. And here he comes home to take a nap!"

He sat undecided in a corner of the cab.

"Hello, Sherman!" came a voice from above.

Sherman, startled, leaned out through the cab door and looked up. Knowlton was leaning out of an open window on the second story of the apartment house he had entered, looking down with an amused grin.

"Won't you come up and have some tea?" he sang out pleasantly.

Sherman's face colored with rage.

"No, thank you, *Mr. John Norton*," he called. Then he turned and shouted at the driver to go on, while his brain whirled with the thousand wild schemes of a baffled and enraged man.

He, too, had noticed Lila's preference for Knowlton. And he understood it, as Dumain did not; for the eye of love are keen. He saw the uselessness of trying to combat that preference, for he recognized Knowlton's superiority; but he hoped to acquire the power to force Knowlton to remove himself.

He believed that he possessed the key to that power, and he had sought in many ways to verify his suspicions, but so far without success. He had begun by attempting a bluff. But Knowlton had called it, and it had failed.

He had started a correspondence with friends in Warton. The information he obtained from them encouraged him; his suspicions were strengthened, but not confirmed. And he required evidence.

Then he had shadowed Knowlton, and seemed ever on the verge of a discovery. But the proof he sought, though ever within his grasp, forever eluded him. He was at last almost persuaded to give it up as hopeless.

He was filled with chagrin, disappointment, and despair, while the sight of Lila's face and his desire for her spurred him on to renewed effort.

Now, as he made his way back to the Lamartine, he resolved on a stroke in the open. He would enlist the services of the Erring Knights, at the same time blinding them as to his own designs.

"They're a bunch of fools, anyway," he thought. "I think I'll tackle the little Frenchman."

Accordingly, when he reached the Lamartine he called Dumain aside.

"What do you want?" Dumain asked shortly.

"I want to talk to you about Knowlton," said Sherman.

"What ees eet?"

"I've discovered something about him that I think you ought to know—something not exactly to his credit."

Dumain stiffened.

"Knowlton ees my friend," he observed meaningly. "Go slow, Sherman."

"If that's the way you feel about it I have nothing more to say," said Sherman, turning to go. "Only I thought you were a friend of Miss Williams."

Dumain looked up quickly.

"And so I am," he declared. "But what is zee connection?"

"Only this: That no one who is a real friend of Miss Williams can possibly be a friend of John Knowlton."

"And why?"

"Because—well, I don't think he intends to marry her."

"*Mon Dieu!*" Dumain gasped. "Has he been—"

"No—not yet. But he will be. And she likes him too well already. Have you noticed what she does with the roses he gives her? And do you know how her eyes follow him all over the lobby?"

"Well?"

"Well, you know what that means. It means that Knowlton can do just about what he likes with her. If not now, it'll come soon. And he'll ruin her. Do you know anything about Knowlton? Listen:

"His real name is Norton. One year ago he was cashier in a bank in a little town in Ohio. One morning they find the safe robbed—dynamited. They couldn't prove Norton was implicated, but everybody knew he was. He beat it to New York. That explains where he got his coin. Now you have it. Should a guy like that be allowed to hang around Lila Williams?"

Dumain sighed.

"We are none of us pairfect," he observed.

"Oh, the devil!" exclaimed Sherman, exasperated

"Perhaps not. I guess neither you nor me is going

publish our diaries. But that isn't the point. To put it plainly, I happen to know that Miss Williams is in love with this Knowlton, and that he fully intends to take advantage of it. You know what that means."

Dumain appeared to be lost in thought.

"But what can we do?" he said finally.

"The same as we've done to a dozen others."

"But zis Knowlton—he is no coward."

"There are six of us," said Sherman meaningly.

Dumain rose from his chair with a gesture of decision.

"I speak to Dougherty and Driscoll," he said as he turned to go.

Sherman watched him cross the lobby.

"The little idiot!" he muttered contemptuously. Then he turned his eyes toward Lila's desk.

As he gazed at her his face burned with desire and his eyes glittered like the eyes of the serpent. Slowly they filled with evil exultation. Then, subduing this outward betrayal of his thoughts, he crossed to her desk, halted uncertainly, and finally reached for a telegram blank.

"You have decided to give me some of your patronage?" Lila smiled.

"Yes," Sherman replied. "Only it won't be in code."

A tinge of color appeared in Lila's cheeks, and a pang of jealousy that stung Sherman's heart made him regret the observation. He placed the telegram blank on the top of the desk and after a minute's thought wrote on it as follows:

MR. GERALD HAMILTON,
    President of the Warton National
    Bank, Warton, Ohio.

In case you wish to find John Norton, try the Hotel Lamartine, New York.

W. S.

Lila smiled as she read it.

"You newspaper men are so mysterious," she observed. Then suddenly she turned slightly pale and glanced up quickly.

"She's noticed the similarity in the names," thought Sherman.

"Why?" he said aloud. "Is there anything so mysterious about that?"

"It sounds like a missing heir or a—an embezzler," said Lila.

"I'm sorry I can't enlighten you."

"Oh, I wouldn't expect you to. I suppose you're full of important and terrible secrets."

"Perhaps." Sherman hesitated a moment, then added: "But there's only one that I regard as important."

Lila was silent.

"It is about you," Sherman continued.

"About me?" Lila's tone was incredulous.

"About you," Sherman repeated. His tone was low and significant as he added, "and me."

His meaning was too clear to admit of any pretense that it was not understood. For a moment Lila's face was lowered, then she raised it and said firmly: "Mr. Sherman, I do not wish you to talk to me—like—that."

"I can't help it. You know it, anyway. I love you." Sherman's voice trembled with desire.

"Must I tell you that you annoy me?" she said, rising to her feet.

Sherman lost control of himself.

"You wouldn't say that to Mr. John Knowlton," he sneered. "And the time will come when you can't say it to me. I want you. Look at me. Do I look like a man who wouldn't take what he wants? You will— you must be mine."

The unexpectedness of it caused Lila's face to turn a fiery red. Then she as suddenly became pale. For a moment neither spoke. They had no words; for Sherman had no sooner spoken than he regretted the rashness of his premature avowal. Lila was the first to recover herself.

"Mr. Sherman," she said calmly, "if you ever speak to me in this way again I shall tell Mr. Dougherty and Mr. Driscoll that you are annoying me. Now go."

And Sherman went.

CHAPTER IV.

DANGER.

DUMAIN PONDERED LONG OVER THE INFORMA-
tion Sherman had given him concerning
Knowlton before he decided to act on it.

The fact is that Dumain was strongly opposed to the
revealing of a man's past. He may have had a personal
reason for this; but let us be charitable. Broadway is
not the only place in the world where they act on the
belief that a man's past is his own and should not be
held against him.

Besides, Sherman had admitted that Knowlton had
merely been suspected. There had been no evidence;
he had been allowed to go free. And Dumain was not
inclined to strike a blow at an innocent man who suf-
fered under the blasting stigma of an unproved accusation.

Still, there was Lila. She must be protected at any
cost. And had not Dumain himself noticed her interest
in Knowlton? What if she really loved him?

And what if Knowlton was the sort of man Sherman had declared him to be? Clearly it meant Lila's ruin. For it is the belief of all Broadway cynics that any woman will do anything for the man she loves. So, early the next morning (that is, early for him), Dumain made his decision on the side of prudence.

He spoke first to Dougherty. The ex-prizefighter was greatly surprised.

"I like Knowlton," he said, "and I believe you're wrong to suspect him. But you know what I think of Miss Williams; and where she's concerned we can't leave any room for doubt. Knowlton must be informed that he is absolutely not wanted."

"Zat ees zee way eet looks to me," said Dumain.

He had met Dougherty on Broadway, and as they talked they strolled to the hotel and entered the lobby. The hotel clerk threw them a familiar nod. Miss Hughes sang out a cheery "Good morning," and Lila smiled pleasantly as they passed her desk. Except for two or three strangers, probably commercial buyers, reading their morning newspapers, the place was empty.

"Sure," said Dougherty, continuing. "When are you going to tell him?"

Dumain looked aghast.

"Tom! Surely you don't expect me to tell heem?"

"Why not?"

"What! How could I? Here are zee facts: Knowlton weighs one hundred and eighty pounds. I weigh a hundred and twentee. It would be absurd. I don't think I am a coward; but I would like to leeve anozzer year or two."

Dougherty laughed.

"All right. Leave it to me. I'll tell him. It's too ad," he added regretfully. "I liked Knowlton."

A few minutes later Knowlton entered the lobby. He walked straight to Lila's desk and wrote out a telegram. Dumain and Dougherty, who were only a few feet away, overheard the conversation.

"You're early this morning," said Lila, as Knowlton handed her a bill from a bulging wallet.

Knowlton glanced at his watch.

"Early? It's past eleven."

"I know. But that's early for you."

"Perhaps. A little," Knowlton admitted. "And how are you this fine wintry morning?"

"Well, thank you," Lila smiled.

Knowlton turned away.

"In the name of Heaven, is there anything wrong with that?" Dougherty growled.

"No," Dumain admitted. "But zee die is cast. Never retract a deleeberate decision. There's your man; go after heem."

The ex-prizefighter started across the lobby. Knowlton turned.

"Hello, Tom!"

"Good morning," said Dougherty, visibly ill at ease.

"Are you on for a game of billiards?"

"No," Dougherty hesitated. "The fact is, Knowlton, there's something I have to say to you."

"Is it much?" Knowlton smiled.

"It's enough."

"Then come over to the corner. It's more comfortable. Hello, Dumain. How's the world?" Knowlton continued chattering as they walked to the leather lounge sacred to the Erring Knights. Then he produced some cigars, offering one to Dougherty.

"No, thanks," said Dougherty stiffly.

"What! Won't take a cigar? What's happened?"

Dougherty coughed and cleared his throat.

"Well," he stammered, "the truth is we—that is, they—they think you ought to go—that is, leave—Oh, darn it all!"

"Easy, Tom," said Knowlton. "Give it to me a word at a time."

Dougherty recommenced his stammering, but a word here and there gave Knowlton an idea of what he was trying to say.

"I believe," he interrupted, "you are trying to tell me that I have become *persona non grata*. In other words, the Erring Knights have seen fit to expel their youngest member."

"Right," said Dougherty, inexpressibly relieved. "If I could have said it like that I would have had no trouble."

Knowlton cut off the end of a cigar and lit it.

"And now," he said between puffs, "what is it— *puff*—you want?"

"That's not the question. It's what we don't want."

"All right." Knowlton waved aside the distinction. "Go on."

"In the first place," Dougherty began, "there's Miss Williams."

"I see her," said Knowlton gravely. "She's sending a telegram. Probably mine. See how the light plays on her hair? Well, what about her?"

"You are not to go near her," said Dougherty with emphasis.

"Ever?"

"Never."

Knowlton blew a cloud of smoke toward the ceiling.

"I see. And what else?"

"You are to stay away from the Lamartine."

"M-m-m. Anything else?"

"That is all."

Knowlton rose, walked to a cuspidor and knocked the ashes from his cigar, then returned to his seat. For another minute he smoked in silence.

"And if I refuse?" he said finally.

"There are six of us," said Dougherty with meaning.

"Then, if I enter the doors of the Lamartine I displease the Erring Knights?"

"You do."

"In that case," Knowlton again rose, "I have to announce that in the future the Erring Knights will be displeased on an average of fourteen times a week. It pains me to cause my old friends so much displeasure, but you leave me no choice." He hesitated a moment, then added: "You should have known better than to try to frighten me, Dougherty." With that he walked away.

Dougherty saw him go to the cigar stand, relight his cigar, start toward Lila's desk, suddenly change his direction, and leave the hotel by the Broadway door. Then the ex-prizefighter hurried over to Dumain.

"I told you so," he said gloomily.

"What deed he say?" asked Dumain.

"Just what I said he'd say."

"Well?" Dumain passed over the fact that Dougherty had said nothing whatever about it.

"He ignores us. He intends to do just as he pleases. We're in for it."

"It seems to me," Dumain retorted, "eet would be better to say he's in for it. We'll have to show him we are not to be trifled wiz. Come on; I have zee idea."

They seated themselves on the lounge in the corner and proceeded to a discussion of the plan of battle.

In the meantime Knowlton was striding swiftly toward his rooms on Thirtieth Street. His face wore a worried frown, and every now and then he glanced nervously to the rear. Occasionally, too, his lips parted in an amused smile; possibly whenever he thought of the quixotic chivalry of the Erring Knights.

The streets and sidewalks were covered with snow— the first of the season. Surface cars clanged noisily; voices sounded in the crisp, bracing air with the sharp clarity of bell tones; faces glowed with the healthful exhilaration of quickened steps and the rush of inward warmth to meet the frosty attack of old winter.

The vigor of the north and the restlessness of the great city combined to supply the deficiencies of the November sun, ineffectual against the stern attack of his annual enemy.

Knowlton turned in at the same door on Thirtieth Street we have seen him enter before, and mounted the stairs to an apartment on the second floor.

Once inside he locked the door carefully behind him, then walked to a wardrobe in a corner of the adjoining room and took from it a small black bag. His hand trembled a little as he placed the bag on a table in the center of the room.

"My good friend," he said aloud, "I am inclined to believe that they are trying to separate us. The little comedy just performed at the hotel must have resulted from the good offices of a certain Mr. Sherman.

"Now, the question is, shall I remain true to you or not? You must admit that you're dangerous; still, I'm willing to give you another chance. We'll leave it to fate. Heads you stay; tails you go."

He took a coin from his vest pocket and flipped it high in the air. It struck the table, bounced off onto the floor and rolled halfway across the room.

Knowlton stooped over and looked at it curiously, picked it up and returned it to his pocket. Then he carried the bag back to the wardrobe and replaced it on the shelf.

As he turned and seated himself in a chair by the table, his face wore an expression of gravity and anxiety that belied the lightness of his tone and words.

To the most casual observer it would have been apparent that John Knowlton was approaching, or passing through, a crisis. But suddenly he smiled; sweetly, almost tenderly.

We follow his thought, and it brings us to the lobby of the Lamartine.

Besides the usual crowd of transient guests and midday idlers, we find the Erring Knights assembled in full force. Sherman and Booth, with two or three strangers, are conversing amiably with the Venus at the cigar stand, Driscoll and Jennings are at a game of billiards down the hall, and Dumain and Dougherty are completing their discussion of the ways and means of war. Lila is putting on her hat and coat to go to lunch.

Sherman detached himself from the group at the cigar stand and walked over to the lounge where Dumain and Dougherty were seated.

"Well?" he said significantly, stopping in front of them.

They looked up at him inquiringly.

"Knowlton didn't show up yet," he continued.

"Yes, he deed," said the little Frenchman.

"What?"

"I say, he deed."

"Then, where is he?"

"I don't know."

"Oh!" A light of evil satisfaction appeared in Sherman's eyes. "Then you spoke to him?"

"Yes."

"Then he's gone."

"So eet seems; but he'll probably be back."

"Ah! And what did he say?"

"In effect, he advised us to go to zee devil."

Sherman seemed taken aback.

"But didn't you tell him we'd get him?" he demanded.

But Dumain and Dougherty rose and went to join Driscoll and Jennings in the billiard room without answering him. Sherman's face colored slightly, but he remained silent, gazing after them with a contemptuous sneer.

"My turn next," he muttered after they had gone.

Within the next hour Dumain spoke to each of the Erring Knights concerning Knowlton; and he was somewhat surprised at the unanimity with which they favored his proposal. Driscoll was the only one who had a good word for Knowlton. But he was easily persuaded.

Then Dumain decided on a little strategy of his own. The result was unfortunate; but he could not have foreseen that. The little Frenchman was well acquainted with woman's weakness; but he knew little of her strength. On that day he was destined to acquire knowledge.

When the others wandered out in search of lunch, leaving the lobby all but deserted, he remained behind. For the sake of moral support he communicated his design to Dougherty, who expressed a fear that something was about to be started which it would be difcult to finish.

"Bah!" said Dumain. "You shall see. Sit here to wait. It will be easy."

When Lila returned from lunch he hurried to her desk and helped her off with her coat.

"Have you been taking lessons in gallantry, Mr. Dumain?" Lila smiled.

"Such a question as zat is insult to zee Frenchman," said Dumain, assuming an injured air. "We do not learn gallantry; we are born wiz eet. I insist on an apology."

"But that is not gallant," Lila protested.

Dumain laughed.

"*Eh bien!* We all have our lapses. And, too, you should not have offended me. I am very sensiteeve. Eet ees not fair. Only today I have rendered you a very great sairvice. Not zat I expect any reward—or even gratitude. But I think you should know of eet."

Lila looked up quickly.

"You mustn't talk like that, Mr. Dumain. You have been good and kind to me—all of you; and you know I am grateful. I can never thank you enough."

Dumain was silent.

"But what is the service you have rendered me?" Lila said presently.

"One zat you may not thank me for," said Dumain.

"But what was it?"

"Killing anozzer dragon—of zee human species."

She frowned.

"I'm afraid I don't understand you."

Dumain stammered something about "men" and "danger," and "the need of a protector." He was finding it harder than he had thought.

"But what do you mean?" Lila insisted.

The little Frenchman gathered himself together and plunged in.

"I mean," he said impressively, "zat we have dropped Knowlton and told heem to stay away from you."

The unexpectedness of it made Lila catch her breath in surprise. Then her face colored gloriously, treacherously. A little tremulous, uncertain laugh came from between her lips.

"That was hardly necessary, was it?" she inquired with a brave attempt at indifference.

"We thought so," Dumain answered, admiring her courage. He was thinking to himself: "She's a thoroughbred. *Mon Dieu!* What a woman!"

"You see," he added aloud, "we found out something about heem that was not exactly to his credit. So, of course, we cut heem. What does that mean?" noticing a curious smile on Lila's face.

"I was just thinking," said Lila slowly, "that it must be a very good man who could afford to say to another man: 'You are not fit to associate with me.' Don't you think so?"

Dumain winced.

"But that wasn't it," he protested. "We were thinking of you. None of us pretend to be angels. But we know you are one."

"But why should you have singled out Mr. Knowlton?" Lila insisted, ignoring the compliment. "He acted just as the rest of you. He is kind to me—so are you, so is Mr. Dougherty. He has never offended me."

Dumain opened his mouth as though to answer; but was silent.

"Why?" Lila persisted.

Dumain stammered something about roses.

"Roses!" exclaimed Lila in amazement. "What do you mean?"

"I mean zat you take hees roses home," said Dumain desperately, "and no one else's."

He should have known better. No one can get a secret from a woman in that manner; provided, of course, that it is her own secret. Lila leaned back in her chair and laughed delightedly. The little Frenchman regarded her with a comical expression of wounded vanity.

"Oh!" Lila cried, as soon as she could speak. "Mr. Dumain, you are positively childish! You must forgive me; but it is so funny!"

It was too much for Dumain; he gave it up.

"Tom!" he called in the tone of a drowning man crying for help.

Dougherty rose from the seat Dumain had assigned to him and came over to them. In as few words as possible Dumain explained his dilemma, telling him that Lila was aggrieved at their attitude toward Knowlton.

Lila interrupted him.

"Not aggrieved," she said. "It does not especially interest me; only it seems unjust. And I see no reason for it."

Dougherty turned to Dumain.

"Why did you say anything about it to her?" he growled.

Dumain, having nothing to say, was silent.

Dougherty turned to Lila.

"And you think we are unjust?"

"Yes," she replied.

"Well, you are wrong."

"I believe I am right."

Dougherty reflected for a moment, sighed for courage, cleared his throat, and said:

"Miss Williams, it is time we understand each other. Now is as good a time as any."

"I don't understand you," said Lila.

"You will before I get through. I only ask you to remember what I—what we think of you.

"You know what we've done—not much, perhaps, but all we could—to show you how we feel. We've been glad enough for the chance. There's not much good in any of us, but we're always anxious to use what we've got.

"Now about Knowlton. As long as he was merely one of us, we asked no questions. He was good enough for us. And I guess he always treated you all right. But that's not the point. We have an idea you're beginning to think too much of him.

"And that won't do. Knowlton's all right to buy you roses, and look after you, like the rest of us. But we ain't fit to touch you, and neither is he.

"That's all there is to it. If you'll tell us you don't think any more of Knowlton than you do of any of the rest of us, we'll admit we're wrong and apologize.

"We have some rights, you know. You've let us stand by you and do things for you. All we ask you to do is this: say you don't love this Knowlton."

During this speech Lila lost her courage. Was everyone in on her secret? Her color rose and fell, her face was lowered, and her hand trembled as she raised it to adjust a stray lock of hair behind her ear. Still, she found sufficient strength to answer:

"I know—I know you have rights, Mr. Dougherty. I know what you have done for me. If it were not for that I would be very angry. You may treat Mr. Knowlton just as you like; the subject does not interest me. And now—go, please."

"But you ought to tell us—"

"Go!" Lila exclaimed. "Please!"

They turned and left her without another word.

And Lila knew she had done right not to be angry with them. Perhaps they had been impertinent; but she knew they had not meant to be.

And she was frightened; rather, vaguely anxious. For she felt that they would never have presumed so far unless they knew more of Knowlton than they had told her.

What could it be? Her heart said, he is worthy. But she had not spent months in the Hotel Lamartine without learning something of the unsightly mess that lies concealed beneath the crust; and she feared.

But after all, why should she trouble herself with thoughts of Knowlton? *He* had shown no interest in *her*. He had treated her with courtesy, of course; he was obviously a gentleman. But he had given her no reason to suppose that he would ever be the instrument either of her pleasure or her sorrow.

The afternoon passed slowly. The telegraph desk at the Lamartine was never overworked; but today it seemed to Lila duller than usual. She tried to read, but found it impossible to settle her mind.

At five o'clock she began to fill in her daily report, and prolonged the task as far as possible in the effort to remain occupied. At half past five she prepared the cash for the collector of the telegraph company, who called every evening.

A few minutes later he arrived.

"Not much for you today," Lila smiled.

The collector, a short, plump man with an air of importance, counted the cash, wrote out a receipt and handed it to Lila. Then he took an envelope from his pocket and drew from it a crisp, new ten-dollar bil¹ which he laid on the desk in front of her.

He leaned toward her with a mysterious air as he said:

"Miss Williams, do you know who gave you that?"

Lila looked at the bill, wondering.

"In the past month," continued the collector, "you have turned in something like a dozen of these. We want to know where they come from."

The oddity of the question had taken Lila by surprise, and she had remained silent, gathering her wits; but now she remembered.

Of course, the bills were Knowlton's. Did he not always pay for his telegrams with new bills? And her receipts were not so large but that she would have remembered any others.

"But why?" she stammered, to gain time.

The collector ignored the question.

"Do you know who gave them to you?" he repeated.

"No," replied Lila distinctly.

"No recollection whatever?"

"None."

He reached in another pocket and drew forth another bill exactly similar to the one he had shown her, saying:

"I just got this out of your cash drawer. You took it in today. Surely you remember who gave you this?"

Lila repeated "No."

For a minute the collector eyed her keenly in silence. Then, returning the bills to the envelope, he said slowly:

"That's odd. Very odd—in a little office like this. I don't see how you could help remembering. Anyway, be sure you keep a lookout from now on. They're counterfeit."

"Counterfeit!" Lila gasped.

The collector nodded, repeated his injunction to "keep a lookout," and departed.

Counterfeit!

Lila buried her face in her hands and sat quivering, horrified.

CHAPTER V.

Two Escorts.

THAT NIGHT WAS AN UNPLEASANT ONE FOR LILA. She perceived clearly for the first time whither her heart was leading her, and recoiled in terror from the dangerous path on which she had already set her foot.

She had lied, and she had been faithless to her trust—which, though a small one, was felt by her to be none the less inviolable. She had lied instinctively, naturally, as a matter of course—the heart commands the brain, if at all, with an awful authority.

And for whom had she made the sacrifice? she asked herself. For a man about whom she knew one thing, and that thing was: she loved him. Perhaps, after all, the Broadway cynic is partly right.

Alone in her room that night she attempted to subject herself to a strict and sincere examination. She asked herself: "Why have you done this thing?" and her heart fluttered painfully, endeavoring by silence to keep its secret; but she felt the answer.

She crept, shivering, from her bed, and buried her face in a tray of withered rose leaves on the table.

Love is no snob. He forces the princess to deceive a court, defy a king, and renounce her royalty, that she may fly to the open arms of her despised lover; he forces the working girl to laugh at justice and law, and sacrifice her dearest possession—even herself. And the one triumph is to him fully as sweet as the other. Love is no snob.

His struggle with Lila was a hard one. She fought with the strength of despair, having forced herself to realize the significance of the battle. Nothing is more horrible to a woman than the fear that she has bestowed her heart on one unworthy; I say, the fear, for when the bestowal is once consummated and admitted, she is more apt to glory in it than to be ashamed of it.

Lila ended by saying to herself: "I have done right to shield him. He is good—I know it—surely my heart would not deceive me? What am I to do? I do not know. But I do not regret what I have done."

And she smiled, and slept.

The following day, at her desk in the Lamartine, she felt her doubts and fears return. She chafed under an indefinable sensation of restlessness and expectancy; she performed her duties absentmindedly and perfunctorily; there was a marked absence of the usual pleasant cheerfulness in her manner; her eyes constantly wandered to the door, and returned again to her desk, filled with disappointment. The lobby of the Lamartine did not see Knowlton that day.

To the Erring Knights this meant a triumph. They believed that after all Knowlton had heeded the warning and decided to obey their dictum. They allowed themselves to become unduly excited over the matter, and as the afternoon wore away their faces took on an expression of jubilant satisfaction. Partly was this owing to their genuinely tender interest in Miss Williams; partly to the inherent vanity of man.

At four o'clock in the afternoon Dougherty was pacing up and down the lobby, past the lofty marble pillars, through clouds of tobacco smoke, with the air of a pitcher strolling to the bench after a victorious inning.

He was superbly indifferent to the amused glances of the loungers seated and standing here and there about the lobby, and was even undisturbed by the biting remarks of the Venus at the cigar stand. Finally he strolled over to the leather lounge where two or three of the others were seated.

"You see," said he, waving his hand grandly, "he does not come. And who was it that told him to stay away? I."

"Wait," said Driscoll darkly. "It's early yet. And then—what will you do?"

"Bah!" said Dumain explosively. "As for me, I theenk he is no coward. He will come. And zen—well, we have our program."

But Knowlton did not arrive. Five o'clock came, and six. At the approach of dinnertime the crowd in the lobby thinned perceptibly, and the Erring Knights disappeared by ones and twos.

Jennings, on his way out from the billiard room, stopped at the corner in search of a dinner companion. He found Sherman seated there alone.

"Thanks," said Sherman in response to his invitation. "I'd like to go, but I have a date. See you tonight."

Jennings nodded and left the lobby.

Lila was still at her desk. It was nearly an hour past her period of duty, and there was nothing, apparently, to detain her; still she lingered. She sat with her eyes fixed on the door, hoping that the figure she longed to see would appear at the last minute.

Finally, she arose and slowly put on her coat and hat. On her way out she stopped at the cigar stand and chatted for a moment with Miss Hughes, who expressed some concern at her pallor and appearance of fatigue.

"It's no wonder you're sick," said the Venus sympathetically. "A dump like this is enough to kill you. I can stand it. I'm used to it. But sometimes it gives even me the willies."

"It's nothing," Lila smiled. "I think I have a headache. Thank you for asking. Good night."

She left the lobby by the main entrance, walked up Broadway to Twenty-third Street, then turned west. The rush hour was past, and the sidewalks were nearly deserted. A few belated pedestrians hurried along as rapidly as the slippery condition of the pavement would permit.

The lighted shop windows shone in the frosty air with a sharp brilliancy. Taxicabs and hansoms picked their way cautiously through the ice and snow, and the crosstown cars clanged noisily on their way to either river.

Lila had got nearly to Sixth Avenue, and was hastening her step at the urging of the cold east wind at her back, when she heard her name called behind her. Turning, she saw Billy Sherman, who advanced smiling, with lifted hat.

Half frightened, she nodded and turned to go, but Sherman stopped her with a gesture. There was a con ciliatory smile on his dark, handsome face as he looked down at her.

"Do you take the Sixth Avenue 'L'?" he asked.

Lila nodded.

"Then we can ride together. I am going uptown. You are ill, and you need some one to look after you. If you would only—"

Lila broke in with a protest, but Sherman paid no attention to it, and walked by her side to the Elevated station and up the steps. He stopped at the window to buy tickets, but Lila took one from her purse and dropped it in the box as she passed to the platform. In a moment he joined her.

"Are you unwilling that I should do even so little for you?" he asked reproachfully.

Lila was silent. A train pulled in, and they boarded it together. On account of the late hour, they had no difficulty to find seats. As the train started Sherman turned in his seat to look at her, and repeated his question.

His manner was respectful, and his solicitude appeared to be genuine; and Lila, wearied and worn by anxiety, was touched by it. After all, she asked herself bitterly, who was she, to despise anybody?

"I don't know," she said doubtfully in answer to his question, which he repeated for the third time. "You must remember—what you have said to me— and how you have acted. I wish—I think it would be best for you to leave me at the next station. You were not going uptown, were you?"

"I beg you to forget how I have acted," said Sherman earnestly. "I know that twice I have forgotten myself, but not without reason. You must know that I am and want to be, your friend.

"I shall not pretend that it is all my desire. But if

you will not allow me to be more than a friend, I will be satisfied with that. I couldn't let you come home alone tonight. You were so weak you could hardly stand.''

He continued in this strain for many minutes, while the train rumbled northward, and Lila sat back in her seat with her eyes half closed, scarcely listening.

His voice came to her in a gruff monotone above the rattle of the train, and against her will filled her with a sense of protection and comfort. The words came to her vaguely, unintelligible; but the tone was that of sympathy and friendship—and how she needed them!

Thus she allowed him to continue, while she remained silent, dimly conscious of the danger she had once felt in his glance and voice.

At the One Hundred and Fourth Street station he rose, and she saw with a sense of surprise that she had reached her destination. At the train gate she turned to thank him, but he assisted her down the steps of the station and started west on One Hundred and Fourth Street at her side.

"You are surprised that I know the way?" he smiled. "You should not be. How many times have I stood in this street looking up at your window, when you thought I was far away—or, rather, when you were not thinking of me at all!"

"Mr. Sherman!" exclaimed Lila warningly.

They had halted at the stoop of an old-fashioned brownstone apartment house, and Lila had mounted the three or four steps and stood looking down at him.

"Forgive me," said Sherman in a tone of contrition. "But you have not answered me—I mean, what I said on the train. There could be nothing offensive in wha I proposed, unless you hate me.''

"No. I think I do not hate you," said Lila slowly.
She was tired, and longed to be alone, and was forcing herself to be polite to him.

"Then you are my friend?"

"I—think—so."

"Will you shake hands on it?"

Lila appeared to hesitate, and shivered—possibly from the cold. Finally she extended a reluctant hand a few inches in front of her.

Then, as soon as Sherman touched it with his fingers, she withdrew it hastily, and, with a hurried "Good night, and thank you," disappeared within the house.

For a long minute Sherman stood gazing at the door which had closed behind her; then, turning sharply, he started off down the street. At Columbus Avenue he entered a saloon and ordered a brandy.

"God knows I need it," he muttered to himself. "The little devil! Well, I can't play that game. It's too hard to hold myself in. The other way is more dangerous, perhaps, but it's easier. Friendship! I'll show you a new kind of friendship!"

He beckoned to the bartender and ordered another brandy, with a knowing leer at his reflection in the mirror opposite. Then, having drained his second glass, he left the saloon and, crossing the street to the Elevated station, boarded a downtown train. In thirty minutes he was back at the Lamartine.

The lobby was almost deserted; it was too early for the evening throng. Sherman wandered about in search of one of the Erring Knights, but in vain; and he finally asked the Venus at the cigar stand if she had seen Knowlton. She replied that he had not been in the lobby, and Sherman departed for dinner, well satisfied with the events of the day.

He was destined, on the following day, to have that feeling of satisfaction rudely shattered and converted into despair.

The next morning the Erring Knights were openly and frankly jubilant. Knowlton had obeyed their warning; clearly, he was afraid of them. They felt an increased sense of proprietary right in Miss Williams.

Dougherty, entering the lobby about eleven o'clock, stopped at Lila's desk to say good morning, and stared in anxious surprise at her pale cheeks and red, tear-stained eyes.

"Are you ill?" he asked bluntly.

"Not I," she answered, trying to smile. "I had a headache, but it is all right now."

Dougherty grumbled something unintelligible, and proceeded to the corner where the Erring Knights were assembled. He was the last to arrive. Dumain, Jennings, and Driscoll were seated on the leather lounge, and Sherman and Booth were leaning against the marble pillars in front of it. They greeted Dougherty in a chorus.

"*Bone jore,*" said Dougherty, with an elaborate bow. "How's that Dumain?"

"Pairfect," smiled the little Frenchman.

"Really," the ex-prizefighter asserted, "I think I'll learn French. I like the way it sounds. *'Monseere'* is much more classy than 'mister,' for instance."

"If you do," put in Driscoll, "you'd better speak it better than Dumain speaks English. If a man could be electrocuted for murdering a language he'd be a storage battery by this time."

"Have your fun," said Dumain, rising to his feet and shrugging his shoulders good-naturedly. "Eet ee a treeck—zat Angleesh. I have eet not."

"Hardly," laughed Jennings. "You don't speak it with the finish of our late friend Mr. Knowlton, for instance. By the way, have you seen him?" he added, turning to Dougherty.

"Who? Knowlton?"

"Yes."

"Well, I should say not." Dougherty grinned as though the idea were absurd. "And, believe me, I won't see him—at least, not in the Lamartine. When I tell a guy he's not wanted, that ends it."

"Don't be too sure," Booth advised. "Just because he didn't come yesterday—you know today is another day."

Dougherty turned on the speaker scornfully. "Listen," he said with emphasis. "If that Knowlton shows his face in this lobby—which he won't—but if he does, we'll eat him up."

"*Diable! Mon Dieu!*"

The exclamation came from Dumain, in an undertone of surprise and alarm. The others turned to him in wonder, and, following his fixed gaze toward the main entrance, saw Knowlton walk down the center of the lobby and stop at Lila's desk!

The action and facial expression of each of the Erring Knights at this juncture was curiously indicative of their different characters.

Driscoll and Dougherty moved forward and glared belligerently; Booth and Jennings glanced from one side to the other as though in search of reenforcements; Dumain sputtered with wrath and indignation, and Sherman's face darkened with a menacing scowl. None of them, however, appeared to be particularly anxious to cross the lobby.

Knowlton had not cast a single glance in their diction. His back was turned to them as he stood talking with Lila, and their conversation was in so low a tone that the Erring Knights heard not a word of it.

For perhaps two minutes this scene, half farcical, remained unchanged. The Erring Knights muttered to each other in undertones and glared fiercely, but they made no move.

Suddenly they saw Knowlton lift his hat and bow to Lila, turn sharply, and leave the lobby even more hurriedly than he had entered it.

Each of the Erring Knights glanced round the circle of his companions; some questioning, others assertive.

"It's up to us," declared Dougherty. "We've got to show him."

They gathered themselves closely about the lounge, and all began talking at once.

In the meantime, what of Lila?

When Knowlton entered the lobby she was busied with some papers on her desk, and therefore did not see him. She became aware of his presence only when he stopped at her side and spoke to her.

For a moment she was speechless with surprise and gladness and confusion. She stared at him strangely, unseeing.

"What's the matter?" smiled Knowlton. "I hope I don't look as fierce as that."

Then, as Lila did not answer, he reached for a telegraph blank, wrote on it, and handed it to her, together with a ten-dollar bill which he took from his wallet.

Lila's dismay and confusion were doubled. The bill was exactly similar to the others he had given her, and to those which the collector had declared to be counterfeit.

What could she say? Finding no words, and feeling that she must do something, she extended her hand to take the bill, then drew it back, shivering involuntari'

Summoning her courage by a violent effort, she faltered:

"Mr. Knowlton, that bill—I—I cannot take it."

And as Knowlton's face filled with surprise and something else that resembled uneasiness, and before he could speak she continued:

"The other day our collector showed me one of the bills you had given me, and asked where I got it. He said they were counterfeit. I thought you would want to know."

Knowlton had turned pale and was staring at her fixedly.

"Well?" he said.

"Shall I tell him?"

"Why—didn't you?" the young man stammered eagerly.

"No. I thought I had better speak to you first. You see—" Lila's voice faltered and ceased, her face reddening to the tips of her ears with shame.

Knowlton picked up the bill he had laid on the counter and returned it to his pocket. His hand trembled nervously, and his voice was low and uncertain as he said:

"If it's all the same to you, I—it would be better not to tell him. I shall not bother you with more of them. And I—I thank you," he added, as he turned away. That was all.

Lila turned to her desk, sick at heart; and when little Dumain bustled over a few minutes later with the intention of learning something of what Knowlton had said to her, he found her in tears.

"*Mon Dieu!*" he gasped. The sight of Miss Williams crying was unprecedented and, to Dumain, extremely painful. "What is zee mattaire?"

"Nothing," said Lila. "I have a headache. For

goodness' sake, don't stand and stare at me!''

Whereupon Dumain retreated to the corner where he had left the others in secret session. He decided not to tell them about Lila's tears, being convinced that if he did so they would proceed to murder Knowlton on Broadway at high noon.

Besides, he had an idea that the tears were caused by Knowlton's having said farewell, in which case there would be no necessity for action on the part of the Erring Knights. Dumain was certainly not a coward; but he was—let us say—discreet.

Lila was overwhelmed with shame and humiliation. She had told Knowlton that she had lied for his sake, which amounted to a confession of her interest in him and regard for him. He must have understood. And he had muttered a perfunctory thank you, and walked away.

But perhaps he took it as a matter of course. Perhaps he regarded her as one of those creatures to whom deception is natural—of loose morals and conscience— whose aid may be depended upon by any stray enemy of society and morality.

This thought was unbearable. Lila clenched her fists tightly till the little pink nails bit sharp rings in the white palms of her hands.

Why had he not explained? It could have been but for one of two reasons: either he was guilty and could not, or he regarded her opinion as unimportant and did not care to.

And if he were guilty; but that was impossible. John Knowlton, the man to whom she had given her heart unreservedly, and forever, a counterfeiter—a criminal? It could not be.

There remained only the supposition that he cared so little about her that her good opinion was a matte of indifference to him. And this, though mortifying, was bearable. Still was she filled with shame, for he had heard her confession, and had made no sign.

Most probably she would never know, for she felt convinced that she would never see Knowlton again. She had been unable to avoid overhearing a great deal of the conversation of the Erring Knights concerning him, and Dumain himself had told her that they had warned him to stay away from the Lamartine.

She smiled bitterly as she thought of that warning. If her anxious protectors only knew how little likelihood there was of Knowlton's taking the trouble either to harm her or to make her happy!

For hours these thoughts filled her mind, confusedly, without beginning or end. It seemed that the afternoon would never pass.

Gradually the lobby filled, and for a time business at the telegraph desk was almost brisk. The Erring Knights strolled in and out aimlessly. From the billiard room down the hall came the sound of clicking balls and banging cues.

Now and then the strident voice of the Venus at the cigar stand rose above all other sounds as she gave a pointed retort to an intimate or jocular remark of a customer. At intervals the bell on the hotel desk gave forth its jarring jingle.

At five o'clock the crowd in the lobby began to disappear. There came intervals in the confused hum of voices and steps. Half past five arrived; and six. Lila put on her hat and coat and arranged the papers on her deck.

She would not linger tonight; that was over, she told herself. Henceforth she would be sensible, and—and forget.

The lobby was nearly empty except for the Erring

Knights, who were gathered in the corner, seemingly engaged in a hot discussion. Lila noticed that Sherman, while apparently attentive to his companions, was watching her covertly, and she surmised that he intended to follow her as he had the evening before, and escort her home.

Why not? she asked herself bitterly. At least he cared.

She stooped to put on her rubbers, and, having some difficulty with one of them, remained for some time with her head lowered. When she sat up, with flushed face and hair disarranged, she found herself looking into the eyes of John Knowlton.

He stood by her desk, hat in hand, with an air of embarrassment and hesitation. Evidently he was waiting for her to speak; but, overcome with surprise, she found no words.

A glance over his shoulder showed her the Erring Knights standing across the lobby, regarding Knowlton with open hostility.

Finally he spoke.

"I feel I owe you an explanation," he said with an apparent effort. "I hope you don't think there was anything wrong about—what you told me this morning."

Lila's wounded pride came to her assistance and gave her strength. This was the man to whom she had given so much, and from whom she had received so little. Worse, he was aware of her weakness. Yet must he learn that she was worthy of his respect, and her own. And yet—why had he returned? She hesitated.

"I don't know what to think," she said doubtfully.

"It will take some time to explain," said Knowlton. "And I want you—if you can—to think well of me.

I wonder if you'd be angry if I asked you to go to dinner with me. Will you go?''

Lila caught her breath, while her heart contracted with a joy so keen as to be painful. Of course she ought not to accept his invitation. She felt that that would somehow be wrong.

Besides, he must not be allowed to believe that her favors could be had for the asking. But how her heart was beating! And she said:

"I—I am not dressed for it, Mr. Knowlton."

"We could go to some quiet little place," he urged. "I know you have been thinking horrible things of me today, and with reason. And of course, if you think I am not—not worthy"—

"Oh, it is not that!" Lila exclaimed.

"Then, will you go?"

And though Lila was silent, he must have read her answer in her eyes, for he picked up her umbrella and opened the gate of the railing for her, and they started down the lobby side by side.

Halfway to the door Lila halted and turned to face the Erring Knights, who had neither stirred nor spoken since the entrance of Knowlton.

"Good night!" she called cheerily.

But there was no response. The six gallant protectors returned her gaze in grim and frigid silence.

A little back of the others Lila saw Sherman's dark face, with his lips parted in a snarl of hate. She shivered slightly and turned to her companion.

"Come!" she said, and in spite of her effort to control it her voice trembled a little.

Knowlton opened the door and they passed out together.

CHAPTER VI.

THE TRANSFORMATION.

A WAITING TAXICAB STOOD OUTSIDE THE HOTEL. Knowlton helped Lila inside and got in after her. "Now," he asked, "where shall we go?"

Lila murmured something about her dress, and left the decision to him. Knowlton leaned forward and spoke to the driver.

"Restaurant Lucia, Thirty-seventh Street, near Sixth Avenue."

The driver nodded and started the cab north on Broadway.

Knowlton sat upright in his corner, intuitively divining Lila's wish for a period of silence to adjust her thoughts. The cab went forward by fits and starts owing to the heavy traffic.

Light and shadow came and went through the windows as they passed glaring cafés and theaters, or darkened shops and office buildings. The air was crisp and tingling.

Lila felt herself transported to a scene in the *Arabian Nights*. Not the gorgeous palaces, or the tricks of magicians, or the dark and mysterious passages, but the spirit of wonder.

This lies not ever in mere things, but in the heart. To ride up Broadway in a taxicab at half past six of a December evening may mean anything, or nothing. To the tired businessman it means a convenient but expensive method of getting home to dinner. To the painted woman it means one of the advantages to be derived from an easy conscience. To Lila it meant love and romance and youth and hope.

She did not stop to analyze her feelings; they surged through her heart and brain tumultuously with a glorious gladness. She was discovering for herself what a great philosopher has called "the sweetness of facts."

She was with Knowlton. He was able to explain the counterfeit bills. He did care about what she thought of him.

She was grateful to him for his silence. Certainly her mind needed readjustment. For two days she had been miserable and unhappy to the verge of despair.

A few minutes ago she had actually been ready to allow Sherman to accompany her home. The smile which this thought brought to her lips was not very complimentary to Mr. Sherman.

And then, with the suddenness of an impetuous Jove, the prince of her dreams had arrived and carried her off in his chariot! Was it not enough to make a girl wish for time to get her breath?

She was so deep in her contemplation of "the sweetness of facts" that she was positively startled by the sound of Knowlton's voice announcing that they had reached their destination.

He helped her from the cab and paid the driver, and they entered the restaurant.

The Restaurant Lucia was one of those places to be found, by the initiated, here and there from the Battery to Harlem, where one may obtain excellent food, well cooked and well served, without the fuss and glitter and ostentation of the "lobster palaces." It does not pretend to Bohemianism, and is therefore truly Bohemian.

As Knowlton and Lila entered the dining room by a door set two or three steps lower than the sidewalk, the orchestra, consisting of a pianist, a 'cellist, and two violinists, was finishing a Spanish melody. They walked down the aisle to the right to the clapping of hands, and Lila turned to observe the little orchestra leader, who was bowing right and left with the air, and the appearance, of an Italian duke.

Knowlton halted at a table near the wall toward the rear, and they seated themselves opposite each other. It was a little early for dinner in the Restaurant Lucia; it was not yet half filled. Lila glanced about curiously as she took off her gloves and gave the inevitable tug to her hat.

Knowlton, being a man, immediately proceeded to business.

"Will you have oysters, or clams?" he asked. "And will you have a cocktail?"

Lila made a grimace.

"I couldn't possibly decide what to eat," she declared. "You select. And I—I don't care to drink anything."

Knowlton regarded her with the usual mild surprise of a man at a woman's lack of interest in the sublime topic of food, and entered into a serious conversation on that subject with the waiter, while Lila amused herself by a survey of the dining room. She was seated facing the door, to which Knowlton's back was turned.

Knowlton, having completed his order, tossed the menu aside and looked across at his companion. Her elbow was resting on the table, with her chin in her cupped hand.

Her eyelids drooped as though reluctant to leave unveiled the stars they guarded, and a tiny spot of pink glowed on either cheek.

Suddenly, as Knowlton sat watching her silently, her hand dropped to the table and she gave a startled movement, while her face filled with unmistakable alarm. She glanced at Knowlton and met his questioning gaze.

"Mr. Sherman," she whispered excitedly. "He just entered the restaurant, and is sitting at a table near the door. He saw us."

Knowlton started to turn round to see for himself, but thought better of it and remained facing his companion.

"The Erring Knights," he said easily, with an indifferent shrug of the shoulders. "Assuredly, they protect you with a vengeance. But I can hardly compliment them on their choice of an emissary."

"But surely it must be—he is here by accident," said Lila. "They would not have sent him."

"Perhaps he sent himself," Knowlton suggested. "I happen to know that he is an adept at the gentle art of shadowing."

Lila's face flushed with annoyance.

"He has no right"—she began impetuously. "I hate him. He has spoiled my dinner—I mean, our dinner."

At this Knowlton, who was hiding his own annoyance, protested with a laugh that it would take more than Sherman to spoil it for him. His enjoyment, he declared, rested only with his companion. Lila sighed and poised her fork daintily over her plate of clams.

"Does the creature eat?" asked Knowlton presently.

Lila glanced toward the door.

"No," she replied. "He drinks."

Knowlton chuckled at her tone of disgust and declared that he felt a certain pity for Mr. Sherman.

But gradually, as the dinner progressed, they forgot his presence. Knowlton exerted himself to that end, and soon had Lila laughing delightedly at a recital of his boyhood experiences in the country.

Under the influence of his sparkling gaiety her cheeks resumed the healthy flush of youth and health, and her eyes glowed with pleasure and animation.

"Not so much—please!" she protested, as Knowlton heaped her plate high with asparagus tips. "You know, I am not a poor, overworked farmer, as you seem to have been. Though, to tell the truth, I don't believe half of it."

"I don't blame you," said Knowlton cheerfully. "In fact, I don't believe it all myself."

For a time there was silence, while Lila listened dreamily to the orchestra, and her companion frowned portentously over the delicate and stupendous task of apportioning the salad.

"And now," Knowlton said presently, placing the spoon in the empty bowl with a sigh of relief, "what about yourself? I shall expect you to be just as frank as I have been. I already know your age, so you may leave that out."

Lila felt a little thrill find its way to her heart. Was it possible he remembered their first meeting so well?

Of course, she did, but that was different. She decided to find out.

"And pray, what is my age?" she asked.

"Twenty," said Knowlton promptly. "Did you think I had forgotten? I guessed nineteen. You said twenty."

Then he did remember! Lila paused a moment to keep a tremor from her voice as she said:

"Then there is little to tell. I get up in the morning and go to work. I go home at night and go to bed. That's all."

"Fair play!" Knowlton protested. "Now that I have a chance to learn something I shan't let you escape. So far I've been able to learn just one thing about you."

"And that is?"

"That you're an angel."

Lila did not know whether to be angry or amused. The smile on her companion's face added to her uncertainty; but Knowlton hastened to relieve her of her embarrassment.

"I had it from Dougherty," he continued. "On the morning of my admission to the charmed circle of the Erring Knights I asserted my right to information. Tom gave it to me something like this."

Knowlton curled his upper lip and puffed out his cheeks, in imitation of the ex-prizefighter.

" 'Listen here, Knowlton. All we know is that she's an angel. And that's all you need to know.' And," Knowlton finished, "as he seemed to know what he was talking about, I believed him."

Lila opened her mouth to reply, then stopped short and gazed at the door. Then she turned to her companion with a sigh of relief.

"He's gone," she announced.

"Who?" asked Knowlton.

"Mr. Sherman."

"Oh! I had forgotten all about him." Knowlton beckoned to the waiter and asked for his check before he continued: "Well, this time we shall follow him—at least, out of the restaurant."

"Oh!" cried Lila. "Must we go?"

"Unless we are willing to be late," Knowlton smiled, glancing at his watch. "It is 8:15. It will take us ten minutes to get to the theater."

"To the theater!"

Lila's eyes were round with surprise.

On his part, Knowlton pretended surprise.

"Surely you wouldn't think of sending me away so early?" he exclaimed. "I supposed that was understood."

Lila shook her head firmly.

"I couldn't possibly," she declared.

"Have you anything else to do?"

Lila did not answer.

"Do you mean you don't want to go?"

Lila said: "I mean I can't."

"Say you don't want to go."

She was silent.

Knowlton looked at her.

"Is there any reason?"

"Dozens," Lila declared. "For one, my dress. I have been working in it all day. Look at it."

Knowlton did so. It was of dark-blue ratine, with white lace collar and cuffs, and its simple delicacy appeared to him to leave nothing to be desired. After a scrutiny of some seconds, during which a flush of embarrassment appeared on Lila's cheeks, he looked up at her face and smiled.

"Is that all?" he demanded.

Lila, after some faltering and hesitation, admitted that it was.

"Then you must go," Knowlton declared. "I won't take a refusal. Your dress is perfectly all right. You look a thousand times more—I mean—I would rather be—"

He covered his confusion by rising from his chair to help Lila with her coat. She, still protesting, drew on her gloves and accompanied him to the door. There Knowlton halted to ask if she would choose the theater. She replied that she had no preference.

"But you will go?"

Lila nodded. Knowlton thanked her with a look as they left the restaurant and started toward Broadway.

At the corner he hailed a taxicab and ordered the driver to drive them to the Stuyvesant Theater, having wrapped Lila snugly in the laprobe, for the night was freezing.

"Are you tired or cold?" he asked, bending toward her solicitously.

"Neither," Lila answered, "but very comfortable. I wish you would take your share of the robe."

Knowlton protested that he was really too warm already, while he bit his tongue to keep his teeth from chattering.

Broadway was sprinkled with cabs and limousines, but the sidewalks were almost deserted. Your New Yorker is no cold-weather man. On moderate days he wears an overcoat, and on cold ones he stays indoors.

Knowlton and Lila arrived at the theater barely in time to be seated before the raising of the curtain, and Lila had not even time to note the name of the play. She looked at her program; the lights were down and it was too dark to read. She leaned over to Knowlton.

"The name of the play?" she whispered.

He whispered back: "It hasn't any."

She looked at the stage, and, in her wonder at what she saw, forgot to wonder at the oddity of his reply.

I shall not attempt to describe the scene. It was the ambitious attempt of a daring manager to stage Gautier's famous fantasy in the eleventh chapter of *Mlle. de Maupin*.

He had succeeded, if not perfectly, at least admirably. There were the glowworms and the pea blossoms and the eyes of dwarfs and gnomes and the distance of apple-green. The characters, with their pointed steeple-shaped hats and swollen hose, wandered aimlessly about with an infinite grace and talked of this and that and nothing in soft, musical tones of carelessness.

To Lila, who had certainly not read *Mlle. de Maupin*, the scene was inexplicable, but wonderful. Throughout the entire act she held her breath in amazed delight, expecting every minute that something would happen. Nothing happened, of course; but she was not disappointed. When the curtain fell she sighed deeply and turned to her companion.

He was smiling at her curiously.

"What do you think of it?" he asked.

Lila answered him with a series of "Oh!" and "Ahs!" and exclamations of delight.

"But," she managed to say finally, "I don't understand it a bit."

Knowlton told her of the origin of the fantasy, and explained that she couldn't very well be expected to understand it, since it had neither beginning nor end, nor cause nor reason.

"It wasn't made to be understood," he finished. "It was made to enjoy."

The two following acts were similar to the first, with

a change of setting and costumes. Throughout Lila sat in breathless delight, with now and then a glance at Knowlton to see if he were sharing her enjoyment.

Always as she looked at him his eyes turned to meet hers, and they exchanged a smile of sympathy and understanding. When the curtain fell for the last time Lila turned to him with a sigh of regret.

"Oh," she said, "if the world were only like that!"

"It would be amusing," Knowlton agreed "But we would die of *ennui*. It would be too easy. No struggle, no passion, no hate, no love."

Lila was silent as they made their way out of the theater. The audience had been small, and they had no difficulty to find a cab at the door. As Knowlton seated himself at her side he leaned forward and told the driver to drive to the Manton.

Lila laid a hand on his arm.

"Please," she protested earnestly. "I must go home, really. I couldn't eat a bite, anyway; and it would spoil the play. I want to stay in fairyland."

Knowlton felt the earnestness of her tone and forbore to insist. He gave Lila's address to the driver, and they started uptown.

"And now to come to the point," said Knowlton suddenly, after several minutes of silence, during which the cab had sped swiftly northward.

His tone, Lila thought, was constrained and forced. It gave her a vague uneasiness and she asked what he meant.

"About the counterfeit bills," Knowlton explained.

He appeared to be speaking with difficulty, like a man who forces himself to mention an unpleasant subject.

Lila realized with a feeling of surprise that she had

forgotten entirely the events that had caused her such great anxiety and pain but a day before.

His words came to her with a distinct shock. She looked at him and wondered at herself for having supposed, under any circumstances, that such a man as John Knowlton could do anything wrong.

"Of course, I must explain—" the young man was continuing, when Lila interrupted him.

"Please, Mr. Knowlton, don't! There is nothing to explain—or rather there is nothing which needs to be explained. I was silly ever to imagine that you could be—I mean, please don't talk about it."

Knowlton tried to insist, but without eagerness.

"But that is what we are here for. It was my excuse for asking you to come. I admit the subject is painful and embarrassing to me, but I promised to explain and I ought to."

"But why?"

"Because I want you to believe in me and be my friend. I—I want you to think well of me."

"Well, I do," said Lila. The protecting darkness hid the glowing color that mounted to her face. "I am your friend. There!" She held out a tiny gloved hand.

Knowlton took it and held it for a moment in his own. But he did not smile, and his manner was uneasy and constrained.

"Please let's forget it," Lila begged. "Do you want to spoil my whole evening?"

Knowlton said "No" without enthusiasm.

"Well, you are doing it," Lila declared with pretended severity. "And if you don't improve within one minute I shall complain of you to Mr. Dumain and Mr. Dougherty and Mr. Driscoll."

This brought a smile.

"I imagine that will be unnecessary," Knowlton observed.

"But I can goad them on."

"That would be unfair. They are already six to one. I had counted on having you on my side."

"And so I would be if you weren't so gloomy."

"Then from now on I shall be Momus himself," laughed Knowlton. "We are already at Ninety-sixth Street, and surely I can wear the mask for three minutes."

He began with an imitation of Pierre Dumain expounding the scientific value of the game of billiards, and soon had Lila laughing unrestrainedly. By the time the cab stopped at her door he was as gay as she.

As the driver opened the door of the taxi Knowlton sprang out and assisted Lila up the steps of the apartment-house stoop. At the door Lila stopped and held out her hand.

"Have you your key?" asked Knowlton.

Lila produced it from a pocket in her coat. He unlocked the door and she passed within. She thanked him and gave him her hand, and fluttered up the stairs. At the top of the first flight she halted. She had not heard the door close.

"Good night!" she called softly, and up to her came Knowlton's voice in return:

"Good night!" Then the sound of the closing door.

Lila entered her room and lit the gas. It seemed strangely unfamiliar. Here she had wept and read and slept and prayed. But here she had never been happy. For two years—since her mother's death—it had been her home. Home! Rather it had been her cage.

But now, as she sat on the edge of the bed without having removed her hat or coat or gloves, the room seemed transformed. The dingy little dressing table, the chairs, the pictures, seemed to have assumed a new form of beauty.

The ticking of the little marble clock on the mantel, that had been mournful and melancholy and disconsolate, sounded a cheerful note of sympathy. For Lila was happy!

Half an hour later she was standing in front of her mirror, gazing at the reflection of a rosy, flushed face and deep, liquid, lustrous eyes. "Why," she said aloud, "that can't be me! I never saw anything so beautiful in my life!"

Then, laughing happily at her own foolishness, she got into bed and snuggled cozily beneath the covers.

CHAPTER VII.

THE ENEMY'S ROOF.

KNOWLTON, HAVING BID LILA GOOD NIGHT, stood irresolutely for a moment with his foot on the step of the taxicab. He thought of walking downtown and mentally calculated the distance—seventy blocks—three miles and a half. He looked at his watch; it was a quarter to twelve, and the cold had increased with the deepening of the night.

Drawing his coat closer round him and stepping into the cab, he gave the driver the number of his rooms on Thirtieth Street.

As the vehicle started forward the face of the man inside was set sternly, almost painfully. His eyes stared straight ahead, his lips formed a thin, straight line, and now and then the muscles of the cheek quivered from the tensity of the jaws.

Thus he remained, motionless, for many minutes; evidence of a conflict of no common strength and importance. He was insensible to the movement of the cab, to the streets through which they passed, even to the nipping cold. He gave a start of surprise when the cab stopped and looked up to find himself arrived at his destination.

He sprang out, handed the driver a bill, and started toward the entrance of the apartment house.

"Wait a minute, mister!" came the driver's voice. "This is a ten-spot."

"All right; keep it," replied Knowlton.

He halted and turned to observe the curious phenomenon—a New York taxicab driver who announced that he had been paid too much! He heard his cry of "Thank ye sir!" and saw him mount his seat and send his taxi off at a speed that carried him out of sight in three seconds.

As Knowlton turned again to mount the stoop he noticed a big red limousine approaching from the east slowly. He glanced at it in idle curiosity as it stopped directly in front of his own door, then began to move up the steps, feeling in his pocket for his key.

Suddenly he was halted by a shout from the street:

"Is that you, Knowlton?"

The voice was Tom Dougherty's.

Knowlton, mastering his surprise, with his hand on his key in the door, turned and sang out:

"Yes. What do you want?"

Three men had got out of the limousine and were standing on the edge of the sidewalk. In front was Dougherty; Knowlton recognized him by his slouch hat. Dougherty made a step forward as he called in a lower tone:

"Come here."

Knowlton understood, of course, what was up. That is, he knew why they wanted him—but what did they want? And, being curious and by no means a coward he decided to find out. He stepped back to the side-walk and across to the three men.

"Well?" he inquired coolly.

Dougherty pointed to the limousine.

"Get in!" he commanded.

The other two men, whom Knowlton saw to be Sherman and Jennings, made a cautious step forward, evidently with the intention of getting between him and the door.

"Take it easy," advised Knowlton, smiling at them composedly. "If I want to go in," he nodded toward the door of the apartment house, "I'll go. And now, Dougherty, what is it you want? I'd advise you not to try any tricks."

"To Hades with your advice!" put in Sherman. "This is our game."

"Shut up!" growled Dougherty. Then he turned to Knowlton. "You know why we're after you. Dumain and Driscoll and Booth are waiting at Dumain's rooms. We'll give you a fair chance in ten-round go with Driscoll. But, believe me, he'll beat you up right. And if he don't, I will."

Knowlton gazed at the ex-prizefighter for a second in silence, then started toward the limousine.

"You say this is a square deal, Dougherty?" he asked, turning suddenly.

Dougherty, amazed at his coolness, replied that it was.

Knowlton continued:

"I'm willing to take you on one at a time, but I don't care to walk into a trap."

He looked at Dougherty for another minute, ap-peared to hesitate, then jumped up on the seat in front beside the chauffeur.

"You'll freeze, man!" exclaimed Dougherty, while

Sherman and Jennings got in the limousine. "Get inside with us."

"No thanks," said Knowlton dryly. "I prefer the cold."

Dumain's rooms were only a few blocks away, and within five minutes the limousine had stopped in front of them. The cold wind rushing against Knowlton with stinging force had set every nerve in his body tingling and filled him with a glow of exhilaration.

Dumain's rooms—on Twenty-first Street a little west of Sixth Avenue—were on the first floor of a four-story apartment house, with an old-fashioned high stoop leading to the door. Up the steps of this went Dougherty, with Knowlton at his side, followed by Sherman and Jennings. In answer to their ring Dumain himself opened the door.

"Did you get heem?" he asked.

"I came," Knowlton answered before Dougherty could speak.

Dumain led them down a long hall and into a room on the right.

Evidently this room—a large one—had been arranged for the expected encounter. It was bare of furniture save for a row of chairs along the further wall. The floor was partly covered with a coarse Wilton rug.

At one end, in the center, was a high mantel loaded down with vases, bronzes, trays, and pasteboard boxes—these latter evidently containing some of the paraphernalia of the palmist. The two windows at the opposite end were closed and the shades drawn.

Driscoll and Booth were seated on two of the chairs along the wall when the newcomers entered.

"All ready, eh?" Knowlton observed, standing in the middle of the room and looking around with an amused smile.

Dougherty regarded him with undisguised admiration.

"By gad, you're a cool one!" he remarked.

Knowlton walked over to a chair and sat down without answering him.

The others were gathered together in a group by the door, consulting in undertones, with occasional glances at Knowlton. Finally, with nods of satisfaction and at a word from Dumain, they crossed the room and seated themselves.

The little Frenchman stood in front of them and spoke:

"We deed not come here to talk. I will say very leetle. I will mention no names. Zat is, I will not mention her name. Eet ees to be a fight for ten rounds by Meester Dreescoll and Meester Knowlton. Meester Dougherty will referee. Meester Knowlton must have what you call a second. Will you be heem, Sherman?"

"No!" Knowlton interposed. "I want no second. I shan't need any."

Dougherty sprang to his feet impatiently.

"Strip, then!" he shouted.

The combatants lost no time. Driscoll carried a chair to the corner of the room near the door; Knowlton carried one to the opposite corner. Then, stripping bare to the waist, each seated himself to await the call of the referee. Booth stood by Driscoll's chair, holding his overcoat. The others were seated in the chairs along the wall.

"Two-minute rounds," announced Dougherty from the middle of the room. He was in his shirtsleeves and was holding a watch in his hand. Then, stepping to one side, he called:

"Time!"

The fighters, as they advanced to the center of the

room, appeared to be evenly matched in weight and build. Their white bodies, trim and supple, glowed from the sudden contact with the air, for even within the room it was chilly.

But a closer inspection revealed a difference. Driscoll was a little too fat; his arms too plump and smooth. And his step to the practised eye lacked elasticity and lightness. His eyes gleamed with a wariness and alertness which it was impossible to communicate to the body, handicapped as it was.

A little murmur of astonishment ran along the quartet of spectators as they turned their eyes on Knowlton, and the referee, in his surprise, nearly dropped his watch.

Here was a man worth looking at. His flesh, white and smooth as his opponent's, showed little muscular ripples as he bent forward in a posture of defense, and his arms, firm and of goodly length, displayed magnificent knots on the inner forearm and from the elbow to the shoulder. His waist was small, and under the skin on the back of the shoulders appeared tightly drawn, steel-like bands of muscle.

Exclamations in undertones came from the row of chairs:

"Heavens! The man's a white hope!"

"I'd hate to be in Driscoll's place!"

"Where d'ye suppose he got it?"

On the face of Sherman, who was silent, appeared a curious expression of mingled fear and hatred.

Really, there was no mystery about it. The athletic records of a certain Western university could have explained all in five minutes. This was the man who had made it necessary for that university to add another cabinet to their trophy and medal room.

But, feeling as they did that their man was hopelessly beaten on form, the Erring Knights nevertheless urged him on with cheering words as the fighters squared off.

"Go to it, Driscoll!"

"Eat him up, Bub!"

"Soak the big dub!"

And Driscoll did his best. He began by trying to outbox his opponent. But within the first twenty seconds Knowlton pulled down his guard with a clever feint and staggered him with a straight punch to the face.

Driscoll came back with a cheerful grin and by fast footwork and taking the fullest advantage of his longer reach, went to the end of the round without further damage. Knowlton went to his corner smiling.

The next three rounds were slow. Driscoll, afraid of his wind, tried once or twice to rush the fighting, but was unable to reach his man. Knowlton, always smiling; took it easy. His breath came as regularly as though he were sitting still.

The smile got on Driscoll's nerves. He knew he was being played with, and that aroused his anger. Time and again he aimed a blow at those lightly parted lips, only to find them a foot out of his reach.

He began to pant heavily and was unsteady on his feet as he walked to his corner at the end of the fourth round. Helpless rage possessed him as he looked across the room and saw Knowlton sitting in his chair with easy unconcern.

At the cry of "Time!" he gathered himself together and rushed at Knowlton with set teeth and glaring eyes. Knowlton, unprepared for the sudden onslaught, was caught off his guard and carried to the floor.

Shouts of encouragement came from the excited

spectators. Knowlton sprang to his feet. The smile was gone.

"Kill him, Driscoll!"

"You've got him going!"

"Put him to sleep!"

Again Driscoll rushed madly. But this time Knowlton was prepared. He stepped aside nimbly as a cat, and Driscoll stumbled and nearly fell. As he recovered his balance Knowlton turned and swung with his right.

It caught Driscoll on the ear and he went down like a shot. He was up at the count of three and, sobbing with rage, rushed again. The onlookers sprang to their feet in excitement.

This time Knowlton met the assault squarely and stopped it with a stiff punch.

"Time!" called Dougherty.

Everybody began to talk at once. Booth helped Driscoll to his corner. Blood was on his face and he breathed in quick, short gasps.

"Cut it, Bub," said Jennings, running over to him. "The big slob'll kill you."

Driscoll tried to grin, but wasted no breath on speech. He leaned back in his chair while Booth waved a towel wildly up and down in front of him. When he heard Dougherty call "Time!" for the sixth round he would have sworn that he had rested not more than ten seconds.

Cries came from the onlookers to "take it easy" and "watch him," but Driscoll heeded them not. His blood was boiling and the face of his opponent appeared to him in a dim and wavering haze.

Toward it he rushed in blind fury. Knowlton stepped back and there was a dull thud as his fist landed on Driscoll's shoulder.

Driscoll staggered, but kept his feet. Again and

again he rushed, and again and again he was stopped by Knowlton's fist. It was evident that Knowlton was putting no force in his blows, but was merely stopping the rushes with extended arm.

This enraged the spectators.

"End it, darn you!" howled Booth.

Knowlton smiled—and ended it. Not waiting for Driscoll's rush, he leaped forward and swung with his right. Driscoll, receiving the blow on his left side, staggered and swayed, then sank to the floor, a limp, helpless heap.

Knowlton gave the prostrate form a single glance, then walked to his corner and sang out coolly: "Next!"

"I'll next you, you bruiser!" The voice, filled with tears of rage, was Dougherty's. He had sprung to Driscoll's corner and was removing his vest and shirt.

The others lifted Driscoll, assisted him to the side of the room, and, wrapping his overcoat closely about him, seated him in a chair. His eyes were closed, and Booth stood at his side to support him.

Jennings ran over to help Dougherty. Sherman sat silent, the muscles of his face twitching queerly. Little Dumain was jumping up and down in the intensity of his excitement.

"I hope he keels you!" he screamed, shaking a fist at Knowlton.

"*Chacun tire de son côte,*" said Knowlton calmly.

"*Mon Dieu! Français!*" shrieked Dumain. "Eet ees degradation!"

Knowlton laughed at him.

Dougherty, stripped to the waist, advanced to the middle of the room and pushed the little Frenchman aside.

"Come on," he said grimly to Knowlton. "We

don't need a referee. This is no boxing match. It's a fight, and you'll soon find it out.

Dumain retreated to the side of Booth. Sherman rose from his chair and stood in front of it. Driscoll opened his eyes for the first time, and kept them open.

The battle that followed was worth the price of a ringside seat at Madison Square Garden.

Within the first minute Knowlton discovered that the man he was facing was by no means a tyro. He had thought that Dougherty, completely out of condition, would be unable to withstand even the crudest kind of attack and had led with a double swing. Dougherty stepped back cleverly, waited the exact fraction of a second necessary, and then lunged forward like a panther.

Knowlton found himself on the floor with blood streaming from his nose, while the onlookers shrieked with ecstasy. He regained his feet warily, and, changing his mind as to the capabilities of his opponent, altered his tactics to suit.

Dougherty was fighting with all the cunning at his command. He realized that he was handicapped by the shortness of his wind, but figured that this was nearly, if not quite, equalized by the fact that Knowlton was not fresh. He did not throw himself away, as he had done in the encounter with Driscoll in the billiard room of the Lamartine. Instead, he called into play all his old-time ring knowledge and relied on superior tactics and skill. He waited for another break on the part of Knowlton.

But Knowlton was not to be caught napping again. He fought cautiously and warily, watching for an opening. He was not a pleasant sight to look at. The blood from his nose covered the lower half of his face and one side of his neck. His hair was matted with sweat, and his damp body glistened as he bent, now, forward, now to one side or the other, dodging, feinting, waiting.

For upward of five minutes they sparred and shifted, neither one gaining any advantage or landing a punishing blow. Then it began to get warmer.

Dougherty's foot happened to alight on an upturned corner of the rug, and as he glanced downward for the merest fraction of a second Knowlton closed in and landed a stinging jab on his face, turning him half round.

Instead of returning, he completed the circle, and, catching Knowlton unaware, staggered him with a left swing. They exchanged blows at close quarters, then clinched for a rest.

Knowlton was beginning to weaken under the prolonged strain. He had played with Driscoll longer than was good for his wind, and by now he was breathing heavily, while Dougherty was comparatively fresh. He tried to hold the clinch to get his wind, but Dougherty broke away.

Then, urged on by the exited and encouraging cries of the Erring Knights, Dougherty started in to finish it. By using his feet cleverly Knowlton avoided close fighting, but he received two body blows that made him grunt.

In recovering from the second of these he opened his guard, and a clean uppercut on the point of the jaw bent him backward and left him dazed.

Dougherty followed it up savagely, landing on the body at will, while Knowlton retreated blindly, covering his face with his hands. The onlookers howled with delight.

"Now get him, Tom!"

"It's all yours, old boy!"

"Keel heem!"

But they did not know Knowlton. Driven into a corner, apparently a beaten man, he felt within himself that stirring of the spirit that comes only on the boundary line of despair.

He had felt it before on the gridiron when, with his body a mass of bruises, he had hurled himself savagely forward and caught in a viselike grip and held the flying figure that sought to reach the sacred white line but a few feet away—on the track when, with aching legs and painful, gasping breath, he had by one last supreme effort passed the streak of white that seemed to his blurred eyes to have been there before him since the beginning of time. It is the spirit of the true fighting man.

He pushed Dougherty away from the corner, merely shaking his head slightly as he received a swinging blow full in the face. Then he fought back stubbornly, desperately, irresistibly.

Dougherty gave ground. It was by inches, but he retreated. Knowlton made no pretense at guarding. He simply fought.

The tide began to turn. Dougherty fell back more rapidly. His breath came heavily.

Perspiration ran in little rivulets down his cheeks and neck and body and stood out in large beads on his forehead. His face became fixed in a sort of unseeing stare, and his blows were wild and purposeless. He seemed unable to see his opponent.

"My God, Tom! Hit him! Can't you hit him?" cried Driscoll.

Knowlton pressed on unwaveringly. He landed blow after blow on his opponent's unprotected body. Dougherty attempted to swing, took a step forward, stumbled, and fell to his knees. It appeared to be the end.

But the end came from an unexpected quarter. As Dougherty fell, Sherman ran to the mantel at the end of the room, took from it a figure of bronze, and, before any one could guess his purpose, hurled it straight at Knowlton. Knowlton turned, threw up his arms, and sank to the floor with the blood streaming from a deep gash on his head just back of the temple.

For a moment there was dead silence, while all eyes were turned on Sherman. He stood motionless by the mantel, his face very white.

Then all was confusion. Dumain and Booth ran and bent over Knowlton, crying to Jennings to watch Sherman. Driscoll, by this time fully recovered, ran to Dougherty. Sherman started for the door, but was stopped by Jennings, whose eyes were filled with a dangerous light.

"Stay there, you——coward!" he bellowed.

Dougherty had pushed Driscoll aside and was kneeling by the side of Knowlton, and he at once took command of the situation.

Dumain was sent off for bandages and returned with a white linen shirt, tearing it into strips. Booth brought water and some towels, and Driscoll sought the telephone in the next room to call up a doctor. Jennings was assisting Dougherty in his attempt to stop the flow of blood.

Thus busied, they entirely overlooked Sherman.

Intercepted by Driscoll in his attempt to get away, he had returned to the farther corner of the room and had looked on at the scene of activity with an assumed indifference which did not entirely conceal his fear.

Moving suddenly, he felt his foot meet with an obstruction, and, looking down, saw Knowlton's clothing lying in a heap on the floor.

Quick as thought, and glancing at the others to see if he were observed, he stooped down and searched the pockets of the coat and vest. A shade of disappointment crossed his face at the result.

All that he was able to find was a long, black wallet in the inside pocket of the coat.

This he transferred to his own pocket and then assumed his former position of indifference.

In a few minutes the doctor arrived. He viewed the curious scene that greeted his eyes with professional stolidity and proceeded to examine his patient, who remained lying on the floor in the position in which he had fallen.

Without a word, save now and then a grunted command for water or other assistance, the doctor examined the wound and washed, stitched, and bandaged it.

At the commencement of the operation of stitching Knowlton opened his eyes, raised a hand to his head, and struggled to rise.

"Easy—easy. Lie still," said the doctor.

"What is it?" demanded Knowlton.

"They opened up your head," answered the doctor, still busily engaged with the bandage. "I'm putting it together again. Can you stand it?"

Knowlton smiled and closed his eyes.

"How about it?" asked Dougherty when the doctor finally arose.

"Very simple. Merely stunned. No danger. Twenty-five dollars," said the doctor.

"Can he go home?" asked Dumain, handing him the money.

The doctor shook his head.

"Bad—very bad. Too cold. Good night."

He opened the door, bowed, and departed.

"He's a talkative devil," observed Dougherty. "But how about Knowlton?"

"I have plenty of room. He can stay here," said Dumain.

Thus it was arranged, and John Knowlton, perforce, slept under the roof of the enemy.

Dougherty offered to stay with Dumain also, and the offer was eagerly accepted. The others departed at once in a body.

No one had anything to say to Sherman; they thought it hardly worthwhile. All's well that ends without the police.

Knowlton walked to his bed, supported by Dougherty. He was barely conscious and very weak.

They rubbed him down with witchhazel and put woolen pajamas on him and tucked him in like a baby. Then they went into the next room and sat down for a smoke.

Fifteen minutes later, thinking they heard a voice, they returned to their patient.

The voice was his own. He was talking in his sleep half deliriously.

"Lila!" he muttered. "Good-by, Lila! You know you are to live in fairyland and—hang you, Dougherty—no, I don't mean that—Lila—"

Dumain looked at Dougherty and said: "Zat is not for us, my friend."

Together they tiptoed silently out of the room.

CHAPTER VIII.

UNTIL TOMORROW.

WHEN YOU THROW A HEAVY LUMP OF HARD metal at a man and hit him on the side of the head you make an impression on him. I am not assuming artlessness or naïveté—I do not mean a physical impression.

What I wish to say is that his attitude and conduct toward you will undergo a sudden and notable change. He will be filled either with fear or with a desire for vengeance.

He will either betake himself to a distance where there is little possibility that you will present him with any more lumps of metal, or he will take firm and decided steps to return the one you have given him.

Of this rule of life the Erring Knights were perfectly aware, and they wondered much as to which of the two courses would be adopted by John Knowlton. As a matter of fact, he adopted neither—but let us not anticipate.

Knowlton's injury had proved even less serious than the doctor had declared it to be. On the morning after the fight Dumain and Dougherty had been amazed on awakening to find him fully dressed and holding his hat and overcoat, standing by the side of their bed.

"Sorry to disturb you," he had said, "but I am going. Thanks for your hospitality, Dumain. And for your—square deal—Dougherty."

Then, before they had time to recover from their surprise or utter a word, he had turned and disappeared.

For three days the Erring Knights had neither seen him nor heard from him, and they had about concluded that he had seen the wisdom of discretion and decided to practise it.

There was a general disposition to overlook Sherman's contribution to the little entertainment at Dumain's rooms. To be sure, they condemned his cowardice and violence. Since, however, it appeared to have had the desired effect on Knowlton without having inflicted any permanent injury, they were inclined to pardon it. Of course they despised him, as the law does its stool pigeon; but still they tolerated him.

It was with mingled feelings of anxiety and quiet joy that Lila lived through the three days during which Knowlton did not appear at the Lamartine. She had heard nothing of what had happened after Knowlton had left her at the door that evening, but she had not forgotten the appearance of Sherman at the Restaurant Lucia; hence her anxiety. She hugged her memory and waited.

On the morning of the fourth day her patience was rewarded by the following note, handed to her at her desk in the hotel by a messenger boy:

DEAR MISS WILLIAMS:
   I had expected to see you before this, but it has been
impossible, owing to an accident I encountered.
   I have been—let us say incapacitated.
   But will you dine with me this evening? I shall call at
the hotel for you at six.
                                   JOHN KNOWLTON.

   Lila flushed with happiness as she folded the note
and placed it in the bosom of her dress, at the same
time looking round for the messenger boy to take her
answer. But the boy had disappeared. What difference? She was to be with him again!

   As she glanced up and happened to meet the eye of
the Venus at the cigar stand she smiled involuntarily,
so brightly that Miss Hughes fairly grinned in sympathy.

   This little incident did not pass unnoticed. Dumain
and Dougherty, seated on the leather lounge in the
corner, saw the messenger boy hand her the note and
her change of color as she read it, and they glanced
at each other significantly.

   "I wonder!" Dougherty observed.

   "Yes," said Dumain positively. "Eet was from
heem. Zat expression of zee face—I know eet. He ees
a what you call eet comeback."

   And when they saw Lila place the note in her bosom
they were sure of it. Dumain sighed. Dougherty swore.
They departed for the billiard room to communicate
the sad intelligence.

   Thus were they not wholly surprised when, at six
o'clock that evening, they saw Knowlton enter the
lobby and walk to Lila's desk.

   There was a small, ugly, black patch over his right
ear; otherwise no indication of the injury he had received at Dumain's rooms.

He escorted Lila from the hotel, while the Erring Knights looked on in helpless silence.

Forthwith they entered into a warm discussion. Dougherty and Driscoll were for immediate and drastic action, though they were unable to suggest any particular method; Dumain, Jennings, and Booth advised delay and caution; Sherman grunted unintelligibly and left the hotel. They argued till seven o'clock, then dispersed and went their several ways without having decided on anything definitely.

Meanwhile Sherman, who had seen Knowlton and Lila enter a taxicab and followed them in another, was acting on his own account. He had his trouble for his pains.

They stopped at a restaurant for dinner, and Sherman shivered for an hour on the outside, waiting for them to reappear. He then followed them to a concert at Carnegie Hall, and kicked his heels in the foyer for two hours and a half—only to find at the end that they had left by another door, or that he had missed them in the crowd.

He swore violently under his breath, dismissed his cab, and walked at a furious pace to his room downtown, consumed by the fires of jealousy and hate.

Thenceforth the pursuit was one of relentless malignity. Sherman saw clearly that he was playing a losing game, and he redoubled his vigilance and activity with the energy of despair.

To see the woman he coveted thus smiling on another man appeared to him to justify any treachery or baseness, however vile; if, indeed, his evil mind were in need of any impetus.

He felt that he had some evidence of the correctness of his suspicions concerning Knowlton—for instance, the contents of the wallet he had taken from his coat at Dumain's rooms; but he knew that was not enough.

There was not a day during the month that followed but found him on the heels of his quarry. He followed him to cafés, restaurants, theaters, and concert halls, often in company with Lila. He followed him home and to the Lamartine, and on endless walks along the drive and through the park. And all without result.

Then there came a sudden change in Knowlton's habits. One weary morning he began calling at real-estate offices.

By the time they had reached the fifth of these, Sherman, who was following him, disguised with a blond wig and mustache, began to suspect that he had been discovered and was being played with. But he continued the chase.

Knowlton stopped in another real-estate office, and another. Here he remained for over an hour, while Sherman lurked in a nearby doorway. Then he emerged with a companion. Sherman will not soon forget what followed.

They led him to the downtown subway.

At Brooklyn Bridge they boarded a Coney Island Elevated train. On this they rode two or three stations past Bath Beach, then left it for a trolleycar, landing finally at a dreary, swamp-like tract of land, with but one or two houses in sight.

The inevitable cheap saloon was on the corner.

Here they remained for three hours—it was a cold, windy day in January—walking up and down the newly laid eighteen-inch sidewalks while Sherman sat in the saloon, trying to warm himself with cheap brandy and watching them through a window. They gave no sign of preparation to depart. Sherman could bear it no longer.

"I wonder what the fool is up to?" he muttered as

he boarded a trolley car. "Is he going to buy a home?"

And that brought with it a thought which caused him to squirm with pain.

He resumed his muttering: "By Heavens, he'll never get her! If I have to I'll see Colly. He can get the gang, and that means——"

A sinister smile overspread his face.

The fact about Knowlton was, he had got a job.

That evening at the Restaurant Lucia he surprised Lila by telling her of the day's occurrences. They were dining together nearly every evening now, though Knowlton was seldom seen at the Lamartine. He called for Lila at her room.

They had discovered a common love for music and books, and spent half of their evenings at concert halls and theaters. And when Lila felt indisposed or too tired to go out, or the weather was inclement, they remained in her room and Knowlton read stories and poems to her in his deep, well-modulated voice. Lila could never decide which she liked the more—the quiet, happy evenings at home or the more exciting pleasures to be found downtown.

But one thing she knew: never before had she tasted life. For the first time she saw its colors and scented its perfumes. Each day was a new delight; each look and word of Knowlton's a new sensation.

Knowlton spoke no word of love, and Lila wondered a little at it in her innocent way. He was attentive and solicitous even to the point of tenderness, and he was certainly not timid; but he never gave voice to any expression of sentiment.

Lila did not allow herself to be disturbed by this, nor did she employ any artifices—knowing none. She merely waited.

"Perhaps," she would whisper to herself at night when he had gone—"perhaps he will—will tell me—when—"

Then she would flush at the half-formed thought, innocent as it was, and brush it aside.

Nor did Knowlton ever talk of himself. Long since he had heard the story of Lila's life—how she had been left alone and penniless at the age of eighteen, and of the resulting struggle, courageous and at times almost desperate, to keep her head above the alluring and deadly waves of the metropolis. But he had given no confidence in return. He seemed forever entrenched behind an impenetrable barrier of reserve, and Lila never presumed to storm it.

Then, on the evening mentioned above, at the Restaurant Lucia, he suddenly lowered one of the gates of his barrier. They had been seated for some thirty minutes and were waiting for the roast, when, after a period of unusual taciturnity, he had suddenly burst forth:

"I got a job today."

Lila stared at him. At her frank surprise he seemed for a moment amused, then embarrassed. He continued, trying to speak lightly.

"Yes, at last I'm going to work. Real work. Something I've never tried before, but I think I'll like it."

"What—what is it?"

"Real estate. Selling a nice wet swamp in lots of twenty-five hundred square feet each to build houses on. Though I believe they are going to drain it." Then, as Lila remained silent, "But you aren't interested."

"I am," Lila contradicted. "But—as a young lady is supposed to say when she is asked a certain question—'this is so sudden.' I know so little about you."

This was almost a challenge, and it was Knowlton's

turn for silence. Then he found his tongue and soon had Lila laughing merrily at his description of the "lots" he was supposed to sell.

"But who will ever buy them?" she demanded.

"Anybody," Knowlton declared. "There are two million people living in Manhattan. Of these exactly one million nine hundred and sixty-nine thousand five hundred and forty-two think they want to live where they can have a vegetable garden and three chickens."

"And how about the other thirty thousand?"

"Oh, they're the real-estate agents. They know better."

But when Lila had finished laughing she became suddenly serious, saying:

"But that is shameful—to take such an advantage of ignorance."

Whereupon Knowlton spent a half hour defending the ethics of his new profession, with only fair success. Lila insisted that the customers were being duped and held to her belief with such tenacity that Knowlton finally became genuinely concerned.

Lila stopped suddenly.

"But, of course, it doesn't matter what I think," she said, and could have bitten her tongue off the moment afterward.

Knowlton colored slightly and opened his mouth as though to protest, then was silent. This increased Lila's embarrassment, and the waiter, approaching with their coffee, relieved an awkward situation by overturning one of the cups on the tablecloth.

From the restaurant they went to a concert.

"Some day, after they're filled in, I'll take you down and show you my swamps," said Knowlton as they parted three hours later at Lila's door. "And it does matter what you think. You know it does. Good night.''

They shook hands gravely, as was their custom.

Thereafter their meetings were less frequent. Knowlton explained that his new position took more time than he had expected and complained considerably of his trials and tribulations in the disposal of swamp lots.

But his appearance and manner contradicted him. There was a new light in his eyes, a new spring in his step, a new note of freedom in his voice. Lila wondered at it.

But he still managed to see her two or three evenings a week, and in one particular it would have seemed to the ordinary mind that he had lost a job instead of getting one.

Instead of taxicabs, they patronized the elevated and subway. Instead of orchids, he sent Lila roses and violets. Instead of *de luxe*, expensive editions his book presents were dressed in ordinary cloth and leather.

''To be perfectly frank, I must economize,'' he had explained one evening.

Lila had exclaimed:

''I am glad!''

Though he attempted all the way downtown to get her reason for this peculiar sentiment, she obstinately refused to give it. The truth was she hardly knew her reason herself, but she felt vaguely that both the fact and his frank confession of it brought them closer together.

This, she admitted to herself, meant happiness—the only happiness she could ever have.

As for Knowlton—well, the troubles of a salesman of real estate belong properly to comedy. That is a fact. But it would be unsafe to declare it in the presence of a real-estate salesman.

Knowlton was having his full share of the usual troubles, plus a few that were peculiar to himself. He will not soon forget that month.

In the first place he was perfectly well aware that he was being shadowed by Sherman. At times he was inclined to regard it as a joke; at others it caused him serious anxiety.

More than once he started for the Lamartine to discover whether he was acting for the Erring Knights or on his own account, but something held him back—perhaps a remembrance of Sherman's attempted bluff on the day of their first meeting. How much did Sherman know?

Then, as nothing resulted from the long-continued mysterious activities of the amateur detective, Knowlton gave him less and less thought.

Besides, he had no time for mysteries or Erring Knights. He was selling real estate. Not trying to—he was really selling it.

One evening when he called for Lila she found a taxicab waiting at the door as they descended the stoop.

"You see," Knowlton explained after they had settled themselves comfortably on the cushions and the cab had started forward, "I am getting to be quite a businessman. Really, I didn't think I had it in me. I'm fast becoming a bloated plutocrat. Someday you'll be proud of me."

"Not for that reason," said Lila.

"Then there's my last chance gone," Knowlton laughed. "For Heaven knows I've nothing else to be proud of—except that you are my friend," he added, suddenly serious.

But Lila, being in a gay mood, refused to humor him.

"Am I your friend?" she said thoughtfully.

"Aren't you?"

"I'm just trying to decide. I do like parts of you. When you are gay you're very jolly company. When you are serious you are impossible. It seems to me that I could get the most out of your friendship by taking a scientific course in the art of titillation."

"Who would you practise on?"

"Oh—my cat. Goodness knows she's grave enough—she needs it. And if it will work with her—"

"Cats never laugh," Knowlton declared solemnly.

"What frightful ignorance!" exclaimed Lila, with immeasurable scorn. "Did you never hear of the Cheshire?"

"Cheese?"

"No. Cat."

"But that was a grin. She didn't laugh. The distinction is subtle, but important."

"Well, anyway," Lila sighed, "it ought to be effective with you."

"But why do I need it?"

And thus they pretended to wrangle, with neither sense nor intention, till the cab stopped in front of the restaurant.

After dinner they attended a concert of one of the metropolitan string quartets. The program was short, and they arrived at Lila's room before half past ten, their hearts filled with the singing magic of Haydn.

"It's early," said Lila at the door. "Won't you come up and read to me—or talk?"

Knowlton replied that he had an engagement downtown at midnight, which left him an empty hour, and that he would rather spend it with her than anywhere else, and if she were sure he wouldn't annoy her—

"Come," Lila smiled, starting toward the stairs. Knowlton followed.

They talked of the concert. Then Knowlton read a portion of *Otho the Great*, while Lila lay back in an easy chair with closed eyes.

Now and then he would stop, asking softly, "Are you asleep?" and Lila would slowly open her eyes and smile at him and shake her head.

The tones of his voice, though lowered, filled the room with the musical cadences of the Poet of Beauty.

At the end of the second act he looked at his watch and closed the book suddenly, observing that he had only twenty minutes to get downtown.

"I suppose you are going to sell a swamp," said Lila, rising from her chair. "But what an hour!"

Knowlton did not answer. He found his coat and hat and said good night. At the door he turned and there was a new note in his voice—of seriousness and deep feeling—as he said:

"Tomorrow I shall have something to say to you. It has been hard to keep from telling you before, but I felt I had no right. Then—thank God—I shall be free. And I don't want to wait till evening. Will you lunch with me?"

Lila said "Yes," and before she could speak further Knowlton continued:

"I will call for you at the Lamartine at twelve o'clock, if that isn't too early. Tomorrow—at noon."

He turned and departed hurriedly, without giving her time to answer.

At the door he glanced at his watch—a quarter to twelve. He had dismissed the cab. He started at a rapid pace for the Elevated station on Columbus Avenue and barely caught a downtown train.

During the ride he kept glancing impatiently at his watch. Beside him on the seat was a late evening newspaper and he picked it up and tried to read, but was unable to compose himself. His midnight engagement was evidently not with a prospective customer.

At Twenty-eighth Street he left the train, walked east to Broadway, and entered a café on the corner.

The café was very similar to a thousand others on that street and in that neighborhood. It was half filled with men and completely filled with tobacco smoke. On the right was the bar; to the rear a series of partitions and doors leading to the inner rooms; on the left, a few tables and chairs and a row of stalls with leather seats surrounding wooden tables.

Knowlton glanced quickly round, noted that the hands of the clock above the bar pointed to a quarter past twelve, then walked slowly down the room in front of the stalls, glancing in at the occupants of each as he passed.

At the fifth stall he halted. The man seated there looked up quickly, and at sight of Knowlton rose to his feet and held out his hand.

"You're late," he said gruffly.

Knowlton, without replying, edged his way into the corner and sat down.

The man gazed at him curiously.

"What's the matter?" he asked. "You look pale."

"Don't talk so loud," said Knowlton, glancing at a group of three men who had halted within a few feet of the stall.

"All right," the other agreed good-naturedly. "Anyway, there's not much to say."

Reaching in his inside overcoat pocket, he drew forth a small flat package about the size of a cigar-box, wrapped in brown paper.

"Here's the stuff," he continued, placing the package on the seat beside Knowlton. "Shove it away quick. The usual amount—two hundred at one-tenth."

"I don't want it."

The words came from Knowlton in a whisper and with an apparent effort; but his manner was calm and unruffled.

The other half rose from his seat.

"Don't want it!" he cried; but at a warning glance from Knowlton he dropped back and continued in a whisper:

"What's up now? Cold feet? I always thought you was a baby. You've got to take it."

Knowlton repeated with calm decision:

"I don't want it. I'm through."

There ensued a controversy lasting a quarter of an hour. Knowlton was quiet but determined; the other, insistent and nervously excited. Several times Knowlton cautioned him to speak lower, as the same group of men remained standing near the stall, and others were constantly passing within earshot.

Finally, finding Knowlton utterly immovable, the man sighed resignedly and picked up the package and replaced it in his pocket.

"If you won't, you won't," he said. "And now, pal, let me tell you something: you're a wiser guy than I thought you was. They're after us. I beat it on the one-thirty tonight for Montreal."

"And yet—" Knowlton began indignantly.

"No, I wasn't." the other interrupted. "I wouldn't have let you sow it here. All I wanted was the two hundred, then I'd put you next. But you was next already."

Knowlton smiled, knowing the uselessness of any attempt to explain his own motives, and rose to depart, when the other, remarking that he was about due at the station, rose also, and they left the café together. In front they parted, with a smile and a good word. Knowlton walked home with a singing heart, thinking and dreaming of the morrow.

Twenty minutes later, in a room not twenty blocks away from the one where Knowlton was sleeping peacefully, two men were conversing in low, eager tones.

One, a tall, dark man with an evil countenance, was sitting on the edge of the bed dressed in pajamas; the other, with overcoat and hat, was standing in front of him.

"He spent twenty minutes at a café on Twenty-eighth and Broadway, talking with Red Tim," one was saying.

"And who is Red Tim?" asked the man on the bed.

"Number something-or-other in the gallery down at headquarters. Known from Frisco to the Battery. Just now he seems to be shoving the queer. He tried to give a bundle to your man, but he said he was through, and wouldn't take it.

"Evidently, though, he has some of it—your man, I mean. I could have taken Red Tim with the goods on, but I was looking out for you. It might have wised your man to the game."

The man on the bed was calm and thoughtful.

He asked some questions, and his eyes lit up with satisfaction at the answers.

"You've done well, Harden," he said finally. "I suspected this, and now I guess we've got him. It's too late to try to do anything tonight. Come round early in the morning; I may need you. Here's a ten. Good night."

The other, who had turned to go, stopped at the door to call back:

"Good night, Mr. Sherman."

CHAPTER IX.

BETRAYED.

THE ERRING KNIGHTS HAD FOR TWO MONTHS been divided into hostile camps, in support of two widely differing doctrines.

One division, consisting of Dumain, Driscoll, and Jennings, advanced the argument that it was no part of their duty to protect Lila against herself, and that if she chose to disregard their solemn warnings against Knowlton it was up to her.

The other division, to which Dougherty, Booth, and Sherman belonged, declared that they owed it to Miss Williams and to themselves to throw Knowlton from the top of the Flatiron Building, or cut him up into very small pieces, or tie him to a rock at the bottom of New York Bay.

They were all pretty good talkers, and they had many wordy discussions, renewed every time they saw Knowlton enter the lobby and take Lila out with him. They concocted many schemes, and at one time even went so far as to consider an offer from Sherman to procure the services of an East Side gang.

But they never did anything. They talked too much.

This was not without its utility. It furnished any amount of amusement to the Venus at the cigar stand.

If Dougherty approached to buy a cigar, or light one, she would whisper mysteriously, "Is he dead?" and pretend unbounded amazement when informed that Knowlton had been allowed to live a day longer. And all that was needed to start Dumain off on a frenzied oration was for her to observe scornfully: "Gee, I thought a Frenchman had some nerve!"

But most successful of all was her conundrum: "Why are the Erring Knights like the Republican party?" The answer, wrung from her after several days of entreaties and threats, was: "Because their protective system is on the fritz."

But to the Erring Knights themselves the thing was no joke. They talked and schemed and discussed and argued. Dumain and Driscoll were strong for moderation, and succeeded in holding the others in check, sometimes even going so far as to threaten to support Knowlton when the others became unusually reckless in their suggestions. But the attacks of Booth and Dougherty, and especially Sherman, were persistent, and they began to weaken.

On the morning following the events narrated in the preceding chapter Dougherty entered the lobby earlier than usual and found Dumain and Jennings talking to Miss Hughes. Walking over to the cigar stand, he grunted, nodded to the Venus, and pointed with his finger to his particular brand.

"A little off-color?" said Miss Hughes, setting the box in front of him on the counter.

"Best you've got?" Dougherty grunted, selecting a cigar.

"Oh, I meant you!" she grinned. "The cigars are all right. You look like you'd been playing the title role at a leather wedding."

"Huh!" Dougherty grunted.

"Let heem alone," Dumain smiled. "He has zee temperament. He ees veree dangerous."

This awakened Dougherty.

"Shut up!" he exploded. "When I'm like I am now I'm bad."

Whereupon Dumain giggled and Jennings roared. Dougherty started for them, and they retreated to the leather lounge in the corner.

Soon Driscoll arrived, and, finding Dougherty gazing moodily out of the window, took him over to join the others, stopping on the way to say good morning to Lila.

"Pipe the gown!" said Dougherty, with a backward motion of the head as they halted in front of Dumain and Jennings.

"Where?"

"Miss Williams. She's lit up like a cathedral. You know what that means."

The others protested ignorance, and he went on to explain:

"She's expecting Knowlton. Don't tell me. I can *see* it. And if that guy comes around here today I'll act up. Believe me, he's through."

That started them. The word "Knowlton" was enough. When Booth entered ten minutes later he found Dougherty holding his own valiantly against Dumain, Driscoll, and Jennings.

Booth brought fuel for the flame. His first words were: "I saw Knowlton last night." Then, seeing that he had their attention, he added: "With Miss Williams."

They stared at him and demanded particulars.

"It was by accident," he went on. "A friend of mine said he had tickets to a show, and asked me to go. I went. Great jumping frogs! He said it was a show. Well, it was in a hall—the hall was all right—on Forty-second Street.

"Four little dagoes came out with violins. For two solid hours they sat there, looking kinda sick. What did they play? Search me. It sounded like a—"

"But what about Knowlton?"

"Oh, yes! Well, when I went in who did I see two rows ahead? Mr. John Knowlton and Miss Lila Williams, side by side. When the dagoes pulled off anything particularly awful they'd turn and look at each other as much as to say: 'I heard that tune the last time I was in Heaven.' And he called it a show!"

"That proves I was right," said Dougherty, rising to his feet and glaring down at Dumain. "He's been going up to her house maybe every night, and we've been sitting here like boobs. Just because he came to the hotel only once a month you thought that was all he saw her. And here he's been—Do what you please. I'm going to get him."

Dumain and Driscoll were genuinely shocked. They had really thought that Knowlton had not seen Lila except the few times he had called at the hotel; Booth's tale was a revelation. Besides, they had already begun to weaken in their support of Knowlton. And perhaps now they were too late.

"Where's Sherman?" Dougherty was saying. "I can count on him."

"And us," chorused the others.

"Wait a minute," said Dumain. "I tell you. We owe something to her. Well, I go and ask her—never mind what I ask her. Anyway, you wait. Eet weel take me only a minute. Go to zee billiard room."

"That's nonsense," Dougherty protested.

But the others persuaded him that Dumain was right and led him off to the billiard room, while the little Frenchman took his courage between his teeth and crossed to Lila's desk.

Lila was indeed, as Dougherty had expressed it, "lit up." She wore a dress of very soft and very dark brown, relieved at the cuffs and throat and down the front of the waist by bits of cream lace.

Her eyes glowed, too, and her lips were parted as though in happy expectancy. It will be remembered that at twelve o'clock she was to lunch with Knowlton.

As Dumain approached her desk she looked up and smiled brightly.

"You are veree *chic*," said Dumain, surveying her with admiration.

"What is French for 'blarney'?" Lila demanded.

"No," said Dumain; "really, you are." Then: "Were you at home last night?" he blurted out.

Lila showed her surprise at the question, answering:

"Why—no. I attended a concert."

Then Dumain plunged in.

"I know," he said. "Wiz zat Knowlton."

Lila was silent. It had been many days since they had spoken to her of Knowlton.

"Were you not?" Dumain demanded.

She said: "Yes."

The little Frenchman continued:

"You must excuse me eef I speak frankly. Long ago we said he was not good, yet you continue to see heem. Dear lady, do you not theenk we know? Eet ees for you we care.''

"But why?" Lila demanded. "You know, Mr. Dumain, if anyone else spoke to me like this I should be angry. But I know you mean to be kind, and I cannot offend you. But I must if you speak this way about Mr. Knowlton. He, too, is my friend."

"Only zat?" Dumain demanded.

"Only—what do you mean?"

"Only a friend?"

"What—what else should he be?"

"*Mon Dieu!*" Dumain exploded, angry at what he thought her assumption of ignorance. "What else? What do you theenk a man like Knowlton wants with a prettee girl like you? Friendship! Ha! Zee kind of friendship zat—"

But the sight of Lila's pale cheeks and flashing eyes stopped him. She did not speak, nor was it necessary. Dumain withstood the fire of her glance for a short second, then fled precipitately.

He found the others waiting for him in the billiard room, which at this early hour—eleven o'clock—was empty. They gathered around him, demanding an account of his success.

"Zee only theeng to do," said Dumain, "ees to finish Knowlton. She ees veree angry. For two months I have thought it best to wait, and now—she loves heem. Eet ees een her eyes. He ees one big scoundrel!"

"That's the first sensible thing I've heard you say for a long time," observed Dougherty.

"I guess I'm with you," said Driscoll.

"I'm on," came from Jennings.

"What did she say?" asked Booth.

"Nozzing," said Dumain. "She just looked. Eet

made a hole through me. Eet ees no good to talk to her.''

At that moment Sherman entered the billiard room.

''No need to convert you,'' shouted Jennings, hailing him.

''What's that?'' asked Sherman, stopping beside the group.

''Why, about Knowlton. We've decided to fix him. He was with Miss Williams last night.''

''Do you call that news?'' asked Sherman scornfully.

''Why, how did you know?''

''I saw them. Do you think because you're blind everyone else is? Also, he was with her Wednesday night and Monday.''

''Where?'' Dougherty demanded.

''Never mind where. Anyway, they were together. I suppose you're ready to listen to me now,'' Sherman sneered. ''After I've done all the work and set the trap for him, you're quite willing to spring it.''

''Don't get heady,'' Dougherty advised. ''What is this trap stuff? And what do you mean by 'work'? If you were so Johnnie Wise, why didn't you put us next?''

''And have Dumain or Driscoll running off to slip the information to Mr. Knowlton?'' sneered Sherman. ''Hardly. I'm not that kind. At last I've got Knowlton where I want him. I'll make him look like a monkey— all I've got to do is pull the string. You guys that love him so much had better hurry around and tell him good-by.'' As he said this last, Sherman, glancing keenly around, could observe no sign of sympathy or pity for Knowlton on the faces that were eagerly surrounding him.

''But what are you talking about?'' they demanded.

"Do you think I'll tell you?" asked Sherman scornfully.

They protested that they were fully as hostile toward Knowlton as he could possibly be, and suggested that he might find their assistance useful. Sherman admitted that they were possibly correct.

"Well, then, what is it?" they demanded. "Where's the trap?"

Still Sherman hesitated. He knew perfectly well that he could easily perfect his plans and carry them out without assistance; but he had a reason, and a strong one, for letting the Erring Knights in on it. The question was, would anyone of them warn Knowlton? He glanced again keenly around the circle of faces, and said for a feeler:

"I know enough to put him behind the bars."

"What's the dope?" asked Dougherty, frowning.

"Counterfeiting," replied Sherman, evidently satisfied with his scrutiny.

"Round ones?"

"No. Paper."

He was immediately besieged with questions:

"Was it tens? He always had 'em."

"How do you know?"

"Is he in with the aristocrats?"

"Does he make it or sow it?"

"He gets it from a Western gang, through a guy called Red Tim," said Sherman. "They've been closing in on 'em for two months, and Red Tim beat it last night. He can't be found this morning, though he was seen on Broadway at midnight. That makes it harder for us."

"How?" inquired Dougherty.

"It makes it harder to get anything on him," Sherman explained. "Red Tim was probably the only one that ever saw Knowlton. He would have peached in a minute; but now he's gone, and the only way to get anything on Knowlton is to catch him with the goods on. And you'd be taking a chance. If you grabbed him he might happen to be clean.''

"But that has nothing to do with us,'' Dougherty objected. "We don't want to grab him.''

"No, I suppose you want him to make his getaway,'' Sherman sneered.

Dougherty stared at him.

"What else would we want?'' he demanded. "Do you think we want to peach? No, thank you. We may be none too good, but we won't hang a guy up, no matter who he is. Anyway, we want him to beat it. Ain't that what we've been after all along—to get him away from here? All we've got to do is to see that he does make his getaway.''

Sherman's face was a study. Filled with chagrin at having miscalculated and with rage at the possible frustration of his designs, he controlled himself with difficulty.

"And you think that will work?'' he demanded, while his voice trembled. "How would you go about it?''

"Easee,'' put in Dumain. "We tell heem either he goes or we what you call eet report. We tell heem what we know. We prove eet to heem. Zen he goes. No more Knowlton.''

"Sure,'' Sherman sneered. "How easy! No more Knowlton, eh? Do you know what he'd do? He'd go home, burn up all his nice little paper, come back, and tell us to go to the deuce.''

"Veree well,'' Dumain agreed. "Zen we make heem go. We would no longer what you call fool wiz heem. Because now we know he ees no fit for her.''

"You tried that once before. Did he go? If it hadn't been for me bringing him down with a piece of bronze he'd have gone out laughing at us," Sherman retorted. "I tell you, the only thing to do is to lock him up."

But at this there was a general clamor. On this point the Erring Knights, with the exception of Sherman, seemed to be all of one mind. They would not "peach."

What they contemplated doing was perhaps a species of blackmail—but we are getting into deep water. With them it was no subtle question of ethics; it was simply an instinctive belief that one was excusable and the other was not.

Sherman found himself the sole member of a helpless minority. He argued and pleaded and threatened, but they were immovable. Too late he realized his mistake in having taken the others into his confidence, and, while prolonging the discussion as far as possible, his brain was busily working to discover a way to retrieve his error.

If he persisted he saw plainly that the others would turn against him and warn Knowlton. Craftily he sought to recover the lost ground.

He began slowly to yield to the others' arguments, and he perceived that they were swallowing the bait.

"I owe him no more than you do," he said in answer to a question from Dumain.

"Then why are you so anxious to see him jugged?" Dougherty demanded.

"I'm not," replied Sherman with a show of exasperation. "All I want is to get him away from here. My way is sure and yours isn't."

"But it is," put in Driscoll. "Dumain and I have been responsible for letting it go as far as it has, but do you think we'll do it again? Anyway, what does it matter what you want? We'll do as we please."

"That's right," said Sherman bitterly. "I do all the work and furnish the information, and this is what I get. Sure, what does it matter what I want?"

"Well, you're right about that," Dougherty admitted. "But we can't see this other thing—we simply can't do it. And our way is just as good if we stick."

"But you won't stick."

"What about it, boys?" Dougherty queried.

There came a chorus of oaths and protestations to the effect that John Knowlton would now, then, and forever find the lobby of the Lamartine extremely uninhabitable.

Sherman appeared to weaken.

"Go slow, go slow, or they'll suspect," he was saying to himself.

The others pressed harder and assaulted him from all sides at once. Finally, "Well, have it your own way," he said with a shrug of the shoulders.

The others applauded.

"But there's one thing I want to say," Sherman continued, "and that is, don't say anything to Knowlton till tomorrow."

"And why?" said Dougherty.

"Because I've got a private detective on his trail, and I want to call him off. And there's another reason, which you don't need to know. What are you going to do—wait till he shows up here?"

"What do you think?"

"I'd wait for him here till tomorrow night, and then, if he hasn't come, go to his rooms. But remember, not a word till tomorrow."

"All right," Dougherty agreed. "And now, who'll be spokesman?"

Sherman rose to his feet, glancing at his watch.

"Count me out," he said, turning to go. "That's your job. Dougherty. See you later."

He sauntered carelessly into the lobby, spoke to Lila and the Venus at the cigar stand, then wandered out into the street.

For a block he strolled along slowly, glancing in at the shop windows, and now and then to the rear. But as soon as he had rounded a corner, out of sight of the hotel, he broke into long, rapid strides.

He had made one mistake, he told himself; he would not make another.

His first thought, after the visit of his detective the night before, was to immediately betray Knowlton to the police. But it was certain that whoever betrayed Knowlton would earn the undying hatred of Lila Williams, and Sherman had therefore sought to bestow that office on one of the Erring Knights.

And they—fools, he said scornfully—had decided to speak to Knowlton instead.

But there was still a chance. He had gotten Dougherty to agree to wait until the following day, and before that time he hoped to have the game in his own hands, if only Dougherty would stick to his agreement, and there was no reason to think otherwise.

He hastened his step. At the subway station on Twenty-third Street he boarded a downtown train.

Fifteen minutes later he was seated in the outer office of a dingy suite whose windows looked out on that curious labyrinth south of the Brooklyn Bridge, and beyond, the East River.

An attendant approached.

"He will see you now, sir."

Sherman rose and followed him to an inner room.

The room was uncarpeted and bare save for two wooden chairs, a massive steel safe, and a roll-top desk. On one of the chairs, placed in front of the desk, was seated a heavy, red-faced man with carroty hair. He dismissed the attendant with a curt nod before he spoke to Sherman.

"What's up now, Billy?"

Sherman, knowing that he had to deal with a busy man, told him in as few words as possible what the reader already knows concerning Knowlton. The other listened to the end with an impassive face.

"You say he was seen with Red Tim last night?" he asked, when Sherman had finished.

"Yes. At Manx's café on Twenty-eighth Street and Broadway."

"And Red Tim had a bundle! Who was the idiot that saw him? Why didn't he arrest him?"

"Private. He was working for me. He didn't want to put Knowlton next."

"Ah! This is personal, then?"

"What if it is?" Sherman returned. "Does that make any difference?"

"No-o," said the other slowly. "But I don't see how we can get him. What evidence have we got? Red Tim can't be found. You say Knowlton refused a bundle last night. Of course, if he had taken that, and had it on him—"

"That isn't necessary," Sherman interrupted. "Why didn't he take that last night? Because he already had all he could handle. He's stuffed with it. Look here." He drew forth a wallet and took from it a stack of bills. "This was his. I got it—never mind how."

"All tens, eh?" said the other, taking the bills. "And beauties!" He examined them curiously. "But how can we prove they were found on him?"

"I can swear to it," said Sherman. "And that isn't

all. He's sure to have more on him now. And he's sure to have a bunch stowed away in his rooms. If you get him there, unexpected, you'll have all the evidence you need and more, too.''

The man at the desk appeared to be lost in thought.

''What is the address of his rooms?'' he asked finally.

Sherman gave him the number of the house on West Thirtieth Street.

''What floor?''

''Second.''

''Do you know anything of his habits? When will he be there?''

''Between seven o'clock and a quarter to eight in the evening.''

''Anyone living with him?''

''No.''

''Flat in his name?''

''Yes. John Knowlton.''

The man at the desk had taken a fountain pen from his pocket and was writing on a pad of paper. He tore off the sheet he had written on, placed it in a drawer of the desk, returned the pen to his pocket, and gazed thoughtfully out of the window for some time.

Then he turned to Sherman, saying:

''We'll get Mr. Knowlton tonight.''

CHAPTER X.

THE END OF THE ROPE.

SHERMAN HAD LEFT THE ERRING KNIGHTS IN THE billiard room of the Lamartine in a state of unrestrained delight.

At last they were to triumph over Knowlton. And it would be, so Jennings declared, a bloodless and well-deserved victory. Dougherty alone appeared to wear an expression of dissatisfaction, and he was urged to explain it.

"I don't like it," declared the ex-prizefighter. "That's no way to fight a guy. Oh, I'll stick, all right, and I'll hand it to him straight, but I don't like it."

"Nobody expects to see you satisfied," Booth observed.

Dougherty, disregarding him, continued:

"And another thing. Why does Sherman want us to hold off till tomorrow? It looks funny. You can't tell what that guy will do."

Dumain put in:

"He said something about zee defective."

"Well, and what about that? He said he wanted time to call off his detective. What sense is there in that? I don't see how it could make any difference when we tell him. It looks funny."

"But what other motive could Sherman have?" Booth demanded.

Dougherty looked at him.

"You know a lot," he observed contemptuously. "You know how wrong Sherman was to have us peach. Well, when he found out we wouldn't, what if he decided to do it himself? And then, to give him time for action, he gets us to promise not to put Knowlton next till tomorrow.

"I don't say that's his game, but it looks suspicious. That guff about his detective is silly. He probably knew it himself, but he didn't have time to think up a better reason."

"Well," put in Driscoll, "it's easy enough to fix it. All you have to do is to see Knowlton today."

"And the sooner the better," said Jennings. "Beat Mr. Sherman at his own game, if that is his game."

"I agree," said little Dumain pompously.

Dougherty slid down from the billiard table on which he was sitting and glanced at his watch, saying:

"Ten minutes to twelve. I wonder if he'd be at home now."

"Probably he's in bed," said Driscoll.

Dougherty appeared to consider.

"I'll go right after lunch," he said finally. "That's settled."

They wandered into the lobby, which by this time was pretty well filled. Dougherty and Jennings stopped in front of a racing bulletin and sighed for the good old days at Sheepshead Bay and Brighton; Driscoll strolled over to the leather lounge in the corner with a morning paper.

Dumain and Booth, joined a group at the cigar stand who were politely but firmly endeavoring to make the Venus admit that she had attempted to improve on nature in the matter of hair. She took it all in fun and good humor and kept them off with a flow of witty evasions. And, incidentally, they bought many cigars.

Driscoll, seated in the corner with his paper, was reading a certain article for the sixth time with an angry frown. The night before he had substituted for the leading man, who had suddenly been taken ill. And this article was not exactly complimentary to the substitute.

He told himself, also for the sixth time, that it was written by an idiot, a Philistine, a man who had no appreciation of true art. Then he threw down the paper, yawning, and glanced round the lobby.

Suddenly he sat bolt upright, staring in the direction of the telegraph desk. Then he looked round the lobby, saw Dougherty standing by the racing bulletin, and ran over to him.

"Look!" he said, laying one hand on Dougherty's shoulder and pointing with the other.

The ex-prizefighter, turning and gazing in the direction indicated, saw Knowlton standing by Lila's desk, helping her on with her coat.

"Now's your chance," said Driscoll.

When Knowlton heard his name called, and, turning, found Dougherty at his side, he uttered an involuntary exclamation of impatience, while Lila looked up in uneasy surprise.

She feared a scene, remembering what Dumain had

said to her an hour or so before. But Dougherty seemed calm enough as he said:

"I want a word with you. Will you step aside a minute?"

Knowlton was inclined to refuse, and would have done so had the request come from any other than Dougherty.

After a moment of hesitation he excused himself to Lila, telling her he would return in a moment, and accompanied Dougherty over to the leather lounge in the corner.

The ex-prizefighter began with a recapitulation of the events of the preceding three months, while Knowlton restrained his impatience with difficulty.

They were seated side by side on the lounge. Across the lobby Lila was seen seated at her desk, drumming on it absently with her fingers. Driscoll and Jennings had joined Dumain and Booth at the cigar stand, and the four were pretending to talk, with occasional furtive glances of ill-concealed curiosity at the two men seated in the corner.

The lobby was full of men smoking and laughing and talking, oblivious of the fact that a near tragedy was being enacted scarcely a dozen feet away.

"And then," Dougherty was saying, "we let you alone. It wasn't my fault, but Dumain and Driscoll wouldn't stand with us. Now they've got to. We've got you marked, and the game's up."

"What is it—another prize-ring entertainment?" asked Knowlton.

"No. I wish it was. I don't like this thing any better than you do. It ain't the right kind of a deal."

Dougherty spoke slowly and with some hesitation as he continued:

"But I promised to stick, so here goes. It's this way:

you leave New York today and give us your word to
let Miss Williams alone, or in you go. We're on.
You're shoving the queer.''

Knowlton didn't blink an eyelash. He sat gazing
across the lobby at Lila's profile in silence, without a
sign even that he had heard. Then he turned his head
and met Dougherty's eyes, saying in an even tone:

''That's pretty bad, Tom. Couldn't you think up
anything better? You've been having bad dreams.''

But Dougherty shook his head.

''It's no use, Knowlton. We know. No matter how,
but it ought to be enough to tell you that you shouldn't
have trusted Red Tim. We've got enough on you right
now to hold you tight. The game's up.''

Knowlton was regarding his companion keenly, and
he saw the truth in his unwavering gaze and air of half
commiseration. Subterfuge was useless. The game was
up.

For a long minute he sat trying to collect his
thoughts. Dougherty's untroubled calmness, the care-
less attitude of Lila seated but a few feet away, the
gaiety of the lobby, all combined to give the thing an
appearance of triviality. He could hardly realize the
fact that the earth was falling away under his feet.

He turned to Dougherty:

''All right, then. You've got it on me. But you can't
do this, Tom. It's not like you. Do you mean to say
you'd actually peach on me?''

''Perhaps not,'' the ex-prizefighter admitted. ''But
I'm not the only one. There's no use talking, you're
up against it, and the only way out is to beat it.

''It's a dirty trick, and I don't like it any better than
you do, but the fact is I'm doing you a favor. The
others all know about it, and they're dead sore, and
they'd do it anyway if I didn't.''

Knowlton's face was expressionless. His eyes stared straight into his companion's, and they held no anger nor resentment nor appeal. But his hand held the arm of the lounge with a grip of steel and the muscles of his jaw were set tensely in his effort to control himself.

Dougherty continued to speak. He explained the conditions under which they would leave Knowlton unmolested—he must leave New York at once and give them his word not to communicate with Miss Williams. And the sooner he left the better, since there was one member of the gang who could not be trusted. It was unnecessary, said the ex-prizefighter, to mention his name.

In the end Knowlton agreed, observing calmly that he was at the end of his rope and had no alternative. In spite of his effort at control, a lifelessness and despair crept into his tone that made Dougherty curse the part he had played. Knowlton gave his promise not to see Lila and said that he would leave New York at once.

He finished:

"Of course, she will know. That's the worst of it, Dougherty. I don't hold any grudge against you; I suppose you couldn't help it. But you were all blithering idiots to imagine that she could ever do anything wrong. She never did and never will.

"I was going to lunch with her today. When I think of—but that's useless, I suppose if I wanted to see her—but I don't want to. It would do no good.

"There's a lot I could tell you, Dougherty, but that, too, would be useless. You've called the turn on me, and I certainly don't intend to whine. Tell Dumain good-by; he was all right. He's a good fellow, that little Frenchman."

Knowlton rose to his feet:

"Is—is she waiting for you now?" stammered Dougherty, glancing across at Lila.

"Yes. When I'm gone, tell her not to wait any longer."

Knowlton hesitated as though about to speak further, then, changing his mind, turned abruptly and without another word passed down the lobby and out into the street. As he passed the cigar stand he heard his name called. He recognized Dumain's voice, but did not halt.

On the sidewalk he stopped and glanced to either side as though undecided which way to turn. Then he started at a rapid stride uptown.

His mind was still a chaos of mingled thoughts. Curiously enough, he felt little surprise.

"I am paying," he kept muttering to himself over and over. "I am paying."

For two hours he walked the streets, unconscious of direction or surroundings, his brain in a turmoil of regret and despair.

Rarely had he so given way to his emotions, but fate had struck him a blow that left him weak and helpless in their grasp. He called it fate. So do we all.

At the end of the two hours he found himself far uptown, on the Drive. It was a clear, crisp February day. Up from the Hudson came a damp, chilling breeze, with the faintest subtle suggestion of the spring about to come; it brought with it the shrieks of tugs and the more resonant calls of ferryboats. Above the factories and piers across the river slanted the descending sun, disclosing the melancholy barrenness of the slope below the Drive.

Knowlton faced about suddenly and retraced his steps downtown. He was fighting the hardest of all fights, and he had had no time for preparation.

He tried to clear his brain of feeling, to think connectedly; he caught himself trying to conduct a mental operation in mathematics in order to prove to himself that he could think, and he laughed aloud. That was a good sign, he told himself: he could still laugh.

He found himself, without knowing how he had come there, at the entrance of the house on Thirtieth Street. He looked at the door for a moment irresolutely, then entered and mounted the stairs to his rooms on the second floor.

He glanced at a little bronze clock on the mantel; it was half past four. His train for the West was to leave Grand Central Station at seven-thirty.

He sat down on a chair by the window, trying once more to collect his thoughts, but in vain. One picture filled his brain to the exclusion of all else.

Remorse, which comes only after suffering, had not yet touched him; he knew only that his every sense, his very reason, had been dulled and obscured by an all-pervading pain.

But if he could not think, he could act, he told himself. As to the course to be followed he had no choice. He had promised Dougherty that he would leave New York, and since his future was decided by that promise there was really no necessity for thought.

He pulled his trunk to the middle of the floor and began to pack, throwing in suits and shirts indiscriminately. From a shelf in the wardrobe he took a package wrapped in brown paper, about a foot square, and stood for some minutes regarding it uncertainly.

"That won't do," he muttered, glancing at the fireplace, long disused, "and I don't dare take it to the furnace." Then, still undecided and placing the package on a table, he resumed his packing.

Finally the trunk was filled and there remained only

to place his toilet articles and a change of linen in his suitcase, together with the contents of a lower drawer in the wardrobe. These items were somewhat curious.

There was a small white glove, two tiny handkerchiefs, a dozen or more letters, two photographs, and several books. These he wrapped carefully and placed in the suitcase, with the exception of one of the books and a photograph.

Glancing at his watch, he saw that it was six o'clock. The cab which he had ordered would arrive in three-quarters of an hour.

The early winter night had long since fallen; the room was dark. He sat down on the trunk to wait.

In the meantime Lila had spent a long and weary afternoon at her desk in the Lamartine.

When she had seen Knowlton, after he had left her for a moment to speak with Dougherty, turn and leave the lobby without so much as looking in her direction, she had been overcome with amazement.

That he, of all men, should be thus openly discourteous, was unbelievable. Well, she thought, of course he would soon return, and when they were at lunch together—

But as the minutes passed by with no sign of his return she grew uneasy. Was it possible he had forgotten his engagement with her? For that he could have deliberately disregarded it was impossible.

Could his conversation with Dougherty have had anything to do with it? She wondered what the exprizefighter had said to him; for she knew that Knowlton had scorned the threats of the Erring Knights.

The minutes flew; a half-hour passed. She told herself that she would wait five minutes more, and then if he had not come, go without him. The five minutes passed, it seemed, as so many seconds; she decided to wait five more. She was glad that Dougherty was not to be seen; she knew that she would have been unable to refrain from asking him to explain.

At one o'clock she forced herself to go.

When she returned from lunch she half expected to find Knowlton in the lobby, and, not seeing him, she burned to ask Miss Hughes or the hotel clerk if he had been there. But she could not bring herself to it, and she proceeded to her desk with a heavy heart.

She was mortified and half angry; but above all, she was uneasy. She told herself that Knowlton would never have thus humiliated her but for some cogent and powerful reason, and she could imagine none, unless—

When Dougherty entered the lobby and joined Dumain and Driscoll in the corner Lila kept herself from calling to him only by an extreme exertion of the will. And, after all, she thought, it might all amount to a mere nothing that could easily be explained and forgiven by a word.

The afternoon dragged slowly by.

You may be sure Dougherty had lost no time in telling the others of his success with Knowlton. They were in high glee.

"But weel he keep zee promise about Mees Williams?" said Dumain.

"As well as you would, my friend." Dougherty was in ill humor. "I'd like to hear you ask him that."

"And now, thank the Lord, we're rid of him," said Driscoll in a tone of finality.

It voiced the general feeling and it was supposed to be Knowlton's epitaph.

They wandered into the billiard room—it was the middle of the afternoon—and began a four-handed game; Driscoll and Booth against Jennings and Dougherty.

Sherman had not been seen since he had left earlier in the day. Dumain, barred from the game on account of his superior skill, took a chair nearby and after each miss explained to the player how easy the shot would have been for him.

But Dumain's mind was only half on the billiard game.

With all due respect to a great people, the fact remains that Frenchmen are as a rule "gabby" little fellows, and Dumain was a true son of his country. They can talk about anything, and at all times with pleasure, and when they really have something to say and somebody to say it to, silence becomes for them a positive pain.

Thus it was that Dumain squirmed in his chair.

Not fifty feet away Lila was seated at her desk, and how he longed to tell her of Knowlton!

The reason he did not run to her at once with the news may be summed up in one word: Dougherty. He knew that the ex-prizefighter would not approve, and he was half afraid of him. Dumain was a little man.

The billiard game lasted until five o'clock, when Booth suddenly ended it by announcing that he had to see a customer and departed in haste.

"That's what comes of having a job," said Dougherty in disgust, as they wandered into the lobby. "How anybody can be a typewriter salesman I don't understand. Why can't he live like a gentleman?"

This seemed to be an unanswerable question, as no one responded. They strolled up and down the lobby, then over to the leather lounge and loafed and smoked like gentlemen. Dumain kept one eye—an eye of impatience—on Lila.

At a quarter to six Jennings and Driscoll rose and announced that it was time for them to depart. They were due at the theater at seven-thirty, and they had yet to dine.

"Where are you going?" Dougherty demanded.

They replied that they intended to eat at Tony's and invited him and Dumain to accompany them.

"Eet ees too early for me," said the little Frenchman.

Dougherty hesitated, giving the matter due consideration, and finally decided to accept. They left Dumain alone in the corner. He watched them through the window till they had disappeared up Broadway, then turned quickly. Now was his chance.

Lila, with her hat and coat on, was arranging her desk, preparing to go home. At Dumain's approach she looked up quickly. Her face wore a tired and listless expression that caused the little Frenchman to hesitate. But only for a moment; then he said:

"So your friend deed not even stop to say good-by! You see I was right about heem. Of course you could not know—but when we told you! And now you see."

Lila looked at him.

"What are you talking about?" she said shortly.

Dumain was undisturbed:

"I mean zat Knowlton—you know eet. Bah! Deed you not see heem run like a dog wiz hees tail between hees feet? Do you know why? We found out about heem. He ees what you call eet a counterfeiter. And when we tell heem he runs."

Lila had clenched her fists on the desk before her and was leaning on them heavily.

"That is not true," she said calmly.

Ignoring her, Dumain went on:

"We made heem to leave New York today. Most

probable he ees already gone. Perhaps now you will admit I know something when I tol' you two, three months ago about zis Knowlton? Bah! You were veree angry. You said I am impertinent.'' He nodded his head sagely: "I am wise."

Lila's face was very white. But her voice, though little above a whisper, was fairly under control as she said:

"You say Mr. Knowlton is going away?"

Dumain said "Yes," while his eyes gleamed with satisfaction at the impression he was making.

"Has he gone?"

Dumain supposed so, but wasn't sure.

Lila straightened herself firmly and a new light appeared in her eyes, of resolve, while she calmly buttoned her coat.

"I thought you ought to know about eet," said Dumain a trifle lamely.

Lila appeared to be little moved. She made no comment on Dumain's observation, but thanked him and turned to go, leaving him staring at her in profound amazement.

"Zee devil!" he ejaculated, snapping his fingers. "She cares not zat much!"

But once outside the lobby Lila's courage forsook her. She grasped at a railing and seemed about to fall.

Then, pressing her lips together tightly and forcing back the tears that sought to blind her, she started up Broadway at a walk that was almost a run. She stopped suddenly. Should she call a cab? But, no, she felt it would be impossible to sit still. Again she started forward.

Darkness had fallen nearly an hour before, and the yellow glare of Broadway lighted her steps. The lull following the close of business and preceding the theater hour was evidenced by the quietness of the street; and the few pedestrians to be seen were hurrying to get home to a late dinner.

But Lila was aware of nothing save a fearful anxiety. Would she be too late? Would she find him gone—forever?

This thought occupied her brain to the exclusion of all else. She did not consider whether Dumain had spoken the truth, nor why she was going, nor what she would do: nor was she conscious of any feeling, one way or the other, concerning the revelation that the man she loved was a criminal. She only knew that she must see him.

At Thirtieth Street she turned westward. In another ten minutes of breathless, rapid steps she found herself at the address to which she had sent his letters.

She ascended the stoop and searched on the letter-boxes for his name. There it was—the second on the left—John Knowlton.

For a moment she hesitated, half conscious for the first time of the recklessness and immodesty of what she was doing.

Then she pressed the bell button firmly.

CHAPTER XI.

THE VOICE OF THE LAW.

THE LATCH CLICKED; SHE ENTERED AND AS-
cended the stairs.

In an open door to the left, peering at her curiously in the dim light of the hall, stood a man. It
was Knowlton. Back of him the room inside was dark.

Lila's anxiety dropped from her as a cloak and gave
way to a sudden and overwhelming embarrassment.
She stood at the top of the stairs looking at him, unable
to speak or move.

Knowlton advanced a step from the door, saying:
"Who is it?"

And then, as Lila did not answer, "Who is it?" he
repeated, advancing toward her. "Did you want—
why—not—Miss Williams! What does this mean?
Why did you come? Speak—tell me—"

"I—I don't know—" Lila stammered in confusion.
"I thought—they told me—you had gone—"

She stood with one hand resting on the baluster, her breath coming in quick gasps.

Knowlton jerked himself together with an effort.

"But this will not do. You must go home at once." He took her arm.

Lila shook her head.

"I want to talk to you. I must. You mean that I should not come to your rooms? Well—I trust you, and what else matters?"

Knowlton, taken by surprise and at his wits' end, tried to insist, but Lila refused to listen. Finally, in despair, he led the way into his rooms. He lighted the gas and brought a chair for her, then seated himself on the trunk which he had just finished packing.

Lila looked at it.

"So what they said is true. You are going away."

He attempted playfulness.

"Yes, I am taking some of my swamps out West to sell to some of my old friends. You must admit, though, I never tried to sell you one."

"And you were going—without saying good-by?"

"I—I had to," he stammered. "It was on very short notice. There was no time."

Lila's face colored, then grew very white. She could not know the effort it was costing Knowlton to play his role; to her his lightness seemed sincere. She rose to her feet uncertainly.

"I do not know why I came," she said breathlessly. "But, yes, I do know. And now I am sorry. I cannot tell you how ashamed and sorry I am."

Her lip was quivering, but her eyes were firm and her voice even.

"Mr. Dumain told me you were in trouble—but I have been very bold—and—and I am sorry—"

She was moving toward the door.

At such times and under such circumstances men forget promises and danger, and throw prudence to the winds. Knowlton sprang to his feet and turned to her.

"Lila!"

She stopped, trembling from head to foot. All that she had longed to hear was in his voice—anguish and entreaty and love.

And now that the gates were broken the flood burst forth.

"Lila! For God's sake don't leave me like this! I can't bear it—I won't! Oh, what a miserable coward I am!"

In another moment she was at his side and in his arms, laughing and crying at once, and placing her hands over his mouth to keep him from calling himself a coward.

"No, no, no!" she kept saying, while he held her closer and closer and covered her hands and wrists with kisses.

"Lila! Tell me—my darling—do you love me?"

She nodded.

"You do love me?"

"Yes."

"Say it."

"I—love—you."

"And I—oh, my dear little girl, I worship you. You have known—you must have known, but I want to tell you. And you love me! It can't be true. Tell me."

"I love you," said Lila. And, oh, the curve of her lips and the light in her eyes and the clinging warmth of her arms!

Knowlton kissed her hair, saying:

"And see! You are my little girl." He picked her up in his arms and carried her to a chair, then knelt before her, muttering, "My little girl!" over and over. He was intoxicated.

Lila's eyes were swimming in tears of happiness. She stroked his hair and pronounced his name with a delightful shyness and made him tell her how long he had loved her.

He said, "Always," and got his reward at once.

There was a long silence, while they gazed into each other's eyes. Then Lila, happening to glance up, sighed and pointed to the trunk.

"And now, what about that?"

Knowlton turned sharply—and awoke. He sprang to his feet.

"My God! I had forgotten! And this—this is madness! Ah! You do not know—and I am a coward."

Lila said simply:

"I know everything."

Knowlton stared at her.

"Mr. Dumain told me why you were going away," she continued. "Did you think I did not know? And I—I have been waiting for you to tell me—" She stopped, coloring.

Knowlton suppressed a groan of anguish and forced himself to speak. The words choked him.

"I am a counterfeiter."

"I know it," Lila smiled.

Still Knowlton could not believe, or would not accept. His hands opened and closed convulsively, his breath came in quick gasps, and his eyes were narrowed with misery. Again he forced himself to speak, and the words came with a painful pause between them.

"But—you don't—understand. I am—a criminal. I am running away."

Lila shivered involuntarily at the word, but the smile did not leave her face as she said:

"I love you."

Then Knowlton burst forth:

"But, Lila, you do not know all! Ever since the day—the first time I was with you, I have been straight. And Heaven knows I have tried to make it up. But you humiliate me—you ask me nothing! Do you think there is no explanation? You do not even ask me why!"

"I guess there is no 'why' in love," said Lila.

"But there is in—the other thing." Knowlton drew nearer to her and spoke slowly and earnestly. "Do you remember I told you last night that I wanted to ask you something today? Well—I was going to ask you to marry me. I would have done that, and I would have kept my secret. But now that you know some of it you must know all."

"No," said Lila, "not that. Of the future, perhaps, but not of the past. What does it all matter now?"

But Knowlton insisted.

"Yes, I must. I want you to know it. It is not that I would give excuses; there can be none. But you must know my weakness and folly, and then if you can trust me—"

He paced the floor nervously as he continued:

"In the first place, my name is not Knowlton. It is John Norton. My father is the wealthiest citizen of a town named Warton, in Ohio. I am his only child. My mother died ten years ago.

"My father made his money in the manufacturing business, and he earned every cent of it. All his life he has worked like a slave. I can remember, when I was a little chap, how he used to come home late at night completely exhausted, and come to my room to kiss me good night. He would always reply to my mother's expostulations with the words, 'It is for him.'

"He wanted me to be a gentleman—in a certain sense of the word—and I was perfectly willing. Still I was not lazy. I studied hard at college, and made as good a showing in the classroom as I did on the athletic field.

"After graduation I made a two years' tour of the world, and at the age of twenty-four returned to Warton with a somewhat exaggerated idea of my attainments and accomplishments and a varied assortment of opinions and theories."

Lila was bending forward to listen, with parted lips and glowing eyes. Knowlton stopped pacing the floor and stood in front of her.

"But my father was by no means a fool. Although it was his dearest wish that his wealth should prevent my toiling and laboring as he had done, he did not intend that I should live a life of idleness. He had at first been desirous that I should enter a profession, but, seeing that I was unsuited for either the law or medicine, he left it to my own choice.

"I chose banking, and he was delighted, declaring that nothing could please him better. He owned a portion of the stock of the Warton National Bank, and I was at once placed in its offices. At the end of six months I was made cashier, and at the end of the year a vice president.

"Of course I deserved no credit for my success, for the work was pleasing to me and everything was made easy for me. But my father was highly gratified, and, saying that my future was assured, began to press me on a point which had for some months been a bone of contention between us."

"He wanted you to marry some one," Lila said abruptly.

Knowlton gazed at her in amazement. "How in the name of—"

"I don't know," Lila smiled. "I seemed to feel it. You see now that you have no chance to keep anything from me. Who—who was she?"

Knowlton's eyes were still filled with surprise as he continued:

"A Miss Sherman. She was the daughter of a very old friend of my father's, and our parents had decided long before that we should marry when we had reached a proper age. But, though I had no particular objection to her, still I did not care for her, and was certainly anything but an ardent wooer. My father had often complained to me on account of my lack of appreciation of her charms."

"What was she like?" Lila demanded.

"Oh, like any girl! She had hair, and eyes—"

"Like me?"

"There is no one in the world like you," Knowlton declared, but as Lila started to rise he protested:

"No—please—let me finish. When I was elected vice president of the bank my father began to insist that I should marry at once. I demurred. We had many hot discussions on the subject, and it ended by my refusing pointblank to marry Miss Sherman at all.

"Naturally, he was disappointed and angry, but if it had not been for Miss Sherman herself the thing would have soon blown over. She developed an unexpected obstinacy, and declared that I was bound by the agreement made with her father, who had been dead for several years.

"To make matters worse, about this time she received a visit from her brother. This brother had some years before been driven out of Warton on account of some youthful indiscretion, and he had left behind him an exceedingly unsavory reputation. He had gone East—it was said to New York—and had not been heard of for some time until he suddenly put in an appearance at the time I mention.

"He immediately began to threaten me with all sorts of calamities and disasters if I did not marry Miss Sherman. I don't know whether this was with his sister's cognizance and approval or not; I doubt it, for she would hardly have so demeaned herself.

"Sherman acted like a sneak. I never once saw him, but he pestered me with letters and messages until I had about decided either to thrash him soundly or have recourse to the courts."

Lila interrupted eagerly:

"This man—Mr. Sherman—her brother—was he—"

"The same as Mr. Sherman of the Erring Knights? I think so; in fact, I am pretty positive of it, though, as I say, I never saw him in Warton. But he recognized me the first time he saw me at the Lamartine, so there is little doubt of it."

He resumed his narrative, while Lila's interest was so intense that she scarcely breathed.

"This went on for two or three months. My father had come over to my side unconditionally. Miss Sherman had prepared to enter a suit for breach of promise, and her brother was making himself as obnoxious as possible. He spread stories concerning me all over the town, and did everything that could suggest itself to his mind—in the dark.

"One night—I shall never forget it—one Wednesday night I was at work in the bank alone. I had been away for the two or three days previous, and a great deal of work had accumulated during my absence. Also, we had that very day received a large shipment of currency from the East, and I had to check that and stow it away in the vault.

"I had just completed this task, and had not yet closed the vault—it was about eleven o'clock—when I heard some one pounding on the outer door. I called out, asking who it was, and heard in a woman's voice a name which astonished me: 'Alma Sherman.'

"Not knowing what else to do, I opened the door, drawing the heavy steel bolts, and she entered. Before I had time to speak or move she seized me by the arm and drew me over to a private room on the left. 'Wait,' I said, 'I must close the door.'

"But she would not let me go. She seemed half insane, clinging to me and entreating—well, I can't tell you what she said. In fact, the whole thing is in my memory as a nightmare, indistinct and horrible.

"I don't know what I was thinking of, not to have insisted on going back to close the door, but she must have carried me completely off my feet.

"Gradually she became calmer, but still was unable to tell me what she had come for or indeed to speak intelligently at all. I had begun to think she was really out of her mind, when she suddenly sprang to the door and disappeared as mysteriously as she had come.

"I looked for her through the window, but the night was very dark and I could see nothing. She had been with me, I think, about twenty minutes.

"I was roused and curious, of course, but I finished my work nevertheless, locked the vault and the outer doors, and went home.

"The next morning the cashier ran in to me with a face of terror and announced that there was twenty thousand dollars missing from the vault."

Lila gasped involuntarily, and Knowlton answered the question in her eyes:

"No, I don't think Alma Sherman had anything to do with it intentionally. But I think her brother did, and that she was an unconscious accomplice. I don't know. I thought at the time that someone happening to pass by had seen the open door and taken advantage of it.

"There is no use in giving you the details of what followed. I shall come to the end as rapidly as possible.

"Of course, all was confusion and speculation in the bank—and as soon as the news got around in the town. At first I was not suspected; I was considered above it. But it was inevitable.

"I had been left in the bank alone, I had locked the vault myself after it had been checked up by the cashier, and there was no evidence of any kind that it had been tampered with. I made no mention to anyone of Alma Sherman's visit; I did not see how it could do any possible good, and I thought the least I could do was to shield her name.

"Even then I did not know that I was suspected. I discovered later that I had been followed and investigated by detectives. A week after the robbery ten thousand dollars of the missing money was found hidden in a closet in my room in my father's house."

Lila sprang to her feet with a cry of astonishment; but Knowlton, not heeding her, continued:

"Of course, that settled it. What need to tell of the terrible scene with my father—his grief and anger, and my protestations of innocence? I stood convicted by facts, delusive and stubborn.

"Now, when it was too late, I told of the visit paid me by Alma Sherman, being convinced that her

brother was at the bottom of the plot against me. I was
jeered at for my pains. They asked why I had not
mentioned it before, and reminded me that I had declared that no one had been with me at the bank on
the night of the robbery.

"I insisted that they search for William Sherman.
His sister told them that he had returned to New York,
and declared that my statement that she had called on
me at the bank was false!

"My father paid the shortage, arranged that I should
not be prosecuted, and then—disowned me and drove
me from his house."

As he said this Knowlton's voice trembled for the
first time. He hesitated, then conquered his emotion
with a visible effort, and resumed:

"Well, there I was. For a time I stayed in Warton,
determined to prove my innocence, or, if that were
impossible, live down the accusation. But everyone
was against me.

"By my youthful assumption of superiority I had
made many enemies, unknown to myself, and they
were implacable. It was unbearable, horrible! I stood
it as long as I could, then came to New York embit-
tered, cynical, and penniless.

"I had one or two friends here, but as soon as I told
them of my troubles—and I concealed nothing—they
promptly forgot me. Getting a position in my own
line—in a bank—was of course out of the question.
They require references. At the end of a week I was
about ready to go down to the sea by way of the Hudson, when I accidentally met Red Tim.

"It doesn't matter who Red Tim is. There are
thousands of him. He is everywhere. We talked for an
hour, and met again the following day. I was still well-
dressed, and I had a fairly good appearance. At our

third meeting he showed me a stack of counterfeit ten-dollar bills.

"You know the rest. I don't want you to think it was all weakness. It was partly bitterness and partly despair, and I think I was even so far gone as to repeat, 'I have the name, I'll have the game.' I think I was temporarily insane; no one can feel more horror at it now than I feel.

"When I met Sherman at the Lamartine I began to devise schemes for revenge and for clearing my name. But what could I do? I had no friends, nor evidence, nor much hope of getting either. Perhaps some day—

"I had been passing counterfeit money for a month when I met you. During the two months that followed my feelings were indescribable. Whenever I looked at you I felt unspeakable self-contempt. But I said bitterly that I wanted to get even with the world.

"Then—do you remember the first evening we dined together? And the play? Well, after that I despised myself indeed. I felt that I was not worthy to speak to you, to breathe the same air with you. But—you know—I could not stay away.

"For another month I wavered and hesitated, then got a position that was at least honorable, though you hardly seemed to think so. You didn't know how happy I was in it, and how I worked to earn the right to ask you—to tell you my love! I—really, I am proud of it!

"One thing more, and I am done. I had met Red Tim once each month. That was my own arrangement—I didn't care to see him oftener. Well, I saw him for the last time last night, and told him I was through.

"But there is still something." He pointed to a package wrapped in brown paper lying on the trunk.

"That is—I had that left. I should have destroyed it long ago. I am going to tonight."

Lila gazed at the package curiously.

"Is it—how much is there?"

"About ten thousand dollars."

She rose and walked over to him and laid her hand on his arm.

"Destroy it now—at once," she said in a tone half frightened.

Knowlton objected:

"But there is no way. It is best to be safe, and I shall take it to the river. Never fear! But you have not told me what I want to know."

Lila questioned him with her eyes, and he continued:

"I have told you my story. And now?"

At first Lila did not understand; then her eyes filled with light and she raised herself on tiptoe, placing her arms around his neck, and kissed him.

"I love you," she said.

"Will you marry me?"

Her head was on his shoulder. She nodded.

"My darling Lila! I—really, I can't believe it."

"Pooh!" said she scornfully. "You have known it all the time."

"No. I have hoped—and feared. But, ah, I could never have lived without you!"

"And yet"—Lila looked up at him quickly—"you were going away."

Whereupon Knowlton protested that she was unkind, and she admitted it and begged his forgiveness with a kiss. There was a long silence. Finally Knowlton gave a deep sigh and spoke of the future.

He began by saying that he would go away somewhere—anywhere—and make a place and a home for Lila. She interrupted him at once:

"No, no! I will go with you. Why should you go alone? Will we not be stronger together? You think I will be in the way? You do not know me, then."

He tried to argue with her, but she would not listen. He pleaded; there were hardships to be endured which he could not ask her to share; it would cost him his newly regained self-respect. He was crushed, he must have time to get on his feet, he was practically penniless.

Lila replied:

"I have saved a little—enough to last until—until you get—"

"Good Heaven!" he cried in utter humiliation. "And you think that I—no, you do not know me. Can't you understand? Call it pride, if you will, and if you think I have a right to any. There are some things I must do myself. Do you think the confession I have just made has not been painful to me? If you only knew!"

Lila murmured:

"I do not want to hurt you, but I want to be happy, and if you leave me I shall not be."

"Dearest, do I not know?" Knowlton forced himself to be more calm. "And without you every minute will seem a year to me. That is why I shall work all the harder and send for you as soon as I can. And then—"

"And then—" Lila repeated.

"And then I will be the happiest man in the world—happier far than I deserve. And as soon as I can get—"

At that moment a bell in the next room rang violently.

Lila glanced round, startled, and Knowlton turned with an expression of alarm, which speedily gave way to one of relief.

He reassured Lila:

"It is nothing. I ordered a cab to take me to the station."

He ran to the front and looked out on the street below.

"Yes," he said, returning, "it is the cab. It is in front. And that's lucky, for it is dinnertime. Shall we go—"

He was interrupted by a loud knocking on the hall door a few feet away.

He thought it was the cabdriver, and wondered how he had gotten in the outer door below.

He called sharply:

"Who is it?"

There was no answer, but after an interval the knocking was repeated.

"Who is it?" he repeated angrily.

Another short pause, during which Knowlton fancied he heard whispering in the hall outside; then came the reply in a peremptory tone:

"Open in the name of the law!"

CHAPTER XII.

THE LONG NIGHT

LILA GAVE A GASP OF TERROR AND SEIZED
Knowlton's arm convulsively, while the young
man stood speechless with surprise and alarm.

What did he see in that one flash of horror and
regret? He saw Lila accused, arrested, dishonored—
and all for him. The thought petrified him; he was
unable to move.

No care for himself or concern for his own danger
could have moved him to anything save reckless courage or stoical acceptance; but it stunned his every
sense to think that Lila would be caught in the net he
had spread for himself.

But Lila, seeing his helplessness, acted for herself.
For a second only she stood rooted to the spot with
terror; then she glanced with a flashing eye round the
room, while her brain worked with the rapidity of
lightning.

She saw, a few feet to the right, a curtained alcove;

then, as she turned, her eye fell on the package of counterfeit money lying on the trunk. With silent swiftness she crossed the room and picked up the package, and as swiftly sped back to the side of Knowlton.

She held her mouth close, very close against his ear, that no sound might reach the other side of the door, and whispered:

"Get them into the other room—all of them—as far away as possible."

She saw that he did not comprehend her meaning, but there was no time to explain further. She must trust to his sagacity as soon as he recovered his wits.

With one last glance about the room to make sure that there was nothing in it to reveal her presence, she pressed his hand swiftly and disappeared behind the curtain of the alcove. All this had taken but three or four seconds.

The knocking on the door and the command to open were repeated. Knowlton turned the knob of the catch-lock and the door flew open.

Three men burst into the room, the foremost exclaiming, "Here he is!" as he ran to Knowlton, who had fallen back several steps from the door.

And then Knowlton understood Lila's plan, simple and admirable. In an instant his brain cleared, and, realizing that Lila had taken the package of counterfeit money—the evidence—with her into the alcove, he decided on his own plan of action.

Turning suddenly, just as the man nearest him was about to grasp him by the shoulder, he sprang aside with the swiftness and agility of a panther and disappeared into the room beyond, toward the rear. As he had foreseen, the three men, all of them, rushed after him and found him standing by a window looking out on the rear court, laughing gaily.

"Why all the excitement?" he queried pleasantly. "Did you think I was trying to run away?"

The leader of the detectives, a heavy, red-faced man with carroty hair, grunted.

"Get him!" he said to his companions.

Then Knowlton had need of all his composure. But he was not thinking of himself. As the two detectives grasped him roughly and handcuffed his wrists and led him back into the room in front, he was saying to himself. "She had plenty of time. But was that what she meant? It must have been. But where did she go?"

He dared not glance at the alcove; he felt that his eyes would have burned a hole through the curtain.

Then the detectives began a search of the rooms.

"I'm sure the stuff is here," said the red-faced man, "and we've got to find it. You might save us the trouble," he added, turning to Knowlton. "What's the use? The game's up. Where is it?"

Knowlton did not answer. He was leaning forward in an agony of anxiety, watching one of the detectives, who had just approached the alcove and grasped the curtain.

He pulled the curtain aside, letting the gaslight stream into the alcove, and Knowlton barely suppressed a cry of joy. It was empty.

Then he replied to the man who had spoken to him:

"If you'll tell me what you want I may be of some assistance. Everything I own is in that trunk and suitcase," pointing to them.

"Huh!" the red-faced man grunted. "Going to beat it, eh? Open 'em up, boys, while I look him over. Got a key for the trunk?"

Knowlton drew a bunch of keys from his pocket and tossed it to one of the men, then submitted himself to be searched. The detective took several miscellaneous articles from the young man's pockets, then a pocketbook. This he opened expectantly; but as he examined its contents there appeared on his face an expression of keen disappointment.

"What the deuce!" he exclaimed. "Where do you keep it?"

"I have said," Knowlton replied, "that I have no idea what you are looking for. If you will tell me—"

"Cut it!" said the other roughly. "I guess you're a wise one, all right, but what's the use? I tell you we've got enough on you already to send you up. You might as well talk straight."

Knowlton was silent. The red-faced man glared at him for a moment, then walked over to aid the others in their search of the trunk and suitcase.

They pulled out clothing and toilet articles and books, and heaped them indiscriminately on the floor, while Knowlton looked on with a grim smile. Now and then oaths of disappointment came from the lips of the searchers.

Suddenly one of them uttered a cry of triumph and drew forth a neatly wrapped brown paper parcel. The leader took a knife from his pocket, cut the string of the parcel, and tore away the wrapper with eager fingers, disclosing to view—a stack of real-estate contracts.

"The deuce!" he ejaculated. "You're a boob, Evans."

Again they set to work.

Soon they finished with the trunk and suitcase and began on the rooms themselves. Nothing escaped them. They took the covers and mattress from the bed and shook each separately.

The couch was turned upside down and examined with probes. The drawers in the bureaus and tables and wardrobes were removed, and the interiors of the articles subjected to a close scrutiny. They raked out the dust and rubbish from the fireplace, and lifted the bricks.

The search lasted nearly an hour. They found nothing.

The red-faced man, muttering an oath, turned to Knowlton:

"Well, we've got you, anyway, my boy. I guess you'll find out you can't play with Uncle Sam."

Then he turned to his men:

"Come on, Evans, we'll take him down. You stay here, Corliss, and look the place over again and keep an eye out. Try the fire escape—we didn't look out there—and the dumbwaiter. The stuff ought to be here somewhere. If you find anything let me know; if not, report at the office in the morning as usual. Come along, Knowlton."

"But where?" Knowlton stood up. "And on what authority? And for what?"

"To the Ritz, for dinner," said the red-faced man sarcastically, while the others grinned delightedly at the keen wit of their superior. "Where d'ye suppose? To the Tombs. I suppose next you'll want to see the paper. Here it is."

He drew a stamped, official-looking document from his pocket and waved it about in front of Knowlton's face.

The young man said nothing further, but allowed himself to be led out of the rooms into the hall.

"Is it necessary—must I wear these on the street?"

he stammered, holding up his shackled hands.

The red-faced man eyed him grimly.

"I guess two of us can take care of you," he said finally. "Take off the irons, Evans."

The other removed the handcuffs from Knowlton's wrists, and they descended the stairs and passed out to the street, one on either side of the prisoner.

Half an hour later Knowlton was pacing the floor of a narrow cell in the Tombs prison, with a heart full of remorse and bitterness and despair.

Yet he had no thought of his own danger, but was possessed of a fearful anxiety for Lila. Where had she gone? What had she done? Alone on the street at night, and with such a burden—the burden of his own crime! He felt that the thought would drive him mad, and he bit his lips to keep himself from crying out.

He thought of her magnificent courage in the awful scene at his rooms, and his eyes filled with tears. How brave and daring she had been! And how it must have hurt her innocence and proud womanhood to have been driven to such extremities for him—a criminal!

He told himself that she would despise him.

"She loves you," said his heart; "do not insult her by doubting it." Yes, but women sometimes despise the man they love. What a weak, blind fool he had been!

He groaned aloud in unutterable anguish. Piercing, overpowering emotion caused him to tremble and shake as a man with the palsy. He threw himself on the floor of the cell by the prison cot and buried his face in his hands.

He remained thus for an hour. Then he rose and seated himself on the edge of the cot.

"After all," he thought, "this, too, is weakness, and I must fight it. She has said that she loves me. Very well. I shall get out of this, and I have a lifetime to prove myself worthy of her. It is useless to waste time on vain regrets. Oh! She has given me strength. Every minute of my life belongs to her. And I said I didn't want to lose my self-respect! If I ever regain it, it will be through her.''

Finally, after many hours of alternate despair and anxiety and resolution, he threw himself face downward on the cot, utterly exhausted, and slept.

We shall leave him there and return to Lila.

Her plan, swiftly conceived and perfectly executed, had worked admirably.

Her hiding place behind the curtain in the alcove exactly suited her purpose, for the curtain was flimsy and transparent, and, placed as it was between herself and the light, she was able to observe what took place in the room without any danger of being seen herself.

She had trusted to Knowlton's wit, and he had not failed her. As soon as the detectives had rushed to the rear of the apartment in pursuit of him she had quietly stepped forth from her hiding place and gained the outer hall, closing the door softly behind her.

There she hesitated. Her first impulse was to descend at once to the street. But what if some one had been left on guard below? Was it not likely that she would be stopped and questioned; and the telltale parcel examined?

She stood for a few seconds trying to decide what to do; then, at the sound of returning footsteps in the room she had just left, fled in a sudden panic up the stairs to the landing above.

She realized the thousand dangers of her position. What if a detective had been sent up to guard the roof and should return and find her? What if some tenant of the house, entering or leaving, should question her?

What if one of the detectives below should happen to ascend the stairs?

And yet, what could she do? Nothing. She must remain where she was and wait. To go either up or down might be fatal.

She tried to think of some way to get rid of the parcel, which weighed on her arm with all the heaviness of fear. She hated it as though it were a human being. Fantastic schemes raced into her brain.

Should she ring the bell of one of the apartments and hand in the parcel as though it were a delivery from some tradesman? Should she place it on the floor of the hall and set it afire?

Suddenly the street door opened two flights below, and she heard footsteps entering and ascending the stairs. She quivered with terror, and felt a wild impulse to rush madly down and hurl the parcel into the street.

Then, just in time to prevent her crying out, the footsteps halted on the landing below, and there came the sound of a key turning in a lock and a door opening and closing. Evidently the person who had entered had been the tenant on the same floor with Knowlton, across the hall. She sighed with unutterable relief.

Many minutes passed, and each seemed to Lila an hour. What could the detectives be doing? Why did they not go, since they could have found nothing? For she thought, in her ignorance, that by her removal of the counterfeit money she had saved Knowlton from arrest. Her ideas of the manner of procedure of the law and its minions were extremely hazy, as those of a young girl should be. She was soon to be undeceived.

She waited, it seemed to her, for years. She felt faint and dizzy from fatigue and anxiety, her body was limp and nerveless, and she was telling herself that she must soon succumb, when she heard a door open in the hall below. At last!

There were footsteps, and Knowlton's voice came up to her:

"Is it necessary—must I wear these on the street?"

Then came the reply of the detective, and the sound of clinking steel, and steps descending the stairs, and the opening and closing of the street door.

Lila stood dumb with amazement. The meaning of what she had heard was clear to her: they had arrested him and were taking him to prison! But why? Was there something else of which she did not know? But she tossed that thought aside impatiently.

Knowlton had told her his story in detail, and she trusted him. But—prison! She shuddered with horror, and felt herself unable to stand, grasping at the baluster for support.

It was the necessity for action alone that sustained and roused her. To meet this new crisis she forgot her weakness of a moment before, and became again the courageous and daring woman she had been at the arrival of the detectives. She no longer hesitated or feared. She had something to do that must be done.

Holding the parcel tightly under her arm, she descended the stairs. As she passed through the hall in front of Knowlton's rooms the detective who had been left behind to complete the search for evidence looked out at her through the open door. Her heart beat madly, but she forced herself not to hasten her step as she descended the first flight of stairs to the outer door.

Another moment and she was in the street—free.

She glanced to the right and left, uncertain which way to turn. What should she do with the parcel? She wondered why it seemed so difficult to get rid of the thing. Surely nothing could be simpler than to dispose of an ordinary-looking parcel, a foot square.

One could drop it in an ash can, or leave it on a bench in the park, or merely place it on a stoop—any stoop—anywhere. But somehow to do any of these things seemed fraught with horrible danger. She could have cried with exasperation at her hesitation over a difficulty apparently so simple.

Suddenly she remembered what Knowlton had said: "It is best to be safe, and I shall take it to the river." Of course! Why had she not thought of it before?

She turned sharply, and as she turned noticed a man standing directly across the street gazing curiously at the house she had just left. At sight of him she started violently, and looked again. It was Sherman. There could be no doubt of it; the light from a streetlamp shone full on his face.

The spot where Lila was standing was comparatively dark, and as Sherman remained motionless she was convinced that she had not been recognized. But she was seized with terror, and, fearing every moment to hear his footsteps behind her, but not daring to look round, she turned and moved rapidly in the direction of the Hudson.

Ten minutes later she entered the ferry-house at the foot of West Twenty-third Street. A boat was in the slip and she boarded it and walked to the farther end.

She leaned on the rail, gazing toward the bay, as the boat glided away from the shore, and almost forgot her anxiety and her errand in contemplating the fairyland before her eyes.

The myriads of tiny twinkling lights with their background of mysterious half darkness, the skeletonlike forms of the massive buildings, barely revealed, and farther south, the towering outlines of the palaces of industry, were combined in a fantastic dream-picture of a modern monster.

Lila looked up, startled to find that the ferryboat had already reached the middle of the river. She glanced round to make sure she was not observed—there were few passengers on the boat—then quickly lifted the parcel over the rail and let it fall into the dark water below.

She could hardly realize that it was gone. Her arm was numb where it had been tightly pressed against the parcel, and it felt as though it still held its burden. She felt tired, and faint, and walked inside and seated herself.

When the boat arrived at the Jersey City slip she did not land. A half hour later she left it at Twenty-third Street. Another half hour and she was ascending the stairs to her room uptown.

Entering, she removed her hat and coat and threw them on a chair. She was tired, dead tired, in brain and body. She wanted to think: she told herself she had so much to think about.

The face of her world had changed utterly in the past few hours. But thought was impossible. She felt only a dull, listless sense of despair.

She had gained love, but what had she lost? Everything else had been given up in exchange for it. But how she loved him!

But even that thought was torture. Her head seemed ready to burst. Tears would have been a relief, but they would not come.

She dropped into a chair by the window, and, pressing her hands tightly against her throbbing temples, gazed out unseeing at the night.

When the dawn came, eight hours later, she had not moved.

CHAPTER XIII.

JJ

THE END OF THE DAY.

WHEN BILLY SHERMAN HAD VISITED DETEC- tive Barrett—the red-faced man with carroty hair—and had heard him say, "We will get Mr. Knowlton tonight," he knew that the thing was as good as done. Detective Barrett was a man to be depended upon.

But Billy Sherman never depended upon anybody. He made the rather common mistake of judging humanity from the inside—of himself—and the result was that he had acquired a distorted opinion of human nature. His topsyturvy logic went something like this, though not exactly in this form: "I am a man. I am bad. Therefore, all men are bad."

And there is more of that sort of reasoning in the world than we are willing to admit.

Sherman did not go so far as to distrust Detective Barrett, but he had an idea that he wanted to see the thing for himself. Accordingly, shortly after six o'clock in the evening he posted himself in a doorway opposite Knowlton's rooms on Thirtieth Street.

He had been there but a few minutes when he was startled by the sight of Lila approaching and entering the house. This led to a long consideration of probabilities which ended in a grim smile. He thought: "If they get her, too, all the better. Barrett's a good fellow, and I can do whatever I want with her."

Soon a light appeared in the windows of Knowlton's rooms. The shades were drawn, but the man in the street could see two shadows thrown on them as the occupants moved about inside.

Suddenly the two shadows melted into one, and Sherman found the thing no longer amusing. Cursing the detectives for their tardiness, he repaired to the corner for a bracer.

He soon returned and resumed his position in the doorway.

After another interminable wait he saw Detective Barrett arrive with his men, and with fierce exultation watched them enter.

Another wait—this time nearly an hour—before two of the detectives emerged with Knowlton. This puzzled Sherman. "Where the deuce is Lila?" he muttered. Then he reflected that the other detective was probably waiting with her for a conveyance.

And then, to his astonishment, he beheld Lila descending the stoop alone.

She was half a block away before he recovered his wits sufficiently to follow her.

On the ferryboat he mounted to the upper deck to escape observation, completely at a loss to account for Lila's freedom, or for this night trip across the Hudson. Looking cautiously over the upper railing, he had observed her every movement as she stood almost directly beneath him.

And then, as he saw her lift the parcel and drop it in the river, he had comprehended all in a flash. Stifling the exclamation that rose to his lips, he shrank back from the rail, muttering an imprecation.

Somehow she had obtained possession of the evidence—the chief evidence—against Knowlton, and destroyed it! And he had calmly looked on, like a weak fool! Why had he not had sense enough to stop her when she had first left the house? These were the thoughts that whipped him into a frenzy of rage.

But Sherman was not the man to waste time crying over spilled milk. After all, he reflected, the damage was not irreparable, since his knowledge gave him a power over her that should prove irresistible. By the time the boat had returned to Twenty-third Street he was once more fiercely exultant.

But he took the precaution of following Lila uptown; nor was he satisfied until he saw her white face dimly outlined at her own window.

Then he turned, muttering: "I guess she'll do no more mischief tonight."

He was determined that he would not make a second mistake. The first thing was to make sure of Knowlton. Perhaps early in the morning— He glanced at his watch; it was a quarter past nine.

At the corner he turned into a saloon and telephoned the office of Detective Barrett, and, finding him in, made an appointment to call on him in three-quarters of an hour.

He was there five minutes ahead of time. The detective was alone in the office and opened the door himself in response to his visitor's knock.

He was in ill humor.

"You've got us in a pretty mess," he began, placing a chair for Sherman and seating himself at his desk. "We got Knowlton all right, but there wasn't a scrap of stuff in the whole place. Unless we can dig up something, what he can do to us won't be a little. That was a beautiful tip-off of yours—I don't think. I don't say it wasn't on the square, but it looks like—"

Sherman cut him short.

"Wait a minute, Barrett. You shut your eyes and go to sleep, and then when you don't see anything you blame it on me. The stuff was there, and it's your own fault you didn't get it."

"Then you'd better go up there and show it to Corliss. He's probably looking for it yet."

"Oh, he won't find it now." Sherman leaned forward in his chair and held up a finger impressively. "When you went in that house Knowlton wasn't alone. There was a woman in his rooms with him, and a big bundle of the queer. And you politely closed your eyes and let her walk out with it."

The other stared at him.

"What sort of a game is this?" he demanded.

"This is straight," said Sherman, "and I can prove it. I know who the woman was, and I know what she did with the stuff. What I can't understand is how she ever got away."

"Do you mean to say she was inside when we got there?"

Sherman nodded emphatically.

The detective looked puzzled:

"Then how in the name of—" He stopped short, while his face was suddenly filled with the light of understanding—and chagrin.

"Well, I'm jiggered," he said finally. Then he explained Knowlton's ruse—or rather Lila's—to Sherman. "It's an old trick," he ended, "but we weren't looking for it. We thought he was alone. But where did she go? What did she do with it? Who is she?"

"She took a ride on a ferryboat and dropped it in the middle of the Hudson."

"Then it's gone."

"Thanks to you, yes."

"But where did you get all this? Of course, she's a—"

"Back up!" Sherman interrupted. "She's a friend of mine."

"She seems not exactly to hate Knowlton," the detective observed dryly. "Who is she?"

Sherman winced.

"What does that matter? She knows enough to send him higher than a kite, and she'll have to come through with it."

The other became impatient.

"But who is she? We ought to get her tonight."

There was a pause; then Sherman said slowly:

"You won't get her at all."

At the look of inquiry and surprise on the detective's face he proceeded to explain:

"I told you she's a friend of mine. Maybe it would be better to say I'm a friend of hers. Put it however you please, but she's not to be locked up. Serve her as a witness, and she'll give you all you need against Knowlton, and more, too.

"I'll see to that. She can't get out of it. Anyway, if you arrested her, what would happen? You couldn't make them testify against each other, and they'd both get off."

"But as soon as we serve her she'll beat it," the other objected.

"Leave that to me. Of course, I've got a personal

interest in this, and you ought to consider it. I don't
have to remind you—''

"No," the detective interrupted hastily, "you don't.
I have a memory, Billy."

"Well, then it's up to you."

The detective finally capitulated and agreed to do
as Sherman wished. Sherman gave him Lila's name
and address, and advised him to postpone serving the
subpoena as long as possible.

"I want to prepare her for it," he explained as the
detective accompanied him to the door. "I'll see her
first thing in the morning. If possible, we want to prevent Knowlton from knowing that she is to appear
against him, and I think I can manage it. You'll hear
from me tomorrow. Going uptown?''

The other replied that he had work to do in the
office that would keep him till midnight, and wished
him good night.

Sherman was well satisfied with the day's work.
With Knowlton in the Tombs and Lila completely in
his power, he felt that there was nothing left to be
desired. As he sat in an uptown subway local he reviewed his position with the eye of a general, and,
discovering no possible loophole for the enemy,
sighed with satisfaction.

At Twenty-third Street he left the train and made
his way to the lobby of the Lamartine.

He was led there more by force of habit than by
any particular purpose. At first he had thought of going
to see Lila at once, but had decided that it would serve
his ends better to allow her to have a night for reflection over the day's events. She would be less able to
resist his demands.

It was but little past ten o'clock, and he found the

lobby almost deserted. Night at the Lamartine began late and ended early—in the morning.

One or two nondescripts loitered about the entrance inside, the hotel clerk yawned behind his desk, and the weary-looking female who took Miss Hughes's place during the hours of darkness was drumming on the counter with her fingers, chewing gum, and reading a newspaper, thus exercising three different sets of muscles at the same time.

Sherman approached her:

"Have any of the boys been in?"

She looked up from her newspaper and regarded him chillingly:

"Huh?"

It was this young girl's habit never to understand questions addressed to her till they had been repeated at least once. It argued a superiority over the questioner; an indifference to common and sublunary affairs.

She condescended finally to inform Sherman that Driscoll and Booth had been seen in the lobby some two hours before. While talking she contrived somehow to lose not a single stroke on the gum.

Sherman wandered about for half an hour, tried to find someone to take a cue at billiards without success, and had about decided to go home when Dumain and Dougherty entered arm-in-arm.

Dumain called to Sherman, and the three proceeded to the bar. Sherman ordered a whisky, Dougherty a gin rickey, and Dumain an absinth frappé. This is for the benefit of those who judge a man by what he drinks. You see what it amounts to.

The ex-prizefighter was a little ill at ease. He felt that he had treated Sherman a little shabbily by breaking his promise not to speak to Knowlton till the following day; perhaps, after all, he thought, Sherman had acted in good faith.

"I suppose you called off your sleuth," he observed.

Sherman looked up quickly.

"What? Oh, yes. I saw him this afternoon. Good thing, too. He was costing me more than a prima donna. Fill 'em up, bartender."

"Then it's all right to speak to Knowlton now?"

"As far as I'm concerned, yes."

"The reason I wanted to know," Dougherty hesitated, "is because I already spoke to him. It wasn't because I wanted to put anything over on you—don't think that. He came in here about noon, and it was too good a chance to pass up.

"Besides, Miss Williams was going out with him, and I had to head him off somehow. I was a little uneasy about it, but since you say it's all right, I'll forget it. And, thank Heaven, we've seen the last of Knowlton. By this time he's probably so far away from little old New York you couldn't see him with a telescope from the top of the Singer Building."

"Well, you didn't do any harm." Sherman was picking up his change on the bar.

"Eet was best," put in Dumain. "Zee sooner zee bettaire. He was a quiet scoundrel. You should have seen heem when Dougherty told heem! He had not a word. He walked out wiz a frown."

Each man lifted his glass in silence. Each had his own thoughts.

"I'm a little worried about Miss Williams," said Dougherty presently. "I wonder what she thought when she saw him walk out without speaking to her? Knowlton asked me to tell her, but I didn't have the nerve. I think they had a date to go to lunch. And all afternoon she kept watching for him. I saw her."

"She'll soon forget him," said Sherman.

"I doubt it," declared Dougherty. "You know yourself he was different from us. And from the way she looked this afternoon—I doubt it."

"Bah!" Dumain snapped his fingers. "She care not zat much for heem. If she did would she not have been—ah, grief—*distrait*—when she hear he was a what you call eet counterfeiter?"

There was a sudden pause, while Dougherty turned and gazed at Dumain keenly.

"When did you tell her?" he demanded finally.

Dumain was silent, while his face reddened in confusion, and Sherman raised his hand to his mouth to conceal a smile.

"When did you tell her?" repeated the ex-prize-fighter, more sternly than before.

"Tonight," Dumain stammered. "You see, Knowlton had left so sudden, and I thought she ought to know. You see—"

"Yes, I see!" Dougherty roared. "You're a darn Frenchman. That's what you are; you're a darn' Frenchman! You can't keep your mouth shut. You ought to be muzzled. If you wasn't such a human shrimp I'd—Bartender, for the love of Mike, give us a drink."

He drained a highball with two prodigious gulps. Dumain took courage.

"But eet was best. She had to know sometime. So tell her at once, zat is what I theenk. Zen I tell her."

"What did she say?" Dougherty demanded.

"Nozzing." The little Frenchman shrugged his shoulders expressively. "I tell you she care leetle for heem. She lifted her eyes upward in surprise"—he rolled his own toward heaven—"and say, 'Has he gone?' like zat. Zen she say good night like any other time and went home.''

Dougherty grunted in disbelief.

Sherman had for some minutes been meditating on the question whether he should tell his companions what he knew—or, rather, what he had done. It would be in the nature of a triumph over them, but would it not be dangerous? He reflected, and could not resist the temptation.

He took up Dumain's last words:

''And what makes you think she went home?''

The others stared at him—a stare that plainly meant: ''Where else should she go?''

''You evidently don't know the lady very well,'' Sherman continued. ''You think she's as innocent as she looks. She went straight from here to Knowlton's rooms, and she seemed to know pretty well how to get there. You can guess as well as I can what she went after. And how many times—''

He stopped suddenly, though not of his own volition. The compelling cause was Dougherty's fingers about his throat, in a grip of steel.

Dumain had hurriedly stepped aside, and the bartender was loudly expostulating in a tone of alarm, while three or four men who were standing at the bar a few feet away looked on with pleasurable expectations. They knew Dougherty.

The ex-prizefighter spoke no word—he never talked and acted at the same time. He pressed his fingers tighter and tighter, till the face of the man who had insulted Lila began to assume a hue of purple as he pawed helplessly at the wrists that seemed to be made of iron.

''You keel heem,'' said Dumain quietly. ''Let heem go, Tom.''

Dougherty did so, and Sherman stood erect. Then, with a single glance charged with malevolence and hatred, he turned to go.

"No, you don't," said the ex-prizefighter grimly, stepping in front of him. "You've said too much. Tell us what you meant."

Sherman opened his lips to speak, but the words would not pass his throat. He gulped spasmodically.

"Here," said the bartender, handing him a drink of brandy. "This'll fix you."

Sherman drained the glass at one swallow, with a grimace of pain.

"Now," said Dougherty, "speak up."

Sherman wanted to defy him, but dared not. He, too, knew Dougherty.

He began:

"I'll even up for this, Dougherty. What I said was the truth."

"Go on. I'll take care of myself."

Sherman spoke with difficulty, but in a tone of sneering satisfaction:

"Immediately after Dumain spoke to her tonight she went to Knowlton's rooms. She was there when the cops came for Knowlton, and she crawled out somehow with a bundle of the queer and threw it in the middle of the Hudson. Knowlton's in the Tombs, where he ought to be."

The others were gazing at him speechless with surprise.

"That's what your innocent Miss Williams has come to." Sherman continued with a sneer. "And it's your own fault. You wouldn't listen to me. And now—"

The look in Dougherty's eyes stopped him.

The ex-prizefighter's tone was threatening:

"Who put them onto Knowlton?"

"How do I know?" Sherman retorted with an assumption of bravado.

"Maybe you don't," said Dougherty grimly, "but I do. Sherman, you're a skunk. I don't want to touch you. You're too rotten. But I want to ask you some questions—and look here! No—look in my eyes. Now talk straight. Who peached on Knowlton?"

The answer was low but distinct:

"I did."

"You say he's in the Tombs?"

"Yes."

"What's the charge against him?"

"Passing counterfeit money."

"Where is Miss Williams?"

"How do I know?"

"Answer!" Dougherty advanced a step. "You know, all right, you sneak. Where is she?"

"At home."

"Who arrested Knowlton?"

"Detective Barrett, of the Secret Service."

"Does he know anything about Miss Williams?"

Sherman opened his mouth to speak, then closed it again and was silent.

"Answer!" Dougherty's voice trembled with his effort to control it. "And look at me! Don't try to lie!"

There was no escape.

"He—he knows all about her," Sherman stammered.

Then, at the look of uncontrollable fury that appeared on his questioner's face, he sprang to one side, bounded to the door, and fled through the lobby and madly down the street.

Dougherty had started to pursue him, but thought better of it and halted.

He turned to Dumain and said shortly:

"Come on; get home and go to bed. We have work to do in the morning."

CHAPTER XIV.

THE MORNING AFTER.

MRS. AMANDA BERRY PAUSED AT THE HEAD of the stairs and looked curiously at a closed door to the right.

"Now, I call that funny," she remarked to herself. "I ain't seen her go out, and it's past nine o'clock. Surely she ain't sick."

She hesitated, glanced again at the door, and started to descend the stairs, then turned suddenly and reascended them, and knocked sharply on the door at which she had aimed her remark.

Mrs. Berry was a curious phenomenon—a *rara avis*. She owned and operated a rooming house on One Hundred and Fourth Street, New York, and she took a personal interest in her roomers. Not that she was inquisitive or—to put it vulgarly—nosy; she merely had a heart. This was so far from being resented by the roomers that they were all a little jealous of one of their number for whom Mrs. Berry had more than once betrayed a decided preference—Lila Williams.

Receiving no response to her knock, Mrs. Berry knocked again. After a long pause there was a faint "Come in."

She entered.

Lila was sitting in a chair by the window. Her hat and coat lay on another chair near the door. The bed had not been slept in.

"Now what's the matter?" Mrs. Berry sang out cheerily, crossing the room. "Another headache, I'll bet a dollar. If you don't—why, what's the matter? Goodness sakes alive, just look at the girl's face! No wonder you didn't go to work! You just wait—"

"Now, please, Mrs. Berry," Lila interrupted, rising to her feet and trying to smile, "don't bother about me. I—I want to be alone. Really."

Her face was deadly white, giving her eyes and cheeks a sunken appearance, and as she stood with one hand resting heavily on the back of the chair she was quivering from head to foot. Mrs. Berry stared at her in wrathful amazement.

"You want to be alone! Look at you! You get right in that bed—and look at it! You ain't been in bed at all—and I know you come in early, because I heard you. So you ain't sick. Then you're in trouble."

She looked at Lila keenly to confirm her diagnosis, and nodded her head. She knew the signs, and she knew the one thing that would help.

Mrs. Berry was a good-sized woman. She walked over to Lila, picked her up in her arms as though she were a baby, and seated herself in a chair.

Then she spoke grimly:

"You're a little fool. If you keep on like this you'll die. Don't you know what tears is good for? Now go on and cry as hard as you can, and hurry up about it."

Lila was motionless and silent. Mrs. Berry folded her arms tighter around her and continued:

"You know, if it's any real trouble I'll help you. Of course I ain't like a mother, but I'll do all I can. Look, dearie, look at me! What is it? Tell me. Tell me all about it. I'm your mother now, you know. Here, put your arm round my neck—that's right. Now what is it, dearie; won't you tell me?"

She felt the slender body tremble in her arms and something hot and wet on her hand that touched Lila's cheek, but she pretended not to notice, and went on:

"You don't need to be afraid to tell me, no matter what it is, because I can stand anything. Lord! I've been through it all. Of course it's a man—it always is. There! That's right. Now! There, dearie—never you mind me—"

Lila was sobbing, with great sighs and shakings of her frame, the sobs that come from the heart. Mrs. Berry held her in her arms, patting and soothing her, while the storm raged. Presently she rose and laid her, all bathed in tears, on the bed.

"There! That'll do you good. You just keep it up as long as you can. Lord! To think you've had that in you all night!"

She moved busily about the room, hanging Lila's hat and coat in the wardrobe, adjusting the window-shades, and moving chairs that were better off where they were. Finally she moved to the door. She started to speak, but thought better of it, and went out softly, closing the door behind her.

Lila remained on the bed for many minutes, while the tempest gradually calmed, and at length left her with only an occasional long, quivering sigh. Then she arose and bathed her face in cold water and arranged her hair. When Mrs. Berry entered a minute later she was putting on her hat, with fingers that trembled.

"Now what?" Mrs. Berry demanded, stopping in the doorway.

Lila answered:

"I am going to work."

"You are, eh?" Mrs. Berry snorted. "Not if I know it! You take off that hat and set right down in that chair—or, better still, go to bed."

"But I must," protested Lila. "I'm all right now, Mrs. Berry; really I am."

"All right, then you're all right. I don't say you ain't. But you ain't goin' to work."

This was said in a tone which had been only too well known by the late Mr. Berry. He had never been able to resist it, nor was Lila. It forbore all opposition; and without knowing exactly how or why, some minutes later she found herself in the chair by the window eating an excellent breakfast brought up on a tray by Mrs. Berry.

During the morning Lila received several visits from the good woman. She came to remove the tray, she came to fetch the morning papers, and she came to "tidy up the room." On her sixth visit she entered somewhat precipitately and announced that there was a gentleman below to see Lila.

"Who is it?" asked Lila, turning quickly.

"He didn't give his name," said Mrs. Berry. "He's a tall, sporty-lookin', mean-lookin' man."

Lila reflected a moment, then asked Mrs. Berry to show him up. She grunted, and departed.

A minute later Billy Sherman entered the room.

Lila sprang to her feet with an involuntary exclamation of surprise and dismay.

"You!" she breathed.

Sherman nodded, laid his hat and gloves on a table near the door, and crossed the room to her side.

"Yes," he said calmly, "I. Aren't you glad to see me?"

Then, as Lila, unable to speak, pointed to the door with a shaking finger, he continued:

"Well, I'm glad to see you. No, I won't go. And when you hear what I have to tell you, you won't want me to go. I've played with you long enough, and it's about time for us to understand each other. Sit down."

Lila was trembling with indignation and fear. She remembered Knowlton's story: this was the man who had caused all her suffering and Knowlton's misfortune. Sherman's person had always impressed her disagreeably; she now shrank from him as from a snake.

She forced herself to look at him.

"Mr. Sherman, if I had known it was you asking for me I would not have seen you. Go—at once—or I'll call Mrs. Berry."

"So you wouldn't have seen me?" Sherman sneered. "Well, you'd have been sorry for it. If it wasn't for me, do you know where you'd be now? You'd be in the Tombs. That trip of yours across the Hudson last night was a little indiscreet."

He smiled grimly at her gasp of surprise and horror as he went on:

"You wouldn't believe I was your friend, but maybe you will now. Couldn't I have turned you over to the detectives last night? Remember, all I have to do is walk to a telephone—it's not too late."

Lila could only repeat:

"Go—go!"

"But that's not what I want," he continued, ignoring her cry. "I'm fool enough to want to protect you. I love you. For months you've laughed at me; now

it's my turn. You can't look at me any more with your
darned pious air of superiority. A girl that goes to visit
a man in his rooms at night had better take what she
can get. Wait! Wait till I finish!''

Lila, her eyes ablaze, had sprung to the door and
begun to open it. But at the tone of Sherman's last
words, menacing and significant, she halted.

"I thought so," said Sherman meaningly. "You're
not the one to break your own neck. Now do as I tell
you, and you can save both Knowlton and yourself."

Lila stared at him in surprise, incredulous.

"Oh, not for you," he continued, reading her
thought. "I'm not that kind of a fool. I put it to you
straight: do you want to save Knowlton?"

"What—what has that to do with you?" stammered
Lila, removing her hand from the door and turning to
face him.

"Just this: I can save him, and I will—on one condition."

"And the—one condition?"

"That you marry me."

"I—marry—you!" The words choked her.

"Yes. The day that you become my wife John
Knowlton is a free man. Otherwise—you know the
alternative. And, my dear, you could make a worse
bargain. As I said, you are not in a position to choose.
And I love you; I will try to make you happy—"

"You—make me happy!"

The stinging scorn of the tone was indescribable.
Sherman winced, and was moved to a sudden fury:

"Well, and if I don't? I'll have you! At last! And
be careful—I may decide not to marry you. After all,
why should I marry you? Knowlton didn't. That
touches you, does it? And what do you think of your

lover now? Why don't you go down to the Tombs and tell him—tell him—''

He sputtered and paused, overcome with jealous rage. Then, recovering himself with difficulty, he said calmly:

"And now I want your answer. You're at the end of your rope, and you may as well talk sense. None of your high-flown, touch-me-if-you-dare stuff will go now—you're up against a stiff proposition and you've got to make good.

"I've got you. Do you understand that? I've got you. You'd do anything for this Knowlton, would you? All right. When will you marry me?''

Lila wanted to cry out, to run from the room, to close her ears and eyes against his insults and his leering face. But she stood glued to the spot, unable either to speak or move.

The man, advancing a threatening step, repeated his question:

"When will you marry me?''

Her lips moved, but there was no sound.

"By Heaven, you will answer me!'' said Sherman through clenched teeth. He reached her side in two long strides and grasped her arm fiercely. "Speak!'' he hissed. "You little black-eyed devil—speak—tell me—''

At that moment there came three sharp knocks on the door—barely in time.

Sherman, muttering an oath, released Lila's arm and turned quickly about. Lila placed her hand on the back of a chair for support, and, between quick, short, breaths, managed to murmur:

"Come in.''

The door opened. Mrs. Berry entered.

"More visitors,'' she announced shortly, from the

doorway. She seemed not to notice Lila's agitation, and Sherman's back was turned. "Mr. Dumain and Mr. Dougherty is down below and asks to see you."

Then she ran over to Lila, and, placing her mouth close to her ear, whispered:

"I don't know what this is all about, dearie, but if I can help you—"

Lila threw her arms around the good woman's neck and kissed her.

"You can help me," she murmured. "Send them up—Mr. Dumain and Mr. Dougherty—send them up at once! Dear Mrs. Berry, hurry!"

Whereupon Mrs. Berry sped from the room and down the stairs with flying skirts.

Lila stood by the open door. Sherman turned, his face livid with rage—or was it fear? His lips moved, but no words came from them. He stared straight at the door, as though stunned by surprise at the sudden check to his plans, and remained so as Lila advanced eagerly to meet the two men who came puffing up the stairs.

"I am glad to see you," she declared, taking a hand of each.

Dumain bowed grandly, in silence. Dougherty gripped her hand with awkward roughness and stammered an unintelligible "Good morning!"

But he soon found his tongue. Lila moved aside, and at the same instant the newcomers caught sight of Sherman.

Dougherty's eyes were filled with surprise for a moment, then they became alight with an unholy joy. He had spent half the night regretting what he considered the leniency of his treatment of Sherman, and here he was delivered unto his hand!

He pointed a finger at him and spoke to Lila.

"What is he doing here?"

But Lila was so relieved by the unexpected succor that she was scarcely able to speak.

"I don't know," she stammered. "I mean—it doesn't matter, since you have come. Only, send him away—please—at once!"

Then at sight of the look on Dougherty's face she grasped his arm.

"No—not that! Don't hurt him! I mean—just send him away."

But the ex-prizefighter shook off her detaining hand.

"Hurt him? Oh, no. No, I won't exactly hurt him. I'll just shake hands with him. Only I'm so glad to see him that I may be a little rough."

His tone was sharp and clear as the ring of steel, and the touch of sarcasm made it only the more deadly. He started toward Sherman, who retreated with his back against the window, crouched halfway to the floor with his teeth showing in an ugly snarl of fear. The sight struck Lila dumb with terror.

It was Dumain who averted the catastrophe. Dougherty had nearly reached the window when he felt the little Frenchman's hand on his arm, and tried to shake it off.

But Dumain only tightened his grip.

"But, Tom! *Mon Dieu!* Look at her! She weel scream—she weel faint. You can't keel heem in zee presence of zee lady. Eet ees not what you call eet polite. Come! Beeg eediot!"

"Do you mean I ought to let him go?" demanded Dougherty, amazed.

"For now—yes. We keel heem later. Come—look at her!"

Lila added her voice:

"Please, Mr. Dougherty, just send him away. I think he won't bother any more."

Dougherty sighed. Such conduct as this was entirely beyond his comprehension. Since the fellow was there, why not give him what was coming to him?

However, he felt that he must bend to the wishes of the lady. Perhaps, after all, it would be a breach of decorum. But he was unable to speak; he merely stepped to one side as a sign that he obeyed the will of the majority against his own.

Sherman attempted to make his exit with dignity. But his step was considerably hurried as he crossed the room, and it degenerated into a run at the head of the stairs; and he forgot his hat and gloves. Dumain saw them on the table and threw them down the stairs after him.

Then Lila sank into a chair and burst into tears.

This rattled Dumain and Dougherty more than the presence of a dozen Shermans would have done. The little Frenchman walked about as though in search of a means of escape, and finally began examining a vase on the mantel with minute care.

The ex-prizefighter was seized with a fit of coughing and went over to close the door, banging it with a force that shook the house. They avoided meeting each other's eyes and kept their backs turned toward Lila.

Dougherty watched Dumain fingering the vase till he could stand it no longer, then burst forth:

"You fool, can't you do anything?"

Whereupon Lila smiled through her tears, and Dumain, turning, saw her, and sighed with immense relief.

"It's I that am a fool," said Lila, dabbing at her eyes with her handkerchief, "but I just couldn't help it. Oh, I am so glad you came! I thank you—thank you, with all my heart. And now he—Mr. Dougherty, why is he so afraid of you?"

"Him!" the ex-prizefighter snorted. "He's afraid of everyone on earth, including himself. What was he doing here?"

Lila stammered, coloring.

"He—he wanted me to do something. It would do no good to tell you. I hope I shall never see him again. He frightens me. I am so glad you came!"

Then she forgot her confusion when she realized that she had not offered them chairs, and begged them to be seated. They obeyed her, Dumain with a flourish, Dougherty awkwardly.

There was a silence. Each of the men was waiting for the other to speak, and Lila gazed at each in turn. Finally she said:

"Did you come from the hotel?"

"Yes," echoed the two men.

Another silence. Dougherty moved about uneasily in his chair. Dumain twirled his mustache. Lila tried to think of something to say, but found her tongue tied by their embarrassment.

It was Dougherty who finally burst forth with a prodigious effort:

"I suppose you know why we came?"

Lila shook her head and invited an explanation.

"Well, we saw you wasn't at the hotel, and we thought maybe you was at home, so we came up to see."

"We thought perhaps eet was eelness."

"You are very kind," Lila murmured.

"And," Dougherty continued, swallowing hard and forcing the words between his lips, "we wanted to talk to you about Knowlton."

Lila turned her eyes full on the speaker, and Dumain threw him a nod of applause and encouragement.

"You see, we saw Sherman last night, and he told us all about it. I don't want you to think we had anything to do with it. We wouldn't peach on a guy, no matter who he was."

"I didn't think you would," said Lila.

"But," continued Dougherty, now fully started, "we ain't sorry he got it. We're glad he's put away where he can't do any more harm. We don't like the way—"

"Did Mr. Sherman say—anything—about me?" Lila interrupted.

The ex-prizefighter looked away from her.

"Yes," he said finally. "We know everything."

"Then why did you come—"

"That's what I'm going to tell you. And that's why I started like I did. I want you to understand that we're dead against Knowlton.

"Now, there's no use talking about what's past. We don't care what you've done; we ain't even going to say, 'I told you so.' What we want is to help you now.

"Knowlton's done for, so there's no use worrying about him, but from what Sherman said last night we was afraid you might get tangled up so you might have some trouble to get loose, and we want to let you know we're right on the job to help you out of it. I guess that's about all."

Lila leaned forward in her chair.

"But you say—you are 'dead against' Mr. Knowlton?"

Dougherty said "Yes" with emphasis, and Dumain nodded vigorously.

"Then—I thank you," said Lila.

Her tone caused the ex-prizefighter to look at her quickly.

"You mean—"

Lila rose to her feet. Tears were in her eyes, and her hands were clasped together so that little spots of red and white showed on them. Her voice, when she spoke, was low and quavering, but it held that depth of tone which is heard only when the words come from the heart.

"I mean—it is useless to talk to me longer, Mr. Dougherty. I am a very wretched girl. And now I shall offend you—I know it, but cannot help it. I can't take your help, because I won't desert Mr. Knowlton."

Dougherty swore, and immediately was on his feet, stammering an apology, while Dumain glared at him fiercely.

Lila paid no attention to the interruption.

"You see—I can't. Oh, don't think me an ingrate— I know how kind you have been—but you don't know as much about him as I do. And I can't leave him without—I can't think of him as you do"—she tried to smile—"because I am going to be his wife."

"*Mon Dieu!*" gasped Dumain. Dougherty was speechless.

"Yes," said Lila—and there was a note of pride in her voice—"we are to be married. So, of course, you know how I feel about it, and I couldn't very well expect you to help me—us. I am sorry, because I do care for you, but you would never understand—"

She paused. The ex-prizefighter and the little Frenchman each heaved a prodigious sigh. They looked at each other, and each read in the other's eyes his own thought. The Frenchman nodded significantly and Dougherty turned to Lila.

He said:

"We're friends of yours, ain't we, Miss Williams?"

She nodded, wondering.

"Old friends—pals?"

"Yes."

"Well, I want to ask you a question. If you don't want to answer it, all right. What I mean is, maybe I've got no right to ask it, but I want to know. Do you love this guy Knowlton?"

Lila's face colored, she hesitated, and then answered simply:

"Yes."

"How well do you love him?"

"As well"—the answer came as promptly as though it were printed in a catechism—as indeed it is—"as he loves me."

Dumain cried *"Bravo!"* and Dougherty grinned. Then they rose, and each extended a hand to Lila, as a "pal."

She understood, but could not speak, and took the outstretched hands, one in each of her own. Then she found her tongue and started to stammer her gratitude.

"Cut it!" said Dougherty rudely. He was unused to emotion of the tender sort, and this had been a trying scene. "The thing to do now is to get him out. And, little pal, leave it to us. It's a cinch. But, believe me, you'll have to pay for it. There's one thing we've got to have."

"A kees from zee bride?" Dumain suggested.

"No, you darned Frenchman. An invitation to the wedding!"

CHAPTER XV.

NUMBER THIRTY-TWO.

AFTER A NIGHT IN HIS CELL AT THE TOMBS Knowlton rose from his cot early in the morning with a racking headache and a poignant sense of desolation and despair.

But his breakfast, which he forced himself to swallow, and his bath, such as it was, considerably refreshed him, and he found that the night had, at least, cleared his brain and left him able to think. He sat on the edge of his cot and considered his calamity, if not calmly, with fortitude and a supply of the dry light of reason.

He tried to keep his mind off of Lila; he could not think of her with fortitude; it filled him with an overwhelming sense of her loyalty and bravery and sweet compassion.

He reviewed in his mind the probable evidence against himself, turning it over and over, trying to discover its value, but it was like groping blindly in the dark. He knew nothing of what was known.

Had Red Tim been captured? Did they have any direct evidence of any of his—he sought a word—transactions? Or had they counted on catching him "with the goods on"—and been foiled by Lila?

All the morning he sat and pondered on these questions when he was not thinking of Lila. He felt little anxiety concerning her; she had given, before him, so convincing an instance of her wit and courage that he felt assured of her safety. He knew she had escaped from the rooms, and though she had carried a dangerous burden she could have found no serious difficulty in disposing of it.

He remembered her embarrassed timidity as she had entered his rooms, her flash of anger at his seeming indifference, the light of awakening gladness in her eyes as he had told her his love—and then, her arms clasped about his neck, her lips pressed to his, her frank, sweet words of surrender.

And now—he glanced at the bare prison walls—this! He shuddered and groaned.

At that moment there came a voice from the grated door—the rasping voice of the turnkey:

"Knowlton! Someone to see you!"

The man on the cot sprang to his feet in surprise. Could it be—But no, surely it could not be Lila, he thought, and, hesitating, stammered:

"Who is it?"

Then he crossed to the door and peered through the grating.

"Dougherty!" he cried, astonished. "What in the name of Heaven brings you here?"

The ex-prizefighter, who was standing in the middle of the corridor, approached the door.

"Hello, Knowlton! You seem to be on the wrong side this time. How's the world?"

Knowlton stood staring at him stiffly, without speaking. Why had he come? Had anything happened to Lila? Had she been arrested?

"What do you want?" he demanded, in a voice hoarse with anxiety.

Dougherty laughed.

"That's a devil of a way to talk to a friend. But I can see you've got the Willies, so I'll excuse you."

"A—a friend?" Knowlton stammered.

"Sure." Dougherty laughed again, possibly to hide a certain embarrassment. "Do you think I'd be here if I wasn't? Among other things, I've got a little note here for you from Miss Williams."

"Where is she?"

"At home."

"Is she all right? Is she well?"

"Yes—both."

"Thank God! And the note?"

"Not so loud." Dougherty came closer to the door. "I'll have to slip it to you on the quiet. And talk lower—you never can tell in this little hotel who's around. Wait a minute—here—quick!"

A tiny roll of paper showed itself through the bars of the door. Knowlton grasped it with anxious fingers and placed it in his pocket.

His voice was tremulous with feeling.

"Thanks, old man. A thousand thanks. You're sure she's all right?"

"Absolutely."

"Thank God!" Knowlton's fingers closed convulsively over the paper in his pocket. "That's really all I cared about. It doesn't matter much what happens to me—anyway, I deserve it. But if she had been—"

"Well, she wasn't," Dougherty interrupted. "And now to get down to business, for I haven't got any too much time. You're going to get out of this thing, Knowlton, and we're going to help you."

"But why—"

"Never mind why. Of course we're doing it mostly for *her*, but she told us some stuff about you this morning that we didn't know, and we feel we gave you kind of a dirty deal, and we want to square up. But mostly it's for her. You are on the square with her, ain't you? That's all we want to know."

The question was humiliating, but Knowlton swallowed it. He felt that he deserved it, and he realized that Dougherty had a right to ask it.

He said simply:

"You know I am. Didn't she tell you?"

"Yes. I know. And say—you're a lucky devil, Knowlton."

Then they proceeded to a discussion of the steps to be taken for Knowlton's defense. Dougherty was surprised to discover that he knew nothing of the nature of the evidence against him, and declared that it greatly increased their difficulties.

He ended:

"But leave that to the lawyer. Dumain has gone after him now—I left him over at the subway—and they'll probably be here this afternoon."

"But—" Knowlton hesitated.

"Well?"

"Why, about the lawyer. I had thought of conducting my own defense. I don't believe he can help us any."

"What's the matter? Broke?" said Dougherty bluntly.

"The fact is—yes. Or nearly so. And I certainly can't take any more favors—"

"Go to the deuce with your favors! Didn't I say we're going to help you out of this? Don't be a fool, Knowlton! But I can't quite understand how you can be broke. I supposed you had a nice little pile stowed away somewhere. You don't mean to tell me you shoved the queer for that gang and got nothing out of it?"

Knowlton almost smiled.

"But I stopped that a month ago."

"I know that. She told us all about it. But didn't you have sense enough to dig a fat little hole somewhere?"

Instead of answering the question Knowlton asked one of his own:

"Didn't you ask me a little while ago if I was on the square with Miss Williams?"

Dougherty nodded, wondering what that had to do with the accumulation of a "pile."

"Well, I'll show you how square I was. I had two thousand dollars put away. After I got to know her, I—disposed of it."

Dougherty stared at him incredulously.

"Do you mean to say you threw away two thousand dollars in real money?"

"Yes."

It took the ex-prizefighter a full minute to recover from his astonishment and find his tongue, after which he stated it as his settled and firm opinion that Knowlton was hopelessly insane.

He added:

"But don't you worry about the lawyer—leave it to us. And everything else. And now"—he glanced at his watch—"I've got to leave you. It's nearly noon, and I want to catch the boys before they go out to lunch. Dumain will be here this afternoon.''

They talked a few minutes longer before the ex-prizefighter finally departed.

Knowlton listened to his footsteps and those of the turnkey as they passed down the corridor, then he crossed to the little barred window and drew forth the note from Lila. It was short:

> DEAR: I have nothing to say, except that I love you, and are you sure you want to hear that? You see, I am cheerful. Mr. Dougherty and Mr. Dumain are very, very kind to me, and to you. We can never repay them. You must be cheerful, too, if you love me.
>
> LILA.

Knowlton read it over many times and pressed it to his lips. And such is the heart of man that the tears of gratitude which filled his eyes were not for Dougherty's offer of practical and valuable assistance, but for this little inconsequential note, which said nothing except, ''I love you!''

Dougherty, on his way uptown, was facing a new difficulty—a little matter of cash. He was reflecting on the fact that it takes money to prove a man's innocence, especially when he happens to be guilty. And where was the money to come from?

He considered all possible sources of revenue, and found the total sadly deficient. He counted his own purse three times—it amounted to sixty-two dollars and forty-five cents. And this was a matter, not of a hundred or so, but of two or three thousands.

A thousand for the lawyer, a thousand for a ''stake'' for Knowlton and Lila, and a thousand for miscellaneous expenses. The ex-prizefighter was determined not to do the thing by halves. But where to get the three thousand?

He had been headed straight for the Lamartine; but instead of leaving the subway at Twenty-third Street he continued to Columbus Circle, and went for a walk in the park to think it over. One idea he had had from the first he dismissed as too hazardous; but as his field of speculation narrowed and revealed the entire lack of anything better, or even so good, he returned to it again and considered it seriously.

It was by no means sure, but it appealed to him—and there was nothing else. He left the park at Ninety-sixth Street and boarded a downtown Elevated.

It was a quarter past three by the solemn-faced clock above the hotel desk when Dougherty entered the lobby of the Lamartine. All of the men he sought—the Erring Knights—were there, except, of course, Sherman.

Dumain greeted the newcomer.

"Deed you see Knowlton?"

"Yes. Did you?"

The little Frenchman nodded.

"Wiz a lawyer. And I gave heem—zee—lawyer—two hundred dollars. Knowlton ees—ees—"

"Broke?"

"Yes."

"I know it. That puts it up to us, and we've got to make good. Have you said anything to the boys?"

For reply Dumain began to give him an account of what had happened in the Lamartine during the preceding hour.

The other interrupted him impatiently.

"I don't care what they thought. The point is, are they with us?"

"Yes. Positeevely. But they don't understand—"

"I don't care whether they understand or not. Where are they? There's work to do. Come on!"

Five minutes later the five were gathered together on the leather lounge in the corner. Dumain arrived last, having gone to fetch Driscoll from the barber shop in the basement.

Dougherty, leaning against a marble pillar in front of the lounge, began:

"Now, is there anything you guys want to know? Did Dumain explain everything to you? Talk fast!"

There being no response he continued:

"All right. You all know the hole Knowlton's in, and that we've promised Miss Williams to get him out. Well, we need three thousand dollars."

There were exclamations of astonishment, and Booth, who was seated on the arm of the lounge puffing a cigarette, was so profoundly shocked that he fell off onto the floor.

"What do you want to do—buy up a jury?" came from Driscoll.

"Never mind what I want to do," returned Dougherty. "I say we need three thousand. Ask Dumain how much the lawyer wants."

They turned to the little Frenchman, who informed them that the attorney's fee would hardly be less than a thousand, and might be more.

"And another thousand for a stake for Knowlton," said Dougherty, "and the rest for—"

"But why should we stake Knowlton?"

"Shut up! I'm not asking you what to do—I'm telling you!" Dougherty roared. "Are we pikers? That's what I want to know, are we pikers?"

The opinion of the majority, expressed somewhat forcibly, appeared to be that they were not "pikers."

"Then listen to me. First, I say that we need that

thousand dollars, and I don't want to have to say it again. We're lucky if we've got three hundred among us, except Dumain, and he's no millionaire. The question is—where'll we get it?''

"And that is what I would call quite some question," remarked Driscoll.

"It is," Dougherty admitted, "but I've got a plan. It requires a little capital. I have here fifty dollars. Everybody shell."

They hesitated for a moment, but Dougherty's tone was one not to be withstood—and they "shelled." The ex-prizefighter tabulated this result:

Dougherty	$50
Driscoll	32
Jennings	13
Booth	65

Said he:

"That's a hundred and sixty. I need two hundred and fifty. Dumain, give me ninety dollars."

The little Frenchman handed it over without a word. He had already given the lawyer two hundred, and it left his purse pretty slim.

"Now," said Dougherty, "my plan is short and sweet, and make or break. I'm going to divide this into five parts. Each of us gets fifty dollars. You can take your choice of anything in town—go wherever you please and play any game you like.

"No two are to go together. We'll meet at Dumain's rooms at midnight, and if one or two of us hasn't scared up a killing somewhere, you can shoot me for a fool. We've got five chances."

The faces of the Erring Knights were alight with joy. They had not expected anything like this. With vociferous applause they proclaimed the greatness of Dougherty, while that gentleman divided the two hundred and fifty among them evenly and gave them sundry advice.

Driscoll and Jennings protested that they had not an even chance with the others, since they had to work from eight till eleven in the evening, whereupon Booth remarked that it was only four o'clock, and that you could lose fifty dollars in fifty seconds if you only went about it right.

They were all optimistic. Dougherty's scheme was an excellent one, they declared—perfect, certain to win. Knowlton was as good as free. Three thousand? It would be nearer ten.

"Wait," said the ex-prizefighter as they left the lobby together, "wait till tonight. It'll be time enough to crow then. I never yet saw a referee count a guy out when he was still on his feet. Remember, midnight, at Dumain's rooms."

They parted on the sidewalk in front of the hotel, each going his own way and sending back a "Good luck!" over his shoulder to the others.

It would have appeared to the casual observer that Knowlton's chance for freedom, if it depended on the success of this hare-brained, desperate scheme of Dougherty's, was a slim one. But yet it was a chance.

There were five of them—they were anything but inexperienced—and they were at concert pitch. True knighthood finds its brightest glory when pitted against seemingly overwhelming odds; and though the ribbon of their lady fluttered not from their buttonholes, yet did they fight valiantly for her.

The hour of midnight found them—all five—reassembled at Dumain's apartments on Twenty-first

Street, in the room which, some two months previous, had seen the triumph of Knowlton and the treacherous blow of Sherman.

The room was not bare, as it had been then. In the center stood a table littered with books and magazines, above which a massive reading globe cast its circle of light downward, leaving the upper half of the room in darkness.

A piano stood in one corner; by the mantel a chess table with the pieces arranged, apparently, at the crisis of an unfinished game; and there were half a dozen easy chairs, of various shapes and sizes. Altogether, a very pleasant spot—Booth declared he was about persuaded to become a palmist himself.

Driscoll, who arrived last, entered on the stroke of twelve. He found the others waiting impatiently—for Dougherty had insisted that each man should keep the story of his success or failure to himself until all were present. Judging from the expression on their faces, there was little to tell.

The little Frenchman waved Driscoll to a chair on the other side of the table and seated himself on the piano stool. Booth threw down a book he had been pretending to read, and Jennings yawned ostentatiously. All looked expectantly at Dougherty as he pounded on the arm of his chair for attention.

"I guess it's time to kill the cat," said the ex-prizefighter gloomily. "For your benefit," he turned to Driscoll, "we've held off on the dope. I will now tell the sad story of my life. Heaven knows I wish it was different. Maybe I was wrong, but we've only lost two hundred—"

"Come on, cut your mutton," Driscoll interrupted. Dougherty glared at him, sighed, and began:

"I hate to tell it. There's not much to tell. At exactly

four-fifteen this afternoon I took a seat at a table of five at Webster's on Thirty-sixth Street and bought a stack of blues. For an hour I fed the kitty, then it began to come.

"I helped every pair I drew to. I couldn't lose. At about seven o'clock I'd cashed in four hundred and had a stack about the size of the Flatiron Building in front of me.

"If I've ever played poker I played it then. But it began to turn. They wouldn't come. I couldn't get better than a pair, and they were never good enough. I boosted twice on a one-card draw to four pink ones, but couldn't get the filler.

"I prayed for 'em and tore 'em up and tried to run away with one or two, but they called me. And then— I had four ladies topped by a little guy on his first pot!"

A universal groan came from the audience.

"That finished me. I fought back as hard as I could, but they rushed me off my feet. At a quarter past eleven I cashed in exactly fifty dollars. Here it is."

There was complete silence as Dougherty held up five ten-dollar bills and sorrowfully returned them to his pocket. Then everybody began talking at once.

"Anyway, you kept your fifty."

"It could have been worse."

"Zat pokaire is zee devil of a game."

"Come on—who's next? Go on with the story!" This last from Driscoll.

Dougherty motioned to the little Frenchman.

"Me?" said Dumain. "I am worse yet than Dougherty. I got nozzing. I lost zee fifty."

"But how?"

"Zee race ponies," answered Dumain, with a fling at the jargon. "I play nozzing but *écarté*, and there is not zat here. I had a good what you call eet teep for Peemlico. Zee fourth race—zee name of zee horse was Parcel-Post.''

"How did you play him?''

"Straight. To win. A friend of mine got a telegram from zee owner. It was certain he should win.''

"And I suppose he got the place?'' asked Booth.

"What does zat mean?''

"It means he came in second.''

The little Frenchman shook his head sorrowfully.

"Oh, no. He came een last.''

There was a shout of laughter from the others, but it was soon stopped by Dougherty, who turned to Jennings with a gesture. He wanted to get the thing finished.

"I'm in the same class with Dumain,'' said Jennings. "I tried your game, Dougherty, and I thought I was some poker player—but good night! They took my fifty so quick I didn't have time to tell it goodby.''

"Where'd you go?''

"Pearly's, on Sixth Avenue. I've sat in there once or twice before, and about six months ago I made a clean-up. But tonight—don't make me talk about it.''

"We're a bunch of boobs,'' Dougherty groaned. "We'd better all go out in the morning and sell lead pencils. Your turn, Driscoll.''

But Driscoll said that he would prefer to follow Booth, and since Dougherty was not inclined to argue the matter, he turned to the typewriter salesman instead.

"I'm willing,'' said that gentleman, "though my tale contains but little joy. Still, I guess we're about even.

"It doesn't matter exactly where I went. It's downtown, and it's in the rear of a two-by-four billiard hall. At any hour of any afternoon you may find there a number of gentlemen engaged in the ancient and honorable game of craps.

"I'll spare you the details—at least, most of 'em. The game is a big one: there's lots of real money there for the man that knows how to get it, and I figured it out that I was just about the man.

"I rolled the bones till my fingers ached and my knees were stiff, and my voice sounded like a Staten Island ferryboat in a fog—I have a little habit of talking to the ivories.

"Well, to cut it short, I played in all directions. At one time I had six hundred dollars. At another time I had fifteen dollars. At half past eleven tonight I had an even hundred, and it was time to go.

"I had the dice, and I decided on one more throw. My hundred—I played it all—was faded before I put it down, and I threw a natural—a seven. I stuck the two hundred in my pocket and said good night."

"Well, we've got our two hundred and fifty back, anyway," observed Jennings.

"And what good will that do?" growled Dougherty.

"You never can tell. Tomorrow's another day."

"It seems to me," put in Driscoll, "that I remain to be heard from."

"Shoot your head off," said the ex-prizefighter, "and hurry up about it. This is awful!"

Driscoll blew his nose with care and deliberation, cleared his throat three times, and arose to his feet. There was something in his manner that caused the others to sit up straighter in their chairs with an air of expectancy. Noticing this flattering increase of attention, he smiled grandly and surveyed them with a leisurely eye.

"In the first place, gentlemen," he began, "I wish to say that I do not regard myself as a genius, in any sense of the word. At poker I am worse than helpless. The race ponies, as Dumain calls them, are a mystery to me. Nor have I that deft and subtle touch required to roll dice successfully."

There came a chorus of cries:

"Cut it!"

"Cheese the guff!"

"Talk sense!"

"Go on with the story!"

Driscoll waited for them to finish, then resumed calmly:

"Do not be impatient, gentlemen. As I say, I am well aware of the fact that I am no genius. Therefore, I realized that if my fifty dollars grew to the desired proportions it would be only by the aid of miraculous chance. I made my plans accordingly.

"When I left you in front of the Lamartine at four o'clock I went straight to my own room. There I procured a piece of paper, and marked on it with a pen the figures from one to thirty-five, about an inch apart.

"I then tore the paper into thirty-five pieces, so that I had each figure on a piece by itself. I placed these in my hat, mixed them around, and drew one forth. It was the figure thirty-two."

Again there came cries of impatience from the audience, who began to perceive that this lengthy preamble meant an interesting conclusion, and again the speaker ignored them and continued:

"That operation completed, I threw myself on my bed for a nap. At six o'clock I rose, went to a restaurant for dinner, and from there to my work at the theater. My first action there was to borrow fifty dollars, thereby doubling my capital.

"At the end of the play I dressed as hurriedly as possible, leaving the theater at exactly a quarter past eleven, and made my way to a certain establishment on Fiftieth Street, conducted by a Mr. Merrifield.

"It is, I believe, the largest and finest of its kind in New York. They have there a contrivance commonly known as a roulette wheel, which has numbers and colors arranged on it in an unique fashion. I stood before it and placed my hundred dollars on the number thirty-two."

The speaker paused, turned, and took his overcoat from the back of the chair on which he had been sitting, while his audience looked on in breathless silence.

Then he finished:

"The result, gentlemen, can be easier shown than told. Here it is."

He drew forth from a pocket of the overcoat a stack of bills and tossed them on the table, crying:

"There she is, boys! Thirty-five nice, crisp hundreds on one spin of the wheel!"

Then and there was pandemonium. They shouted and danced about, and clapped Driscoll on the back till he sought a corner for refuge, and spread the bills over the table to gloat over, and generally raised the devil. Dumain was sitting down at the piano to play a triumphal march when Dougherty suddenly rushed over to him and clasped his shoulder.

"Did you notice that number?" he asked excitedly.

The little Frenchman looked up at Dougherty.

"What number?"

"The one that Driscoll played on the wheel."

"Yes—thirty-two. Why?"

"Sure," said Dougherty. "Number thirty-two. Don't you remember?—you was down there this afternoon. That's the number of Knowlton's cell in the Tombs!"

CHAPTER XVI.

ALL TOGETHER.

WHEN LILA REACHED THE LOBBY OF THE LA-
martine at nine o'clock on the following
morning she found the Erring Knights already assembled in their corner.

For a moment she forgot everything else in her surprise; she had thought that nothing less than the end
of the world could possibly have roused these gentlemen of leisure from their beds at so early an hour.

Dougherty hastened over to her desk and demanded
to know why she had left her room.

"Why not?" Lila smiled. "I feel all right, really.
And, anyway, I had rather be down here than up there
alone. Did you see him?"

The ex-prizefighter grunted an affirmative and proceeded to give her a detailed account of his conversation with Knowlton on the previous morning. He
ended by saying that they had engaged a lawyer, and
that the sinews of war in the sum of three thousand

dollars had been entrusted to Dumain as treasurer.

"But Mr. Dougherty," Lila exclaimed, "we can't possibly use that! I thought—you see, I have saved a little—"

Dougherty interrupted her:

"Now see here. We're doing this, and you've got to let us alone. Anyway, it's not really costing us a cent. I won't explain how, but you can take my word for it.

"Everything's all right, and you don't need to worry, and for Heaven's sake don't begin any of that stuff about you won't take this and you won't take that. If we're going to help you we've got to help you. What did you think I meant yesterday morning—that I was going to carry a note to Knowlton and then go home and sit down with my fingers crossed?"

Whereupon, giving her no time to answer, Dougherty turned and rejoined the others across the lobby.

This was the beginning of a campaign which lasted a little over a month.

The duties of the Erring Knights were varied and arduous. Each morning one of them conducted Lila to the hotel, and took her home each evening, this escort being necessitated by the fact that Sherman had twice accosted her on the street. He had also called at her home, but there was no necessity for a male guardian there. Mrs. Amanda Berry was a legion in herself.

Dougherty was the official messenger between the Lamartine and the Tombs. At first Lila had insisted on going to see Knowlton herself, but he had begged her to spare him this final humiliation.

The prisoner wrote:

> I long to see you; you know it; but it is enough to have the picture of this place imprinted on my own memory—I can't bear that you should see me here.

Whatever your imagination shows you it cannot be as dreadful as the reality. If I obtain my freedom I shall not feel that I have cheated justice. Heaven knows I could not pay more dearly for my crime than I have already paid.

Knowlton stubbornly refused to allow his lawyer to procure his release on bail. The lawyer said he was quixotic; Dougherty used a stronger and commoner term, but they could not change his decision. He gave no reasons, but they understood; and the lawyer, who was at least as scrupulous as the average of his profession, declared to Dumain that for the first time in ten years' practise he was defending a guilty man with a clear conscience.

As for the case itself, it appeared to be by no means simple. The fact that they had no knowledge of the evidence held by the prosecution made them uneasy, and they bent their efforts mainly to attempts to discover its nature.

There was no danger, they found, from Red Tim, who had got away safely the night before Knowlton's arrest. And he was the only one of the gang whom Knowlton had ever seen or dealt with.

The evidence which the lawyer feared most was that concerning any specific operations, and in relation to the wallet which Knowlton had missed the day following the fight in Dumain's rooms. Knowlton suspected Sherman, but thought it possible that he had lost it on the street.

"Well," said the attorney, "the best we can say is that we're on our guard. We must keep our wits about us and fight it out in the courtroom. We won't know much about what they know before the day of the trial. It's a fight in the dark for us; but remember, they have to furnish the proof."

Dougherty was openly optimistic. After winning a one to thirty-five shot on the number of Knowlton's cell—he had recited the tale to the prisoner with great gusto—he refused to believe that their efforts could possibly culminate in anything short of glorious victory.

"Think of it; just think of it," he would say to Knowlton in a tone which partook of awe. "He drew the blooming number out of his hat—that was the first shot. Then he plays it single, and wins—that was the second. Why, we can't lose. We'll beat 'em both ways from the middle."

"Thanks, old man; I hope so," Knowlton would reply.

Thus three weeks passed by and found them marking time, waiting for the day of the trial. Dougherty spent the better part of two days seeking for Sherman, but without success. They had heard nothing from him, save the times he had accosted Lila on the street, nor seen him since the morning in Lila's room.

"He's surely round somewhere," said Dougherty to Dumain as they met in the lobby one morning. "In fact, I know he's in town, because he's still got that room on Thirty-fourth Street. But I can't get in, and I can't get him either going or coming."

The little Frenchman shrugged his shoulders and glanced across the lobby where Lila sat at her desk talking to a man who had just approached—probably a customer.

"Bah! Let heem alone. So long as he ees not bother Mees Williams that ees all we want."

"It's not all I want," said Dougherty. "I want to punch his face, and I will. He's a low-down, dirty—"

He was interrupted by a call:

"Mr. Dumain!"

The voice was Lila's. They turned. She was standing in front of her desk, her face very white, holding in her hand a sheet of printed paper. Dumain hurried over to her, gave one look at the paper which she thrust at him with a trembling hand, and called to Dougherty.

The ex-prizefighter crossed the lobby:

"What is it?"

"Look!" Dumain held the paper before him. "A what you call eet—subpoena—for Mees Williams! *Mon Dieu!* Eet is all up!"

"Shut up," growled Dougherty, taking the subpoena. "Do you want the whole lobby to know about it? You get excited too easy."

"But what am I to do?" faltered Lila.

"Be a sport. Don't let 'em floor you with a little thing like this. They want you for a witness, do they? It's a good job. I'd advise you to take it."

Lila gazed at him, amazed at his levity concerning what appeared to her to be the destruction of all their plans.

Dougherty read over the subpoena with a smile.

"The fact is," said he, "that I'm surprised they didn't spring this before. I've expected it all the time.

"Sherman knew all about your being at Knowlton's rooms—he told me and Dumain—and what's more, he told us that he'd told the Secret Service about you. Now, why did they hold off so long? That's the only part I don't like."

"But what am I to do?" Lila repeated.

"There's only one thing you can do—go on the stand."

"But Mr. Dougherty! Don't you see? They will ask

me about that night, and about the—the money. And
he will be convicted."

Dougherty appeared to be greatly surprised.

"And how so? Let 'em question you from now till
doomsday and what will they find out? Simply that
you went straight home from the hotel and spent the
evening in your room reading *Pilgrim's Progress*. The
only one they'll have against you is Sherman, and if
a jury wouldn't rather believe you than him I'm a
liar."

Still Lila did not understand. She protested:

"But I didn't spend the evening in my room."

"Don't you think I know it? I'm talking about evidence, not facts. As far as the jury's concerned you
did."

Lila gazed at him in horror.

"Do you mean I'd have to lie?"

"Well, that's a pretty strong word," said Dougherty, "but you can call it that if you want to."

"But I couldn't—I couldn't!"

"You'll have to."

Lila looked at him:

"No. I know I couldn't. If I am a witness, and they
ask me about—that evening, I couldn't tell them anything but the truth."

It was the tone rather than the words that caused
Dougherty to force back the protest that came to his
lips and convinced him of its uselessness.

Here was an obstacle, indeed! And utterly unexpected. Dougherty was not up on feminine psychol-
ogy, and he couldn't understand how a girl could do
for a man what Lila had done on the night of Knowlton's arrest, and then refuse to lie for him.

"Besides, it would be useless," Lila was saying. "I
ink it was Mr. Sherman who saw me, but it may not

have been. Some of the others may have seen me also. And now I remember: the man they left in the room did see me as I passed the door. He might not recognize me, but how can we know? And if he did—''

''All right,'' Dougherty interrupted; ''then there's no use talking about it. We're in a he—we're in a mess; but we'll find a way out, somehow. Dumain, find Driscoll and Booth. I'll get Jennings. Leave it to us, Miss Williams. Don't you worry about that thing''—pointing to the subpoena—''for a minute. Hurry up, Dumain!''

And ten minutes later the Erring Knights, five strong, were assembled in their corner, holding a council of war over this new and dangerous complication.

Booth was ready to throw up the sponge.

''What's the use?'' he demanded. ''They've got him fifty ways from breakfast. And this thing finishes it. If Miss Williams goes on the stand and tells what she knows, he doesn't stand a chance.''

''You don't say!'' observed Dougherty ironically. ''What's the matter—cold feet? And what do you think we're here for? It's up to us to fix it so that she don't go on the stand.''

''Tell me one thing,'' said Driscoll. ''Why haven't they arrested her?''

''Easy enough.'' This from Jennings. ''Because if they did they couldn't force her to testify against Knowlton, and they couldn't force Knowlton to testify against her. They figure that one is better than none.''

''Come on, boys; talk business.'' Dougherty pulled Jennings down on the lounge and glared at Booth. ''We have enough trouble as it is, without trying to figure out why we haven't got more.''

But their wits refused to work. No one had anything to suggest that was worth listening to, unless it w-

Driscoll, who was strongly in favor of avoiding the subpoena by the simple expedient of running away from it.

"The trial is only four days off," said he. "Convey Miss Williams to some safe and sheltered spot till it's over, and let Knowlton join her there."

"But then there'd be a warrant out for her for contempt," Jennings objected.

"Well, you can't have everything," retorted Driscoll.

Dougherty told them to wait a moment and crossed the lobby to Lila's desk. Soon he returned, shaking his head negatively.

"She won't do it," he announced.

"She's darned particular," growled Booth. "What *will* she do?"

But the ex-prizefighter stood up for Lila:

"No, you can't blame her. She looks at it different from us. We'll have to think up something else."

There was a silence. Driscoll lighted a cigarette, offering one to each of the others, and soon the corner was decorated with spirals of smoke. Finally Dumain spoke, for the first time.

"I tell you," said he, "as soon as you feenish this foolishness, what I will do. You know nozzing. I weel ask Siegel."

"And what can he do?" demanded Driscoll. "He'll want to fix up an alibi for her, and she won't stand for it, and then he'll try to bully her."

But the others signified their approval of Dumain's suggestion, especially Dougherty, and the little Frenchman was soon on his way downtown to the attorney's office, while Dougherty left for his daily visit to the Tombs.

Driscoll strolled over to Lila's desk and told her that

Dumain had gone to consult their lawyer.

"But he cannot help us," she faltered. "There is nothing I can do, is there, Mr. Driscoll? Tell me."

"You can keep up your courage," returned the young man. "As Tom would say, be a sport. And this Siegel is a shrewd man; he'll get us through safely, never fear. Dumain ought to be back before noon."

But Lila was completely terrified, and refused to be reassured. The formal phraseology of the subpoena had impressed her with the power of the law; it seemed to her to smell of courts and prisons; and her woman's mind was affected more by the document itself than by the very real danger it threatened.

Throughout the remainder of the morning she sat with her eyes glued on the entrance to the lobby. At eleven o'clock Dougherty returned from the Tombs with a note from Knowlton, but an hour later the little Frenchman had not arrived. Lila put on her hat and coat to go to lunch with a heavy heart.

The day was one of brilliant sunshine, with a saucy, freshening breeze coming in from the bay. Lila ate little and hurriedly, then strolled along the walks of Madison Square.

The grass plots were beginning to turn green, and the trees were covered with brown, damp buds, and in the center of the square a gardener was raking the newly turned earth. The gladness of the approaching spring was in the air.

Lila found it intolerable. She returned to the Lamartine.

Dumain rushed to meet her as she entered the door.

"Mees Williams! I've been waiting for you. Such a plan! Zat lawyer ees a genius!"

The lobby was accustomed to Dumain, and paid little attention to his gesticulations and shrill, high pitched tones; but Lila flushed with embarrassment as they walked to her desk. She felt that everyone was in on her secret, wherein she was unjust to the loyalty and discretion of the Erring Knights.

But this was nothing to the deep, rich crimson that flooded her cheeks as the little Frenchman, in low, excited tones, unfolded to her the plan of Lawyer Siegel. And with it came a smile, curiously tender, as Dumain expressed a doubt as to her willingness to act upon it.

He finished:

"You see, he don't know if you will do eet, and I am to telephone heem at one o'clock; so eef he must—"

"But I will," said Lila. "Oh, I will! But are you sure I won't have to testify? Are you sure?"

"Positeevely."

"Then—couldn't we do it today instead of to-morrow?"

"No," Dumain smiled. "Eet weel take till to-morrow morning to get zee bail for Knowlton. Dougherty ees down to see heem now. Tomorrow afternoon eet will be—remember. I must go to see Siegel for zee bondsman."

And he trotted off, leaving Lila with face still flushed and the shadow of a doubt in her eyes, but with her lips parted in a trembling, wistful smile.

But the plan of Lawyer Siegel, clever and effective as it was, nearly caused a disruption in the ranks of the Erring Knights.

For Dumain and Dougherty alone were in the secret, which they refused to divulge; and the three others strenuously objected. Booth and Jennings threatened, half in earnest, to go over to the prosecution and tell all they knew, while Driscoll made many pointed and cutting remarks concerning the source of the money they were using. But the little Frenchman and the ex-prizefighter were as adamant.

"It's Miss Williams's secret," said they, "and it wouldn't be fair to her to tell it. The fact is, she asked us not to."

This last was not true, but Dougherty knew they wouldn't ask Lila.

"And all we're good for, I suppose, is to sit round with our hands in our pockets," said Driscoll bitterly. This was on the day after the plan had been consummated. "You get Knowlton out on bail and don't show up in the lobby for a day at a time, and when you come back expect us to clap you on the back and tell you how well we like you. It's not a square deal."

"Now, listen here," said Dougherty; "don't be a sorehead. The trial is day after tomorrow; can't you wait that long? Besides, you fellows have had your share. You've been bringing her to work every morning and taking her home every evening, and, believe me, that's some job.

"And here's another. If Knowlton gets out—and he will—there's going to be a little dinner for him and Lila in Dumain's rooms Friday evening. The trial can't last more than one day. We'll leave that dinner to you and Booth and Jennings. When Dumain comes in this afternoon he'll give you the keys to his flat and all the money you need. Go as far as you like."

"For how many?"

"Seven. Us five and them two."

Driscoll grunted, and departed to consult with Booth and Jennings.

On Thursday evening, the day before the trial, Miss Williams was escorted to her home by Dougherty him-self. She was depressed and nervous, and his repeate attempts to rally her spirits were unsuccessful. They dined at a little restaurant on Columbus Avenue, and from there walked to One Hundred and Fourth Street.

"Brace up," said Dougherty, as they stopped at her door. "This time tomorrow night you'll be ready to start on your honeymoon. Don't you like the idea?"

"What do you think he is doing now?" asked Lila, with apparent irrelevance. She had learned to talk to Dougherty as to a chum.

"Reading your letters," said the ex-prizefighter with conviction. "He always is. And now you go up and get to bed and sleep. None of this endless night business."

Lila was standing in the open door.

"I'll try," she promised, smiling. "Good night, and thank you. I'll be waiting for you in the morning."

CHAPTER XVII.

THE TRIAL.

"**M**AY IT PLEASE YOUR HONOR, MR. FORE-man, and gentlemen of the jury—" The speaker was a United States assistant district attorney; the scene, a Federal courtroom in the post office building on Park Row. John Knowlton, alleged counterfeiter, was on trial before twelve of his peers.

The room was old and dingy—the building itself has been called the ugliest in New York. The jurybox, the benches, the railings, were blackened by time and use; the clerk appeared to have been fastened to his desk for many years. A dreary, melancholy room.

The spectators' benches are by no means filled; most of the faces are familiar ones. In a group at the right are Detective Barrett and his two men, with Billy Sherman. Seated side by side on the front row of benches are Driscoll, Booth, Dumain, Jennings, and Dougherty. Toward the rear of the room Lila is seen and by her side—Mrs. Amanda Berry! There are some dozen others—hangers-on, sensation-seekers, and young lawyers.

Knowlton, who was seated by the side of his attorney and engaged in a whispered consultation with him, looked up quickly as the prosecuting attorney rose to address the court and jury. The clock on the wall pointed to half past eleven; ninety minutes had sufficed for the preliminaries, including the selection of the jury. Lawyer Siegel had proven extraordinarily easy to please, thereby earning the gratitude of the judge.

"May it please your honor, Mr. Foreman, and gentlemen of the jury—"

The assistant district attorney proceeded with his opening speech. He was a young fellow—perhaps eight and twenty—and he spoke with the earnest enthusiasm of youth, with forceful, sounding phrases.

The prisoner felt his cheeks burn more than once at their sting. He wound up with the assertion that he would produce sufficient evidence to convict ten times over.

Lawyer Siegel turned and whispered to his client: "He didn't let anything out—he's a slick one."

Before Knowlton could do more than nod in response Siegel had risen to his feet and begun the opening speech for the defense. It was surprisingly short; it entered not at all into details, or even the nature of his evidence, and amounted, in fact, to little more than a general denial. But as he stated that the accused would not be called to the stand in his own defense Knowlton perceived a swift, almost imperceptible, expression of doubt and disapproval flit across the faces of the jurors.

As Siegel sat down the prisoner turned for a fleeting

glance at Lila; she smiled at him brightly.

The prosecuting attorney called his first witness: "James Barrett!"

The detective had little to tell. He identified Knowlton and gave an account of his arrest, dwelling pointedly on his flight to the rear of the flat as they entered.

Siegel, for the defense, did not cross-examine.

The second witness for the prosecution was Billy Sherman.

"What is your name?"

"William Sherman."

"Your business?"

"Journalist."

"Your address?"

He gave a number on West Thirty-fourth Street.

There followed some questions concerning the length of Sherman's acquaintance with the prisoner and the amount of time he had spent in his company; then the prosecuting attorney asked:

"Did you ever see Knowlton pass, or offer to pass, counterfeit money?"

Instantly Siegel was on his feet with an objection.

"Sustained," said the judge.

This was the beginning of a battle royal between the two lawyers. Time and again the prosecuting attorney tried to make his point, approaching it from every possible angle; and time and again Siegel objected that the witness was incompetent to answer.

Finally the judge himself became impatient and addressed the assistant district attorney with some severity:

"Mr. Brant, this witness has not qualified as an expert. You must give up this line of questioning or dismiss him."

Siegel seated himself with a triumphant smile. The

prosecuting attorney frowned and cleared his throat. Knowlton cast a glance over his shoulder at the spectators' benches and sent a smile to Lila.

Dougherty leaned over and whispered to Driscoll:

"I don't know what the deuce they're talking about, but that cagey little guy looks like he'd just stopped a swing on the jaw and was hanging over the ropes."

But young Mr. Brant had another cartridge in his belt. He asked that an exception be noted on the ruling of the court, then turned to the witness:

"Mr. Sherman, where were you on the evening of the 11th of December last?"

"At the rooms of Pierre Dumain, a palmist."

"Where are those rooms?"

"In West Twenty-first Street."

"What is the number?"

"I don't know."

"Who was there with you?"

"The defendant, Knowlton, and four or five others."

"What are the names of the others?"

"Tom Dougherty, Pierre Dumain, Bub Driscoll, Sam Booth, and Harry Jennings."

"What were you doing there?"

The witness hesitated a moment before he answered:

"Having a fight. You see—"

"No; answer my questions," interrupted the lawyer. "Were you fighting?"

"No, sir."

"Who was?"

"Knowlton and Driscoll. Knowlton knocked him out."

"And then?"

"Then Knowlton and Dougherty fought. It lasted ten or fifteen minutes and—"

"Now tell the court and the jury exactly what happened."

"Well, Knowlton was getting the better of Dougherty and had him up against the wall, when all of a sudden somebody threw a piece of bronze or something at Knowlton and hit him on the head. He dropped like a shot."

"Then what did you do?"

"I ran over toward the door, where Knowlton was lying on the floor, and so did the others. As I was standing near him I saw a wallet sticking out of his hip pocket, and I knew they—"

"You mean Knowlton's pocket?"

"Yes. And I was afraid one of the guys might take it, so I stooped down when no one was looking and pulled it out of his pocket—it was nearly out already—and put it in my own, thinking to keep it for him. Dumain had sent somebody—"

Mr. Brand interrupted.

"Never mind the others. What did you do?"

"I waited till the doctor came, and when he said Knowlton's injury was not serious I went home. I believe Knowlton stayed at Dumain's rooms all night. When I got home I put his wallet away—"

"Why didn't you return it to him before you left Dumain's rooms?"

"Because he was still half unconscious. He was in no condition to talk to. Then the next afternoon, I think it was—"

"Aren't you sure?"

"Yes," said the witness, after a moment's hesitation, "it was the next afternoon. I took the wallet out of the drawer where I had put it away, thinking to tak‹

it round to Knowlton's rooms, and as I put it in my pocket I happened to look into it, just out of curiosity, and I nearly fell over when I saw it was full of counterfeit—''

Lawyer Siegel sprang to his feet:

"I object, on the ground that the witness is incompetent.''

"Sustained," said the judge.

"Exception," said Mr. Brant.

The judge turned to the witness:

"Confine yourself to a recital of your own actions.''

"Did you return the wallet to Knowlton?'' asked the prosecuting attorney.

Sherman answered: "No, sir."

"What did you do with it?''

"I kept it awhile, then I took it to Detective Barrett, of the secret service.''

The prosecuting attorney took something from a leather case on the desk before him and, handing it to the witness, asked:

"Do you recognize that?''

"Yes," said Sherman. "It's the wallet I've been talking about.''

"Is it the one you took from Knowlton's pocket?''

"Yes, sir.''

"Inspect the contents. Are they the same as when you first saw it?''

There was a pause while the witness examined each of the compartments of the wallet, then he answered:

"Yes, sir.''

"Everything the same?''

"Yes, sir.''

Mr. Brant stepped forward and took the wallet from Sherman and handed it to the clerk of the court:

"Your honor," said he, "I wish to introduce this

wallet as evidence, with its contents. I shall call an expert later to prove that they are counterfeit."

This was a blow to the defense which, though not entirely unexpected, appeared to be serious. The Erring Knights looked gloomily at each other, but forbore to speak.

Lila was scarcely breathing in the intensity of her anxiety, while Mrs. Berry patted her hand soothingly. The accused was whispering excitedly to his attorney, who listened with keen interest, nodding his head with satisfaction at intervals. The result of this conference was to appear later.

The prosecuting attorney asked his witness a few more questions, for the most part unimportant, then turned him over for cross-examination.

Lawyer Siegel rose to his feet. He had not an impressive appearance, but as he stepped directly in front of Sherman he shot at him a glance so severe and terrifying that the witness involuntarily recoiled.

The tone was no less severe:

"How long did you keep this wallet before you turned it over to Detective Barrett?"

Sherman's answer was low:

"About two months."

"Why?"

But Mr. Brant objected to the question, and was sustained.

Siegel resumed:

"You say somebody hit Knowlton on the head with 'a piece of bronze or something.' Who was it that threw that bronze?"

The witness was silent.

"Who was it?" repeated the lawyer.

Sherman stammered:

"I did."

"I see. Had you been fighting with him?"

"No."

The attorney was shouting his questions with great rapidity, giving the witness barely time to answer, and no time at all to think. Sherman was nervously grasping the arm of his chair.

"Were you standing very close to Knowlton when you threw the bronze at him?"

"No, sir."

"Across the room, weren't you?"

"Yes, sir."

"And as soon as he fell Dumain and Dougherty ran over and knelt down by him, didn't they?"

"Yes, sir."

"And Jennings stopped you when you started to leave the room, didn't he?"

"Yes, sir."

The questions were coming like the rattle of a Gatling gun.

"And he forced you back to the corner?"

"Yes, sir."

"Then he went to help the others with Knowlton?"

"Yes, sir."

"You were over in the opposite corner alone?"

"Yes, sir."

"And when you found the wallet, was it in the coat or the vest?"

"The coat."

"Which pocket?"

"The insi—" Sherman began; then, realizing suddenly what he was saying, stopped short with a look of horror.

He was trapped.

The reason for his previous story of having taken he wallet from Knowlton's hip pocket as he lay on the floor could be found only in the tortuous channels of Sherman's treacherous brain.

Undoubtedly, he had thought to make his evidence stronger by making it appear that the thing had actually been taken from the person of the accused, and had anticipated the difficulty of proving that the coat was Knowlton's. And now he was fairly caught.

Siegel pursued his advantage relentlessly. He hammered the witness with questions, and Sherman stammered and grew red in the face with helpless anger, and finally admitted that his first story had been false. That was all Siegel wanted; he sat down with a smile of triumph; his forehead was covered with beads of sweat.

On redirect examination the prosecuting attorney made a valiant attempt to bring his witness out of the hole he had dug for himself, but in vain. Sherman was hopelessly confused; he made matters worse instead of better, and ended by refusing to answer at all. He was dismissed by the court with a reprimand, and at a sign from Mr. Brant seated himself on the front row of benches.

For a few moments the progress of the trial was halted by a conference between the prosecuting attorney and Detective Barrett, while Knowlton whispered animatedly to his counsel and the faces of the Erring Knights beamed with joy.

"What did I tell you?" said Dougherty to Driscoll *sotto voce*. "Didn't I say he was a slick guy?"

Then the prosecuting attorney turned to face the courtroom:

"Miss Williams, please take the stand."

There was a silence. No one moved. Knowlton kept his eyes fastened on the desk before him. Three of the Erring Knights glanced accusingly at the other two.

Mr. Brant, whose temper had not been improved by the discrediting of Sherman's testimony, looked directly at Lila, who had remained in her seat, and repeated his question.

"Will you please take the stand?"

Lila rose and faced him.

"Do you mean me?" she asked.

"Yes. I called your name. Take the stand."

Lila did not move.

"I beg your pardon, but you did not call my name."

"Aren't you Miss Williams?" said Mr. Brant testily.

Lila answered clearly:

"No."

The attorney started with incredulous surprise. Driscoll, Booth, and Jennings looked around at her in amazement, while Dougherty and Dumain smiled in their superior knowledge. Knowlton did not move.

Sherman sprang from his seat and, crossing to the side of Attorney Brant, whispered excitedly:

"That's her, all right. They're up to some trick. Call her up. She won't lie on the stand."

But Mr. Brant shook him off, and after a moment's hesitation again spoke to Lila:

"Then what is your name?"

Lila sent a single fleeting glance to the prisoner, who had turned in his chair to face her; then looked directly at the questioner. Her answer was low, but distinct and half triumphant:

"Mrs. John Knowlton."

Then she sat down and buried her face in her hands; and, as everybody stared at her in consternation, surprise, or wonder, Lawyer Siegel rose to his feet and addressed the listening judge:

"Your honor, this woman is the wife of the accused; and, therefore, may not be called as a witness by the prosecution. Your honor sees that she is in distress. May I ask that counsel be instructed not to question her further in court?''

But Mr. Brant turned on him angrily:

''Your proof! Show us your proof!''

''Of course,'' said the other, taking a paper from his portfolio, ''I expected you would demand it; I do not expect courtesy from you, sir.'' He handed the paper to the judge. ''That is the marriage certificate, your honor.''

There was a breathless silence throughout the room while the judge adjusted his eyeglasses and inspected the large, stamped document. He looked at the date and the signatures, and glanced at Attorney Siegel searchingly; then turned to Lila and asked her to step to the witness stand.

''I object, your honor—'' began Lawyer Siegel, but the judge stopped him with a gesture.

Lila was in the witness chair. The clerk of the court administered the oath. The judge turned to her.

''Are you the 'Lila Williams' mentioned in this certificate?''

Lila barely glanced at it before answering:

''Yes, sir.''

''Are you the wife of the accused, John Knowlton?''

''Yes, sir.''

''Do you wish to testify for the people in this action?''

''Yes, sir.''

''That is all,'' said the judge; ''you may go.''

Then, as Lila glanced at him gratefully and rose to return to her seat, he handed the certificate back

Lawyer Siegel and turned to speak to the prosecuting attorney with judicial calmness:

"Call your next witness, Mr. Brant."

But the trial had become a farce; a huge joke—on the prosecution. Of his two chief witnesses, one had been discredited and the other disqualified; and Attorney Brant stammered in angry confusion that he had no others.

He recalled Sherman to the stand to give a recital of Lila's movements, as observed by him, on the evening of Knowlton's arrest; but Sherman could tell little, and it was easy to perceive by the expression on the faces of the jurors that the little he could tell was not believed.

Mr. Brant also called an expert, who testified that the bills in the wallet in evidence for the prosecution were counterfeit; then the prosecution rested.

The defense rested without calling a witness.

Then came the closing speeches.

Young Mr. Brant stammered and hesitated for a quarter of an hour, and, considering the paucity of his material, made a very creditable effort; but it was thrown completely in the shade by that of Lawyer Siegel, which may be given in full:

"May it please your honor, Mr. Foreman, and gentlemen of the jury: Without any desire to be flippant, I can only state that since I am confined to the evidence, and since there has been no evidence worth speaking of, I have nothing to say."

And five minutes later, without leaving their box, the jury returned a verdict of "Not guilty," and John Knowlton was a free man.

It was Lila who reached his side first, but the Erring Knights were not far behind; and Knowlton found mself the center of an excited, laughing group of faces filled with goodwill and friendship and—one of them—with love.

In one of his hands he held both of Lila's, and gave the other to each of the Erring Knights in turn; but his lips were silent. Before all these faces, at that moment, he could not trust himself to speak.

"But I was so frightened," Lila was saying. "Oh, I was *so* frightened!"

"Bah!" said Dumain. "At what, madam?"

Lila's cheek flushed at the title, and Driscoll, observing it, put in mischievously:

"Yes; that really isn't very complimentary to us, Mrs. Knowlton."

"Oh!" said Lila helplessly, while the flush deepened.

"And now," said Dougherty, "where's that guy, Siegel? I want to ask him to come up to the dinner tonight. I wonder where—What? Look at that!"

He was pointing excitedly across the room. The others turned and saw Billy Sherman being escorted to the door of the courtroom by two police officers in uniform.

"Probably some of his friends," observed Booth.

"No," said Driscoll; "it's more likely that little slip-up in his testimony. I believe they call it perjury."

At that moment Siegel approached the group.

"Come on," he called gaily; "they're going to clear the room. And I guess we'll be glad enough to go, since we don't have to leave anyone behind. And, by the way, did you notice our friend, Sherman? He seems to be having a little trouble of his own. They just arrested him."

"What is it?" asked Booth. "Perjury? They certainly didn't lose much time."

"No. It isn't that. That was merely a lapse of mem

ory. They came from the outside. I didn't hear what they said, but from the expression on Mr. Sherman's face I wouldn't be surprised if it was murder. We caught him prettily, didn't we?''

They had left the courtroom and were standing at the head of the stairs in the corridor.

"Well, let's forget him," said Driscoll. "He was bound to hang himself sooner or later. Maybe he's done it already. Come on—everybody."

They moved down the stairs and out to the sidewalk, chattering and laughing, still nervous and ill at ease from the restraint and anxiety of the courtroom.

Lined up along the curb were three big gray limousines.

"Now," said Dougherty, stopping in front of them, in the tone of a general marshaling his forces, "here's where we separate."

He pointed to the first of the limousines. "Dumain, you take this car with Knowlton and take him to your rooms. He'll find there what he needs.

"Can't help it, Mrs. Knowlton; it's only for an hour or two. Driscoll, you are to take Mrs. Knowlton to One Hundred and Fourth Street, and get her trunk and bags. The rest of you come with me. And remember: six o'clock at Dumain's rooms. No later. Come on, boys!"

"But what—" Knowlton began.

"Listen here," Dougherty interrupted sternly; "are you going to obey orders or not? Hereafter Mrs. Knowlton can boss you. It's our turn today."

In pretended fright Knowlton turned to Lila and bade her *au revoir* with a pressure of the hand, then sprang into the automobile beside Dumain.

"That's right," said Dougherty. "Here you go,

Mrs. Knowlton. Help the lady in, Driscoll. Come on, Siegel, with us. What's that? Yes, you will—come on! All ready, boys? Let 'er go! So long! Remember, six o'clock!''

CHAPTER XVIII.

WESTWARD HO!

EIGHT GILT CHAIRS WITH EMBROIDERED SEATS and backs surrounding a table covered with snowy linen and shining silver; four diminutive Swiss waiters with quick eyes and silent feet; roses everywhere—on the mantel, in vases on the table, clustered over the door, red and white; candles—hundreds of them—placed wherever there was an inch of space to hold them; such was the scene prepared by Bub Driscoll and his aids for the joy dinner in honor of Mr. and Mrs. John Knowlton, in that apartment on West Twenty-first Street which we have seen twice before.

Lila was escorted to the dining room on the arm of Lawyer Siegel, after an extended and heated controversy among the Erring Knights as to which of them should have that honor.

When it appeared that the matter was apt to be argued till the dinner was ruined, Siegel stepped in and settled the question by offering his services, which were gladly accepted.

Pierre Dumain, as host, sat at one end of the table; Knowlton at the other. On one side was Lila, between Dougherty and Driscoll; opposite them Booth, Jennings, and Siegel.

"What a shame!" said Lila. "I'm so excited I can't eat."

Driscoll observed:

"Now, that's just like a woman. For two months you've been as cool and collected as a cake of ice, while you've had enough trouble to scare an army; and now that everything's over, and you're just at the beginning of a lifelong siege of matrimonial boredom, you're so excited you can't eat!"

"I never did a harder day's work in my life," declared Dougherty, "and I'm hungry like a bear. What do you call this, Driscoll? I'm no bridegroom—I can't eat roses."

But he was promptly squelched by the master of ceremonies, and everybody talked at once till the soup arrived.

Never was gayer company. Lila was at first a little embarrassed at finding herself the eighth at a table with seven men, but that did not last long; no longer, in fact, than when Dougherty, at the finish of the fish, arose to his feet to give an imitation of Miss Hughes chewing gum, powdering her face, and waiting on three customers at the same time.

"She never did," declared Lila, when she could speak for laughing. "That's a slander, Mr. Dougherty."

"What?" exclaimed the ex-prizefighter. "I'll admit it's not true to life; it's too delicate and refined.

Not that I don't like her; the Venus is a good sport. And if there's any—What's this?''

"Sweetbreads in tambo shell, *m'sieu'*," murmured the waiter.

After which Dougherty was silent—and busy—for ten minutes.

Then Lawyer Siegel related some of his court experiences, both humorous and tragical, and Dumain described the mysteries and secrets of the gentle art of reading palms, and Jennings explained that his contract with Mr. Frohman would probably not be signed till the following day, and Dougherty described his first prizefight with an animation and picturesqueness of language that left the others in a condition bordering on hysteria.

"There's one thing," said Driscoll, turning to Lila, "for which I shall never forgive you—that you didn't invite me to the wedding."

"Here, too," put in Jennings. "I call it snobbish."

"Where was it, anyway?" Booth wanted to know. "How did you manage it?"

Dougherty explained:

"Easy. You know we got Knowlton out on bail for one day. Well, he got a license and I got a preacher, and Dumain let us use his French parlor, and stuff was all off in fifteen minutes, But you may get to see a wedding, after all."

Dougherty glanced at Knowlton. Knowlton nodded. Then the ex-prizefighter continued:

''We all know that our friend Mr. Knowlton is traveling sort of incog. His real name is Norton, and that fact demands what you might call supplementary proceedings. The big show is on tomorrow, and if you treat Mrs. Knowlton right she's very apt to give you a bid.''

"Hurrah!" shouted Driscoll. "In at the death is all I ask."

"What an expression!" said Lila. "Mr. Driscoll, I'm offended."

"I beg your pardon," said the gentleman gallantly. "I didn't mean it, I assure you. Waiter!"

"Yes, sir."

"If I order another bottle of white wine—"

"Yes, sir."

"I say, if I order more white wine—"

"Yes, sir."

"Don't bring it."

"Yes, sir. No, sir."

The table grinned, and made a concerted and valiant attack on the dessert, while Jennings and Booth accused each other with some heat of being the cause of Driscoll's order.

Presently Driscoll rapped on the table for attention, and glared fiercely at the disputants till he got it.

"Lady and gentlemen," said he, "I must ask your kind favor and indulgence. Unlike the rest of this proud assembly, Mr. Jennings and myself are workingmen. We earn our bread by toil."

Cries of "Hear, hear!" came from Jennings, while the others jeered.

"Howbeit," continued the speaker, silencing the interruptions with an imperious gesture, "we must be at our tasks by eight o'clock. It is now seven-twenty.

"I understand that Mr. Dumain has a surprise in store for us, and that Mr. Knowlton has kindly consented to make a speech. In the interests of equality and justice I demand that these ceremonies begin at once."

Applause, continued and vociferous, from Jennings. Booth and Siegel each grasped one of his arms and held him quiet. Driscoll turned to Dumain and demanded an answer.

"All right," said the little Frenchman, "I'm ready."

"What about it?" Driscoll turned to the others. They signified their approval. Knowlton, who had been silent throughout the dinner, nodded. Dumain rose to his feet, pushed back his chair, and cleared his throat.

"About zee surprise," the little Frenchman began; "eet ees a pleasant surprise. We are here this evening—"

"Hear, hear!" murmured Jennings.

"Silence him!" ordered Driscoll. Booth and Siegel obeyed, and the speaker continued:

"I say we are here this evening because our hearts are glad for our friend Mr. Knowlton and our very dear lady—God bless her!—zee Lady Lila!"

"To her!" shouted Dougherty, springing to his feet and raising his glass on high.

"To Lady Lila!" came in a deafening chorus, while Lila rose to her feet, trembling and confused.

They drank the toast amid cheers and applause.

"And now," continued Dumain, when they had reseated themselves, "for zee surprise. I must go back a leetle, and I do not speak zee Angleesh so well, so you must have zee patience.

"About Knowlton eet ees—only hees name ees Norton. I can only tell what I know. From what Sherman and our very dear lady have say to me I add zis to zat, and I know nearly all.

"I know he was officer in a bank in Warton, Ohio, and zat money was missing, and zat our friend was what you call eet suspicioned. And about zis Sherman tol' me, and from what he look at me I theenk to myself, aha! Sherman know more zan he say.

"Well, I theenk very little about all zat—I nearly forget eet because we are all busy wiz trying to put Knowlton away from all. For many weeks I forget eet."

Dumain paused, glanced at his audience with the assurance of a man who holds a high trump, and continued:

"All zis we all know. Well. Today I take Knowlton here to my rooms where ees hees trunk I brought. But he needs something—we go out. I stop in zee Lamartine to wait for heem—I go to zee telegraph desk, I go to zee cigar stand, I go to zee front desk, and Geebson call me and say, 'Telegram here for a man named John Norton. Do you know heem, Dumain?'

"I say, 'Yes, I will take eet to heem,' and he give eet to me, and I open eet and read eet to make sure. What I theenk, eet ees for Knowlton. Right. Here eet ees."

He took a yellow telegraph form from his pocket and waved it in the air. It was extra size—the telegram was a long one.

They shouted, "Read it!"

But Dumain tossed it to Knowlton, who, after reading it through, let it fall from his hands to the table and turned a white face to Lila.

"What is it?" Lila faltered.

Dougherty snatched up the telegram and read it aloud:

"Mr. John Norton, Hotel Lamartine, New York. Alma Sherman has confessed all. I was a fool not to believe you, but come home. Her brother got the money. They have wired to the New York police. Come home at once. Letter follows, but don't wait for it. Wire me immediately.
"FATHER."

"Oh!" cried Lila. "And now—and now—"

In the confusion that followed, while the others applauded and shouted and clapped Knowlton on the back, Dougherty had to place his mouth close to her ear to make her hear:

"And now what?" he demanded.

"And now," Lila answered, "he—he doesn't need me, after all."

The ex-prizefighter sprang to his feet.

"Ha!" he cried in a tone of thunder. "Silence! Shut up, you! Knowlton, do you know, what your wife is saying? She says that now you won't need her!"

Another moment and Knowlton was at her side, holding her in his arms.

"Lila! Dear little girl! We shall go home—home—together. Darling! Not need you? Look at me!"

For the next five minutes the Erring Knights and Lawyer Siegel were occupied in the next room, chased thereto by Dougherty, who commanded them to make as much noise as possible.

Presently Knowlton's voice came:

"Come back here! What are you doing in there? I say, Dumain! Dougherty!"

They came through the door backward, in single file, and Lila was forced to laugh in spite of herself.

"That's better," said Dougherty approvingly. "This is an occasion of joy, Mrs. Knowlton. No tears allowed."

Lila smiled at him.

"But say!" put in Driscoll, as he lit a cigarette—Lila had long since commanded them to smoke—"do you know what? That's what they took Sherman for at the courtroom!"

"They didn't waste any time," Booth observed.

"Oh, I know how he knew that," Lila was saying

to Knowlton and Dumain, who had expressed their wonder at his father's knowledge of his address. "It was Mr. Sherman who told him."

"Sherman!" they exclaimed.

"Yes," Lila asserted.

Then she told them of the telegram Sherman had sent to the president of the Warton National Bank concerning John Norton, and Dumain and Knowlton hastened to inform the others of the fact that they owed the receipt of the telegram to the enemy himself, thereby doubling their joyous hilarity.

Then they surrounded Knowlton and demanded a speech. He protested; they insisted. He appealed to Lila for assistance; she commanded him to do his duty.

There was no escape; he motioned them to be seated, and began:

"Boys, I know this is no time to be serious—for you. You're having a good time. But you've asked me to talk, and to tell the truth, I'm glad of the chance to relieve my mind. If you don't like what I say it's your own fault. I know you're good sports, but there are one or two things I have to speak about.

"First, money. You've spent about sixteen hundred dollars on my defense, and you've given me a thousand for a stake. There's been nothing said about it— you've turned it over to me without a word—but I want you to know that the first thing I'll do when I get home—when we get home—is to send you a check for the twenty-six hundred. Now, don't think I'm refusing a favor; it isn't that. The Lord knows I've accepted enough favors from you without your insisting on that one, too."

"Oh, of course, if you're rolling in wealth—" put in Driscoll.

"Then that's settled. I'm not going to try to thank

you; if I talked all night I couldn't make it strong
enough. Lila and I are going out West where they like
to say you find nothing but good, clean Americans,
and I've always thought the boast was justified; but
wherever we go, and whoever we see, we'll never
meet as good men, or as straight sports, or as true
friends as the Erring Knights.

"Here's to you, boys! God bless you!"

Knowlton's voice was trembling so that he could
scarcely speak, and his eyes shone with tears as he
drained the glass and threw it on the floor, where it
broke in a thousand fragments.

The following afternoon the bride and groom were escorted to Grand Central Station by the Erring Knights.
And there they received their reward if they had felt
they needed any. For after Knowlton had shaken hands
with each of them and arranged for a grand reunion
when he and his wife should next visit New York, as
they stood lined up at the entrance to the trackway,
Lila approached Dougherty, who happened to be first,
with a farewell on her lips.

He held out his hand. She ignored it, and, stretching
on tiptoe, placed a hearty uncompromising kiss on his
either cheek! And before he could recover she had
passed on to Dumain and repeated the operation, and
then to the remaining three.

In another moment she was walking down the platform by the side of the train with her arm through that
of her husband, preceded by two porters loaded with
bags and suitcases and flowers and candy; and every
now and then she turned to look back at the Erring
Knights, who were waving their handkerchiefs frantically in unrestrained and triumphant glee. And then,
throwing a last kiss from the car platform, while

Knowlton waved his hat, they disappeared inside, and a minute later the train pulled out.

It happened, by a curious coincidence, that that train held two sets of passengers for the little town of Warton, Ohio.

In a day-coach, seated side by side, were two men. The face of one, dark and evil looking, wore lines of sleeplessness and despair and fear. The other, a small, heavy-set man with a ruddy countenance, was seated next the aisle, and had an appearance of watchfulness as he kept one eye on his companion while he scanned the columns of a newspaper with the other. William Sherman was going home to pay.

But a few feet away, in a Pullman, sat the man he had tried to ruin and the girl he had tried to wrong.

They were looking at each other, they felt, almost for the first time. Between them, on the seat, their hands were closely clasped together.

Thus they sat for many minutes, silent, while the train passed through the city, crossed to the west, and started on its journey northward along the banks of the glorious Hudson.

"Dearest," said the man in a caressing tone.

The girl pressed his hand tighter and sighed happily.

"They're good fellows," the man continued, "every one of them. And to think what we owe them! Everything—everything."

"Yes," said the girl, "everything. We must never forget them."

But the truth was, as was clearly apparent from the tone of her voice and the melting of her eyes into his, that she had forgotten them already!

Out of the Line

Out of the Line

MRS. SAM ROSSINGTON PULLED ASIDE THE curtain of her bed and gazed out upon the world beneath the window-shade which her maid had drawn only a minute before.

Then, as she stretched out her hand toward the chocolate tray on the table at her elbow, her mouth opened with the deep, frank yawn of solitude, and she propped herself comfortably against her pillow to sip and to ruminate.

Today was Mrs. Sam's—or Agatha's—birthday, and she was paying the white-bearded Father his inevitable tribute of regret and consideration. Old Time is never discreet or tactful.

At this moment he was reminding Agatha with brutal frankness that she had passed her thirty-first summer, and that henceforth his sickle would descend with increasing rapidity and more disastrous stroke. For Agatha, comparatively young as she was, had already reached that melancholy point in life where one's thoughts lean rather to the past than to the future.

Though, to be sure, Agatha's fluttering brain was seldom long disturbed by anything so uncomfortable as thought. Like one who "wandered in a forest aimlessly," she had taken life as it came—and taken all she could get—with hardly a thought for yesterday, and with none at all for tomorrow.

Like most human lives, which are in their development of soul and sensation curiously similar, however they may differ in incidents and experience, Agatha's existence had been distinctly divided into periods.

The first, which might be called the Romantico-Innocent, she had almost completely forgotten, save where here and there the fragrance of some sweet remembrance had refused to succumb to malodorous disillusionment.

The second, or Domestic-Hypocritical, she remembered, but with a shudder. Willing as she had been to be amused, Sam Rossington had come near being too much for her. Agatha had been for him neither a wife nor a friend, but merely a sensation; and, since she had originally been planned by the Creator for something a little better than an ornament or a plaything, she had more than once repented of her blindness and folly.

Having married Sam Rossington for the sake of his wealth and the worldly comfort and security it represented, she had stuck to her bargain with commendable constancy, and it must be admitted that he got his money's worth; on the other hand, it is true that Agatha had not been wholly free from regret.

It had taken various forms, having at times ascended even into the region of pious aspiration, but being more often distinctly of the flesh. In short, Agatha was one of those unfortunate beings who are endowed with a soul, and then left without a will to support it. Nothing is quite so uncomfortable as a loose conscience.

The passing years had blurred, but not effaced, the past. Disturbing glimpses of it now and then visited her dreams, though they no longer caused any deeper emotion than a mild wonder as to whether her life could, after all, have been made to contain any more happiness than she had known.

One face, which always appeared to her white and drawn with suffering, was of most frequent recurrence in her visions. Even yet she wondered that she had been able to dismiss such a man as John Carter; and even yet she admired his manly ways of accepting defeat.

To be sure, he had signified his intention of going straight to the devil as rapidly and thoroughly as possible, after the immemorial custom of disappointed youth; but he had really been very decent about it.

Ah well! Agatha sighed as she rang for her maid—what had she, a sophisticated widow, to do with youthful fancies? That had been ten years ago. For seven of them she had lived with her husband, when he had suddenly shown an unwonted consideration for her by contracting a fever during the festival at Havana, and dying in less than a week—an act which Agatha felt had almost justified her choice of him.

"And the funny part of it is," said she aloud, as the door opened to admit her maid, "that I have really missed the poor devil!"

"I beg your pardon?" said Jeanne.

"Nothing," said Agatha. "Take away the tray. Was there no mail?"

"No. Mrs. Cranshaw and Miss Carson telephoned,

and there are some roses and a basket of orchids—
shall I bring them up?"

"Lord, no!" said Agatha. "The room already smells
like the Temple of Allah." She lay back on her pillow
and watched the girl silently. "Jeanne," she said suddenly, "do you know that today is my birthday?"

"Certainly, *madame*," came the answer from the
depths of a closet.

"Well, aren't you going to congratulate me?"

Jeanne emerged from the closet carrying a gown,
which she placed on the arm of a chair.

"Why—" she began uncertainly, embarrassed by
this unwonted display of friendliness on the part of
her mistress, "I—I wish you many happy returns of
the day, *madame*."

"Thanks," said Agatha dryly. "I suppose I could
hardly expect you to be enthusiastic about it." She
regarded Jeanne curiously, as though seeing her for
the first time. "I have never given you much encouragement, have I?" she said.

"You have been very good to me, *madame*."

"Perhaps—in a way," said Agatha, pondering. "It is
curious," she continued impersonally, "that I have
never taken the trouble to know you. Sam used to say
I was unsympathetic. Perhaps that is why I have no
friends. I tell you, Jeanne, I am growing old; for I am
beginning to be lonesome—this morning I am positively unhappy. What was Mrs. Cranshaw's message?"

Jeanne looked up from the dressing-table, where she
was arranging the articles for a somewhat complicated
toilet.

"To ask if she could expect you this evening. The
bath is ready, *madame*."

Agatha did not find her usual delight in the cold,
bracing water, nor in the mysterious and fragrant cer-

emonies which followed her emergence; and by the time Jeanne began to dress her hair she was almost irritable.

This was alarming; Agatha was anything but a creature of moods; and Jeanne, who possessed a sensitive soul, found herself speculating on the possible reasons for this unexpected development of nerves.

Meanwhile her deft fingers moved rapidly, arranging the golden brown coil of which Agatha was justly proud, while Agatha gazed absently at the array of bottles and jars on the table before her.

"Jeanne," she said suddenly, "I shall not go to Mrs. Cranshaw's tonight."

The maid was silent.

"I am sick of it all," Agatha continued presently, half to herself. "It is so utterly idiotic—though, thank the Lord, it's not respectable. This is a fit, Jeanne— and the first I've ever had. I'm just beginning to realize that I've wasted ten years and I suppose I'll waste the rest. It's a habit. And yet—today—"

She interrupted herself suddenly—"Jeanne, if you were me, what would you do with a birthday?"

"I don't know, *madame*," the maid stammered, hesitating.

"No, you must answer," Agatha persisted, "I'll leave it to you. I am *Haroun Al Raschid*, and you're my grand vizier. But I warn you I'm devilish melancholy, and you'll need no little imagination. I want a positive adventure. Come! What shall it be?"

The maid laughed uncertainly.

"*Madame* might give a party," she suggested.

Then, at Agatha's impatient gesture of derision, she walked round and in front of her chair stood looking down at her.

"If *madame* is serious—" she began.

"I am," Agatha declared.

Whereupon Jeanne, in her capacity of grand vizier, and with a preamble which, though interesting enough, has nothing to do with this story, made a most unique suggestion. As she concluded, Agatha rose and clapped her hands gleefully.

"Jeanne," she cried, "you are positively a jewel! Better than that, you are right! For the first time in my life, I shall try to make someone else happy!"

In more ways than one, New York is a city of distances. At midnight in winter it is, for instance, a million miles from Tenth Street and Broadway to West End Avenue, where Agatha's cozy apartment was situated.

At exactly half past eleven in the evening of her birthday Agatha, closely wrapped in furs and attended by Jeanne, entered a limousine at her own door and startled the chauffeur by directing him to drive to Tenth Street and Broadway. A minute later they had turned south from Ninety-Sixth Street and begun their journey.

This Broadway is easily the most interesting street in the world. It contains the world—in miniature and caricature. The Lucia of Naples, the Champs Elysées of Paris, the Muski of Cairo, the Grove of Damascus— all are to be found here, if you only know where to look for them. With an open eye and a ready soul you can circumnavigate the globe in one night between the Battery and Washington Heights.

Even Agatha, who had been partially awakened by Jeanne's unexpected eloquence of the morning and the excitement of her own unusual errand, felt a new sense of interest and life as the limousine sped southward past endless rows of apartment houses, darkened shops, shabby moving picture theaters and glittering cafés.

On through the Circle, dominated by a screaming advertisement of a Sunday newspaper and a general appearance of loud vulgarity; past Fifty-Third Street, darkened by the L tracks overhead and the dusky skin of its inhabitants underneath; into the realm of fur-lined overcoats, painted faces, dazzling lights, and popping corks.

Then through a quiet length of a mile or so, bursting suddenly into the cheaper and noisier gaiety of Four-teenth Street, the car carried them, now rapidly, now more slowly, until at last they passed into that strip of comparative darkness which is left by right to the tender mercies of the watchman and policeman.

Agatha, buried deep in her furs and lost in thought, was roused by a touch on her arm.

"Look!" said Jeanne, pointing to the right. "There they are, *madame!*"

There they were, indeed; a line of silent men, in single file, beginning at the corner of Tenth Street and reaching up Broadway almost a full block. There could not have been less than eighty or ninety of them. In the semi-darkness—the street is dimly lighted here—it was barely possible to perceive that they were poorly and scantily clothed, and shivering from the cold, and that their faces presented a haggard, almost a sinister, appearance.

They had been waiting here in the bitter cold, some of them, for over an hour; it is easy to believe that they were really in need of that for which they waited; miserable in themselves, and companions of misery. One would hardly go through such an experience for the sake of a fortune; they were waiting for a chunk of bread and a cup of coffee.

By now they shuffled and stamped with impatience; for the hands of a clock in a nearby window pointed at five minutes to twelve, and midnight was the hour for which they waited.

"Poor devils!" Agatha shuddered.

Then she leaned forward and spoke to the chauffeur, and the car came to a stop close by the curb at the head of the dark line.

As the door of the limousine opened and Agatha stepped to the sidewalk, a policeman who had been pacing up and down beside the line approached her and touched his cap respectfully.

Agatha accosted him; he nodded; and as she continued somewhat hurriedly, explaining the nature of her errand, his face broadened with an expansive grin and he wagged his head appreciatively.

"Lord, ma'am!" said he. "There's no objection in the world. Sure, and I'm glad to see you make the poor devils happy. I'll keep watch down the line so as to make sure they don't repeat on you. They're sly ones."

"Thank you," said Agatha. "And now if you'll tell them—"

"Sure," said the policeman. He turned to the line and raised his voice. "Men," he said, "here's a lady givin' a birthday party, and she wants to play a little game of 'Hold fast to all I give you.' The rules are to stay in line till it's over. You won't have to go around the corner tonight."

As Agatha stripped a crisp new bill from the package she held under her cloak and handed it to the man at the head of the line she felt a curious fluttering of her heart, unlike anything she had ever before experienced. And as she saw the man's eyes fill with tears and heard his fervent "God bless you," her hand trembled with so unusual and divine an emotion that it could scarcely find the pocket inside her cloak.

And so with the second and the third and the fourth—on down the line she went, while she gradually controlled her fast-beating heart and began to give words of cheer and good wishes along with her bounty.

Half the men in the line—those white, drawn, haggard faces—were in tears; she felt half smothered by the shower of blessings and gratitude. Never before had she been so utterly happy.

She was about three-quarters of the distance down the line when one poor fellow, on catching sight of the figure on the bill she gave him, fell on his knees at her feet and began mumbling incoherently his thanks and blessings. Agatha patted his shoulder and added her tears to his own. And then, as she turned to the next man in the line and looked up into his face, she uttered a cry, tottered backward, and probably would have fallen but for his prompt spring forward to her support.

"John!" she breathed. "God in heaven! John!"

The man shook her rudely.

"Fool!" he whispered. "Don't recognize me!"

Then, as the policeman came running up, "She stumbled," he said sullenly.

The policeman returned to his position. Agatha, by a supreme and violent effort of the will, controlled herself and, taking a bill from the package, held it out to the man.

"Take it," she said as calmly as possible. Then, pressing closer to him, "Listen," she whispered rapidly. "Come to me—tonight—at once—" and then,

at the look of refusal in his eyes, "you must. I shall
not leave till you promise." The man next him in line
leaned forward curiously. "For God's sake, John!"

He shook his head and opened his mouth to speak,
then, hesitating, glanced around at the white, strained
faces peering intently at them through the dim light.
When he turned to Agatha his face wore a grim smile,
and when he spoke his voice, low and grave and
strained, was tinged with a bitter humor.

"I will come," he said. "The address?"

Agatha whispered it in his ear; he nodded his comprehension and turned an impassive face to the policeman, who approached to inquire the cause of the
delay. Agatha passed him, unheeding, to continue on
down the silent line, and five minutes later she reen-
tered the limousine.

"Jeanne," she said calmly, "I want to cry. Let us get
home!"

"But, *madame*," said Jeanne as the car turned about
and started up, "you are so pale—surely—what has
happened?"

"Nothing," said Agatha shortly. "Only—I have seen
a ghost. Please Heaven—" she broke off and laughed
bitterly.

"Well, at least I shall see him. After all, what does
it matter?"

She sank back into her corner, motionless and silent,
while the car sped on swifter than before. Once more
they passed through the glare of Fourteenth Street, the
glitter of Times Square, and the monotonous irregu-
larity of upper Broadway.

Arrived in her rooms, Agatha threw off her furs and
turned to her maid. There was a feverish restlessness
in both her manner and tone; her eyes glowed with

excitement; from head to foot she quivered with repressed emotion.

"Jeanne," she said, "I expect a caller—Mr. Carter. He will probably be here at any moment. When he comes, show him in."

Then she went into her own room and sat down to wait.

Five, ten, fifteen, thirty minutes passed—tense, strained with suspense and expectation; minutes during which thought and feeling were so closely packed and of so intense a nature that they resulted in a sort of numbness or nothingness, and left both brain and body wearied to exhaustion.

Then came the reaction; for Agatha was quite old enough to be cynical. She walked over to a mirror and surveyed herself critically, a cold, sarcastic expression in her eyes.

"Lord, what a fool!" she said aloud. "Sam was right, after all. If he could only see me now, how amused he would be! And he wouldn't care a hang!"

Then the door opened and closed; and she raised her eyes to meet those of John Carter.

The man before her was well worth a study. Here, in the glaring, penetrating light, many things were revealed that had been mercifully hidden in the dimness of the street. His suit was shabby and ill-fitting, but clean; his shoes, that had at one time been tan, were spotted and cracked; his linen though white, considerably the worse for wear; and the hat under his arm was a shapeless mass of dirty felt.

But at the sight of his face these items were forgotten. The square jaw, the hollow cheeks, the white, sloping forehead, the severely straight nose, all were dominated by the fantastic, bitter humor and grim inscrutability that looked out at you from the steady steel-gray eyes.

Knowing, cynical, and yet somehow expressionless, they gazed steadily at Agatha until she was forced to turn aside nervously and motion him to a chair.

Carter remained standing.

"Here I am," he said quietly. "What do you want?"

Agatha, hearing his voice and looking into his eyes, began to understand why she had been unable to forget John Carter. And she began to be afraid—of what, she could not have told.

"Won't you sit down?" she said, advancing toward him with outstretched hand. "You haven't even said 'Good evening,' " she laughed nervously.

Carter regarded the hand for a moment quizzically, then, taking it in his own, led her to a chair and seated himself beside her.

"Perhaps you are right," he said, after a pause. "It may be better for both of us to have it out. But what is there to say? As for you, I know all about you; and as for me, you know all about me, too—after tonight. I had forgiven you, and you had forgotten me. What else is there to say?"

"Perhaps," said Agatha, looking directly at him— "perhaps I had not forgotten."

Carter laughed mirthlessly.

"My dear Atha," he said, "it is useless for us to pretend. Especially for you. I am no longer twenty-five. In some ways, I am no longer a man. If I am bitter, you will please remember who sowed the seed for me. Against my will I promised to come here to-night to save you from your own folly—you were completely unnerved, and you were capable of any-thing. Why did you ask me? Was it merely curiosity? Or pity?"

"I don't know," said Agatha. "I think—I wanted to help you."

For some minutes there was silence. Carter sat motionless, his face turned away from Agatha, expressionless and grave. Then, suddenly, he felt the touch of a hand against his cheek, and the sound of a voice—the merest trembling whisper—sounded in his ear.

"Jack! I don't want to help you! I want you—to help me! I have not forgotten you Jack—I have never forgotten you, Jack—I have never forgotten you! Oh, I am silly and helpless, and I love you; I have always loved you—"

Agatha was crying silently on her knees by the side of Carter's chair, her head resting against his shoulder. Her arm crept around his neck, and she clung to him, quivering.

With an effort Carter controlled his voice. "Atha."

There was no answer. For a moment the man sat silently staring straight ahead, the merest quiver of an eyelid betraying the battle that was raging within; then, placing his hands on Agatha's cheeks, he lifted her head from his shoulder and arose, trembling, to his feet.

"By God," he said quietly, "you almost got me. Listen, Atha. There was a time when I wanted just what you want. But now—you're too late."

To Agatha, still kneeling by the chair he had left, the words came as in a dream. The strain under which she had labored for two hours; the reaction from ten years of repression and restraint, left her numb almost to the point of unconsciousness.

She heard, but she was incapable of movement. And Carter's voice, grave and measured, came to her as from a distance, and as though it were the voice of fate itself.

"You think you want me, Atha, but you are mistaken. The man you're looking for died ten years ago—you know best who killed him. You and I are as far apart as the poles—we'd hate each other in a week.

"You want to bring back the past—well, give it up. It's the most hopeless and utterly impossible task in the world. We had our chance; we'll never have another. We're through, you and I.

"I don't love you; I don't even pity you; for you are not the Atha I loved—you are not Atha at all. My life is not the only one you've ruined. Don't think I am deceived by your display of emotion and feeling, and don't deceive yourself. It's all a lie.

"It's merely a yearning for the past; a desperate and hopeless effort to make your dreams come true; a memory; an echo of what once was, and can never be again. There's nothing left to either of us but bitter experience and perhaps a passion or two; and we were not made to satisfy each other's passions."

The voice ceased suddenly, with a little throb, a catch of pain. Agatha heard his steps approaching, and was aware that he stooped above her, though she felt nothing; then she heard his steps again receding, and the door open and close.

He was gone.

She struggled to her feet with an effort; then stooped and picked up something which her movement had shaken from the chair by which she had knelt.

It was the bill she had given to Carter in the line. Summoning her strength she called Jeanne, then sank back into the chair, while the bill fluttered from her hand to the floor.

Agatha gazed at it stupidly as it lay crumpled at her feet.

"He might have taken it," she said plaintively, wearily. "He might have taken that."